Roses

Roses

G. R. Mannering

Sky Pony Press
New York

Sky Pony Press books may be purchased in bulk at special discounts for sales promotion, corporate gifts, fund-raising, or educational purposes. Special editions can also be created to specifications. For details, contact the Special Sales Department, Sky Pony Press, 307 West 36th Street, 11th Floor, New York, NY 10018 or info@skyhorsepublishing.com.

This is a work of fiction. Names, characters, places, and incidents are either the products of the author's imagination or used fictitiously.

Sky Pony® is a registered trademark of Skyhorse Publishing, Inc.®, a Delaware corporation.

Visit our website at www.skyponypress.com.

10 9 8 7 6 5 4 3 2 1

Library of Congress Cataloging-in-Publication Data

Mannering, G. R.
 Roses / G.R. Mannering.
   pages cm
 Summary: "A darker retelling of Beauty and her Beast, set in the fantasy land of Sago amid a purging of all the magics in the land"-- Provided by publisher.
 ISBN 978-1-62087-988-7 (hardcover : alk. paper) [1. Fantasy.] I. Title.
 PZ7.M31516Ro 2013
 [Fic]--dc23
                                      2013027916

Printed in the United States of America

Map of the Western Realm illustrated by Danielle Ceccolini.

In memory of Richard Hayton

Contents

Part One

She panted into the chilled air. Snowflakes fluttered around her like ashen butterflies, clinging to her lashes and to the hood of her thick cloak. Champ, her warhorse, tore through the night's darkness with clouds of warm breath, and his flanks heaved after the rush of the ride.

Before them in the enchanted quiet stood a castle. It was just as it had been described to her, and she grimaced slightly, for she had hoped that it was not real. The snowflakes whirled around its facade without settling, brushing against the latticed windows and marble arches. It was vast and rich with numerous turrets of coppery bricks that appeared to rise higher and higher until they were lost in the white of the snowstorm. Its outline flickered against the magenta sky and shifted under her gaze, as if it almost was not there.

She swallowed hard and pressed her heels into Champ's sides. The pair made no sound as they approached the gates; the blanket of snow muffled all noise, and Champ's hooves sank deep into its cushioned whiteness. He flicked his ears. She knew that he did not want to approach, but they could not turn back. She leaned forward and laid her cold, raw hand on his sweaty flank to reassure him.

She was not surprised when the iron gates swung silently open of their own accord. She gritted her teeth as she urged Champ on and reminded herself that she was saving the life of a man who had once saved her own.

As the gates clicked shut behind them, she heard the distant roar of a beast.

CHAPTER ONE

The House of Rose

When she was born, the midwife screamed. It was a reaction she was later familiar with. A child with amethyst eyes, silvery skin, and white hair is abnormal in Pervorocco. The combination is startling and with the later addition of a surly demeanor, she became quite frightening.

But even in babyhood, with the gentle air of innocence, she had terrified the midwife. The young woman held the pale, slippery bundle in her outstretched arms and screamed. The silver skin was so light it was almost translucent, and mauve webs of veins glinted beneath its surface in the shadowed room. The baby was unnatural and freakish to an olive-skinned, dark-eyed race of people, and the midwife's fingers began to tremble. At that moment the bells at the nearest temple clanged to mark midnight.

The midwife immediately thought the bundle a gypsy's child, a sorcerer's child, a cursed child—born at the bewitching hour to steal her soul. She looked up, intending to thrust it into the arms of the mother, but the mother had vanished. This produced a second scream.

A doctor darted into the room and scanned the beds of dying patients in the yellow glaze of the oil lamps. His eyes finally alighted on the last bed in the corner, where a midwife stood alone, clutching a ghostly child, and he pressed his thumb and index finger together instinctively in the sign of the gods before immediately reproaching himself. Nobody believed in the gods anymore.

"What is it?" he asked, moving reluctantly toward her.

The midwife blinked, but did not answer. She vaguely knew the doctor, as she knew all of the staff at the paupers' hospital, but names were never shared. There were too many dying people for such trivialities.

The baby began twitching and moaning.

"What is it?" he repeated, wiping his damp brow. Though it was the spring season, Sago was muggy and hot. It would remain like this through all four seasons—the heat never ceased.

"It is . . . " the midwife trailed off, lost for words.

"Where is the mother?" the doctor asked.

An empty bed with unsoiled sheets stretched tightly over a straw mattress stood before them without the faintest indent to suggest that someone had lain there, let alone given birth.

"She was here," the midwife gasped. "She was here . . . I'm sure of it."

"Where is she now?"

"I . . . I do not know."

"What did she look like?"

It would not have been the first time that a mother had given birth and then tried to escape the paupers' hospital without her child. In the suffocating throng of downtown Sago—the capital of Pervorocco—children were an unnecessary expense and the shantytown orphanages were overflowing.

The midwife creased her brow and licked her chapped lips as if to explain, but then a vacant look passed across her face and she stared off down the ward.

"I do not know," she said at last.

The baby began crying louder and its tiny, translucent cheeks turned red. It was the red of blood and not the rosy blush of a normal child. The doctor had treated a few Rurlish in his time—a pale, fair race—and yet none of them had looked silvery like this beast.

"How long have you been on your shift?" he asked.

In the swamp-like squalor of the paupers' hospital it was not unusual to work a whole day and night without rest. The doctor had been rushed off his feet since yesterday lunchtime and he had various streaks of rusty brown down the front of his shirt to prove it.

"I have just come on my night shift."

The doctor glanced at the baby nervously. It would not be admitted to any orphanage looking the way it did and there would be little use trying to find its mother—whatever gave birth to this creature had surely flown back from whence it came. He did not know what they were to do with such a thing.

"Perhaps it is from The Neighbor?" the midwife whispered hopefully. "They let anything across the borders now."

"I do not think so. I have birthed Magic Bloods before and this is different."

"A Magic Being?"

"I think not."

The midwife shuddered and the baby's wailing grew louder.

A dying patient in a nearby bed groaned.

"Quiet the thing!"

The midwife clumsily grasped some nearby stained swaddling and wrapped the creature in it. It looked somewhat better when she had finished, but still her fingers shook.

"What are we to do?" she asked.

The doctor rubbed his forehead. Born in an outer city, some crazy notion had brought him to Sago seasons ago to seek work. He had been young then, without the softness about his belly that had arrived with middle age, and he had been full of dreams to singlehandedly raise the healthcare of the impoverished shantytowns that swept the edges of downtown Sago like a lady's full skirt. Those hopes had long been lost in a never-ending sea of sick and dying people. The doctor was tired and most of his compassion had been wrung out of him. His first thought was to leave the baby outside the front door, but just as he considered this, something at the side of the bed caught his eye.

He bent down and picked up a hexagonal amulet from the floor, instantly recognizing it.

"I know where this thing is from!" he gasped, the relief in his voice palpable.

The midwife nodded.

"I spoke to a gentleman about it—the House of Rose. I would not have recognized it otherwise, but the crest is so distinct."

He brushed his thumb across the carved rose at the center of the amulet, feeling the hard undulations of its heavy petals. Family amulets were a dated concept and now rarely seen in the streets of Sago or its surrounding towns. They belonged to the Houses and those with ancient ancestry.

A few days ago, the doctor had rushed out of the hospital's front door and into the muddy street to gasp as much fresh air as the putrid, humid atmosphere allowed. He had been removing the gangrenous leg of a child with no sedation and he had needed a moment away from the young boy's tortuous screams.

"Are you all right?" a voice had asked.

The doctor had looked up to see a gentleman, although the exact appearance of the man was unclear to him now. He could only remember that he had been surprised, first to be addressed by anyone in that street, and second that such a smart individual should be wandering among lowly beggars and prostitutes.

"Yes," he had found himself saying. "I just needed some air."

It was then that he had glimpsed the amulet around the gentlemen's neck, clearly on show for all to see. It was a heavy, gold, hexagonal disk with filigree twisting its borders and an intricate, carved rose at its center. It was possibly the most beautiful thing that the doctor had seen in a long time and he immediately advised the gentlemen to hide it, for thieves stole openly in the city's center.

"Thank you," the gentlemen had said, and he had possibly tipped his hat, if he had been wearing a hat, the doctor thought, trying desperately to remember.

"It's magnificent," the doctor had replied, unable to think of a better word.

The gentlemen had nodded and said, "It is my family, the House of Rose," and his eyes had flashed. They had flashed with a color that could have been silver or gold or violet. Or, maybe it was just the light.

Then the stranger had walked away.

It was funny that such a thing had stuck in the doctor's mind; his never-ending line of patients usually eclipsed all else in his life.

"Are we to send it to the House of Rose then?" asked the midwife, keen to get away from the freakish baby.

The doctor nodded. "I will take it to the nearest town hall and ask them to send it to a House of Rose relation."

"Fancy such a thing being from one of the Houses . . ." muttered the midwife, but she was too pleased to be rid of the baby to make anything of it.

Despite it being the dead of night, the town hall would be open. The constant stream of drunken criminals, homeless orphans, and illegal gamblers left Sago's town halls with no opportunity to close their doors. It was a running joke that the overflowing shantytowns never slept—night or day, it was all the same to their inhabitants.

The midwife passed the swaddled bundle to the doctor, who grimaced and held it awkwardly in one arm, trying not to look at the mewing package. As he hurried out of the ward, a little part of him was glad that he had an excuse to leave. He was too distracted in his thoughts to notice a well-dressed gentlemen brush past him in the hall with eyes that might have been silver or gold or violet. Or, maybe it was just the light.

CHAPTER TWO

The Youngest Daughter

The House of Rose was easily traced through the town hall system to Ma Dane Herm-se-Hollis, its last surviving member. Her own amulet hung in her drawing room so that guests might see that she was of good breeding, but she no longer wore it around her neck like a prize, as she had done in her youth.

Good breeding was all Ma Dane had had then, for she was plain looking and thick shaped even as a girl, with the addition of a disagreeable temper. She had used the amulet to attract a painfully rich husband, the merchant's son, Pa Hamish Herm-se-Hollis, who was desperate to marry ancestry. Pa Hamish could hardly believe his luck when Ma Dane House of Rose made eyes at him at a dance, and their wedding was arranged soon after.

Since the House of Rose was sinking into a swamp of poverty, Ma Dane's widowed mother was only too happy to marry her youngest daughter off to anyone, let alone a considerably wealthy family. The widow had wondered how on earth her plain-looking child had managed to attract such a suitor, but upon making inquiries, she soon realized that Houses in better financial positions had dismissed Pa Hamish on account of his ugly exterior, social ineptitude, and shady dealings. However, Ma Dane's mother had slowly been dying for some years, often worrying about what would become of her youngest daughter once she was gone, so she had wisely turned a blind eye to these shortcomings, passing away with relief a few days before the wedding.

After a honeymoon on an island off The Neighbor, Pa Hamish and Ma Dane had moved into Pa Hamish's father's mansion, intending to care for the bed-ridden, foul-tempered old man in his last days. The mansion sat on the seafront of Sago's richest, most extravagant boulevard and was everything that Ma Dane had ever wished for in the cramped, stinking boarding houses of her younger years. It had an extensive fleet of servants, vast chambers, and a two-story ballroom. To complete the idyllic fairy tale, Pa Hamish's father promptly died after the couple had been living there but one season and the whole contents of his boundless estate passed to his only son and domineering daughter-in-law.

That was when Ma Dane stopped wearing her amulet and instead hung it in her drawing room, realizing that the dated emblem would inspire respect in high society, but never acceptance. To be accepted one had to conform to the nouveau riche lifestyle and Ma Dane desperately wanted to be accepted. She spent the next several years plotting her way up Sago's social ladder, using her wealth, her good breeding, and her husband's formidable family business as leverage.

Such distractions were exactly what Ma Dane needed to forget her past and she succeeded in escaping it for many seasons. Even the death of her mother had left little impression on her, for she had known that the widow would die and she had feared it. The House of Rose had no other family in Sago and no inheritance to speak of, thus Ma Dane had no possibility of making her own way in the realm. Her father, before he had dissolved into gambling and drink, had refused to let his children pursue an occupation, arguing that they were gentry and could survive on their breeding and family wealth alone.

As a child, Ma Dane had watched as all the belongings of the House of Rose were gradually sold to pay off her father's crippling debts and finally the grand mansion itself, which was knocked down to build new housing. After her father committed suicide, well-to-do friends gave her mother needlework and they survived on the small earnings she could make, living in boarding houses and eating broth. It was one of those well-to-do friends who had taken pity on the lonely, plain Ma Dane and had invited her to a ball in the summer season, and it was at this ball that she had met Pa Hamish.

It was no wonder with a beginning such as this that Ma Dane did not like to dwell on her past. Her present and her future were too distracting, full of parties, gowns, entertaining, and preserving the lavish, seafront mansion. Ma Dane managed to forget her childhood until a strange, ghostly baby appeared on her doorstep, like a message from her past.

———⟨∞⟩———

That fateful day had started like any other in the grand Sago mansion named Rose Herm—a name combining good breeding and fabulous wealth, which the powerful couple had hoped would impress guests. The seaside capital was awaking with its usual hum of seagull cries and silvery peal of temple bells (the temples still remained in Sago as a tourist attraction, though its inhabitants had long decided that religion was passé). The humidity was high for the late spring season and the fierce sun was already burning off the mist from the sea.

A rude knock sounded at the oak, double front doors. Since the death of her father-in-law some forty seasons past, Ma Dane had been splashing the inheritance about by unnecessarily refurbishing Rose Herm. Those oak double doors were her latest addition.

A passing maid approached the porch curiously, as it was only guests who entered there and no one was scheduled to arrive until noon. She unbolted the latch and heaved on the heavy oak slabs until they gave way with a groan. Wiping her moist brow with the back of her hand, she looked on to the deserted front gardens with their ornate flower displays and miniature fountains. Her first thought was that a spell, escaping from one of the passing circuses, had splattered itself against the oak paneling. It was not an unusual occurrence, especially in the late springtime when the circuses would descend on Sago for summer pickings, filling the crowded streets with their colored streamers, bizarre Magic Beings, and pesky spells. The maid was about to turn away when she heard a whimper.

She looked down and screamed.

Another maid came rushing out of the breakfast room at the end of the hall. Such noise was not permitted in the morning at Rose Herm, since Pa Hamish was always grumpy before noon and Ma Dane was grumpy every hour of the day. The second maid skidded to a halt on the marbled floor and followed the gaze of her fellow servant.

Rather than scream, she squeaked loudly and made the sign of the gods with her thumb and index finger.

The silver newborn baby wriggled and moaned, weak from lack of food and comfort.

"What is it?" boomed the unmistakable voice of Ma Dane from the breakfast hall. She had seen the second maid rush out after the first maid's scream and Ma Dane was in the mood for shouting at someone.

The maids gasped at one another and silently conveyed their mutual horror.

"What *is* it?" yelled the voice of Ma Dane. She had been troubled by dreams and old nightmares these past few nights and her short temper was close to exploding.

It was then that one maid noticed the amulet placed beside the swaddled baby and she jumped, startled. She was sure that she had seen the same amulet in the drawing room just an hour ago as she plumped the cushions. She pointed at it and the other maid dropped her expression of alarm, looking puzzled.

"Is it the same?" one whispered.

The other shrugged.

"Get in here *now!*" screeched Ma Dane, and the sound of a fork hitting the breakfast room wall could be heard.

The maids were far more afraid of the wrath of Ma Dane than the hideous baby, and one scooped it into her arms with a shudder as the other carried the amulet, and they hurried to their mistress. They entered the breakfast room with cheeks flushed, fearful and uncertain.

Ma Dane was seated at the head of the table, seething. Master Eli was beside her, kicking his legs in his highchair, and Pa Hamish was perched on an armchair in the corner, wiping sleep from his eyes, a grouchy frown on his face.

"What have—" began Ma Dane before the words vanished from her lips.

Her brown eyes flicked between the bundle of swaddling and the rose amulet. Her puffed bosom, which had been heaving with anger and spilling over the confines of her bejeweled gown, stilled. Her cheeks turned pale. She looked instantly ill. In all their years of service at Rose Herm, the maids had never seen their mistress appear so.

A deadly silence thickened the air. Ma Dane, who was never quiet, sat motionless, and Eli made no sound. Even Pa Hamish paid attention for once and opened his sleepy, brown eyes wide.

"What is it?" he asked finally, disgusted.

The baby mewed.

"Please, Ma, it was on the doorstep—" began one maid.

"—with this," finished the other, holding up the amulet.

Ma Dane shivered, though it was stiflingly hot.

"That hangs in the drawing room!" cried Pa Hamish. "Is this some trick?"

At the raised voices, Eli began to make a fuss, but for once, Ma Dane did not notice. She swallowed hard and gasped, trying to regain her composure.

"Where—" she began, but she was not able to continue.

"You should not touch such things!" shouted Pa Hamish. "Put that back where it belongs!"

"No, please, Pa," cried the maids. "We just found them!"

"Liars! Thieves!"

Ma Dane abruptly pushed back her chair and stood, juddering the table and causing all of the china to rattle. Her husband fell silent and Eli stopped his blubbering.

"Is it a girl?"

One maid pulled back the swaddling before nodding.

Ma Dane's cheeks turned a shade paler.

"What is the meaning of this?" scoffed Pa Hamish, but his wife was not listening.

Ma Dane's dark eyes darted about the room feverishly as she clenched and unclenched her fists into her skirt, biting the soft flesh of her cheek. She had tried to ignore the signs, she had willed it not to be real, but here it was. Here *the thing* was.

The blistering orange glow of the morning sun was streaming through the broad crystal windows and outside she could hear, among the screeches of seagulls and ringing of bells, the gentle sucking of the sea. It brought back an unwelcome memory and she licked her sweaty, thin lips. Many, many seasons ago, she had stood at the edge of Sago's shore and made a young, desperate promise. She wished that she could not remember, but it hung as heavy as a gold amulet around her neck.

"Take it upstairs and give it to the wet nurse," she commanded in an unusually weak voice.

The maids exchanged frightened looks.

Pa Hamish's mouth dropped open.

"Put the amulet in my rooms," Ma Dane carried on. "And do not speak of this again or you shall lose your places."

She sat down.

The maids silently thanked the gods they were always told not to believe in and rushed out, fearful that their mistress might change her mind.

Ma Dane rang the bell for the next course and servants appeared, carrying platters of fresh omelets from the kitchens.

Pa Hamish stared at her, shocked.

"What by gods was—"

"*Silence!*" hissed Ma Dane.

And like the obedient, downtrodden husband he was, Pa Hamish never mentioned it again. In fact, he did not see the child until she was sixteen seasons old and could no longer be confined to the nursery. He had forgotten her existence and when he saw the freakish thing roaming one of Rose Herm's long corridors, he screamed.

CHAPTER THREE

The Baby with Amethyst Eyes

The evening following that awful arrival, Ma Dane retired to her rooms after a fretful day pretending to listen to her visitors while her head was filled with the horrors of her past. Traipsing into her dressing room, she let her restless dress-maids unlace her gown before dismissing them. She wanted to be alone. That baby had awakened something inside her—something that she had long buried. She could feel it fizzing through her blood. She clutched her head, trying to convince herself that it was only a headache, but she knew that it was more than that.

Staggering into her vast bedroom, she stood before her gilded looking glass and pulled at the pins in her hair. She had been so eager to be left alone that she had forgotten to let her dress-maids take it down. She entertained the thought of firing them for such negligence—that would give the servants something new to worry over. It seemed a good idea.

Suddenly, her dark hair tumbled down her back, the pins falling free. She froze, her reflection in the mirror pale and aghast. The pins moved themselves into a neat line on the dresser beside her and her hairbrush alongside them began to twitch.

Ma Dane stamped her hand over it. She had worked so hard over the years to control herself—she would not give in now.

"Asha!" she spat. "Asha, what have you done?"

Picking up the brush, she threw it to the floor, and her rage consoled her. Marching over to the bed, she snatched up the rose amulet that had been left with the baby. It was different from her own—heavier, darker, and more powerful. The weight of it in her hand suddenly gave her a rush to her head, and her anger was about to be replaced with fear when her stubbornness took over.

This was *her* house.

With the amulet burning a Magical heat into her hand, Ma Dane walked into her dressing room and opened a back wardrobe where her old collection of dresses was kept, the ones her mother had made for her trousseau when she first married Pa Hamish. She had not let go of them in all those seasons, though they were wildly dated and almost absurd now. With a hiss of rage, she threw the amulet into the closet and slammed the doors.

———⊸⊷∞⊶⊷———

News of Rose Herm's new addition spread and Ma Dane's high society friends began asking probing questions, wondering if the abnormal child that they overheard their maids whispering about was real. Rumors circulated through drawing rooms and dance halls, people speculating whether the child was Ma Dane's or simply a curse rooted in the dodgy dealings of the Herm-se-Hollis past. Oddly, Ma Dane was more concerned about the former assumption.

The arrival of the baby also unsettled the servants at Rose Herm. From the first instance it crossed the threshold, there was a noticeable anxiousness in the air, even in the kitchens. Ma Dane did not know if it was simply her imagination, but her day-to-day dealings with the house staff in the following moon-cycle felt strained. Sensing something, Eli forever blubbered in her presence and Pa Hamish disappeared as often as he could to his men's club. He had never broached the subject of the baby since Ma Dane had summoned him to silence, but it would be some time until he forgot it completely.

Another moon-cycle passed before—worn down by rumors and terrified servants and sick of waiting for the event to brush over of its own accord—Ma Dane decided to take matters into her own hands. She arranged an early summertime ball in the lush, expansive back gardens of Rose Herm and invited all of Sago's high society.

The evening was well underway with heaped platters of food and the hum of a full orchestra when Ma Dane called the guests to attention. It was a typical, stifling hot Sago day and everyone thought the beads of sweat dripping down Ma Dane's round face were due to the punishing sun.

As smoothly as she could manage, Ma Dane addressed the rumors that had been buzzing through Sago's social scene concerning the new arrival at her house. She even managed to provoke a titter from the crowd when recounting one particular story that a winged moorey had flown through her drawing room windows. But she assured everyone that this was not the case and described her new cause to take in the beggar children of prostitutes. Thus, her high society friends and the servants of her household—even her husband—swallowed the lie that the baby was a street urchin, born mutilated as a result of its mother's under-realm ways, and life returned to normal.

But that night, and every night for the following moon-cycle, Ma Dane dreamt that Asha was crying.

—∞∞∞—

It was lucky that a wet nurse was still employed at Rose Herm when the newborn arrived. Master Eli was past the age of needing one, but Ma Dane had been considering a second child (she quickly decided not to after the arrival of the amethyst-eyed baby), and so she kept the woman on, not wanting her to be snatched up by another household.

It was also lucky that the wet nurse was from a largely Magic Blood family in The Neighbor, and therefore was not so repulsed as everyone else when she was presented with the newborn. She still whelped upon seeing it, but after she had recovered from the initial shock, she would let it rest in her arms and feed from her, seeing how weak and malnourished it was. She was kind natured and the tales of Magic Blood cousins born in her home country with various strange goings on left her assured that the baby's blood would settle soon and she would look like a true Pervoroccoian in time.

The wet nurse was the baby's sole nurturer for many seasons. To avoid upsetting everyone in the house, the child was confined to the nursery and allowed outside only once every four days, when the wet nurse would take her around the gardens. She was absolutely forbidden to venture away from Rose Herm itself; Ma Dane was too fearful that her appearance would spark old rumors.

Thus, the child grew into a shy, quiet toddler, seeing only the wet nurse and a few other servants who happened to pass on their walks. She was dressed in the old clothes of Master Eli and never seen by the Herm-se-Hollis family.

When sixteen seasons had passed, the wet nurse knew it was high time that she left the household and that a proper nanny be employed. She had long stopped feeding the baby herself and was now purely a babysitter. Though she had come to love the lonely child, there was little more she could give her and she was restless to move on. After several petitions made through other servants to meet with Ma Dane were ignored, the wet nurse handed in her resignation. Only then was she summoned one winter's morning to Ma Dane's office, and she decided to take the baby with her.

Ma Dane's office was a spacious room at the back of the house on the ground floor filled with books and a long, wide desk that she sat behind to do business. She liked to spend an hour in her office every morning, attending to the needs of servants and managing the household's accounts. Pa Hamish never concerned himself with such things, leaving all the monetary and household management to his wife.

It was a warm morning with a fresh, salty breeze whistling in from the sea. The residents of Sago generally exalted in its short winters, it being the only time that they could venture outside without parasols. Soft, glowing light seeped through the windows of Ma Dane's office as the wet nurse entered, the light silhouetting Ma Dane's bulky form bent over her desk. The wet nurse walked into the middle of the room, and Ma Dane finally looked up.

She jumped. Her eyes locked on the baby toddling at the wet nurse's side. In some way she had imagined it frozen in time, forever to remain a silvery bundle and she could not fathom the toddler before her.

"I trust you received my letter of resignation, Ma," the wet nurse said, after a long silence had ensued.

Ma Dane roused herself and a deep shudder traveled down her body.

"She is harmless," the wet nurse added, mistaking the shudder for one of disgust. "In fact, if I may be so bold, Ma, I think she looks mighty better."

She was right and Ma Dane could see that. Once you recovered from the shock of the thing, its large violet-colored eyes and pearly silver skin could almost be endearing. It was also chewing on the nail of its right thumb in a way that reminded her painfully of Asha.

"Anyway, I must resign, Ma," carried on the wet nurse, taking Ma Dane's silence as indifference. "I think the child will need a nanny and . . . I am not sure how much longer she will stay in the nursery, Ma. She is a curious little thing."

"Yes, you must go," said Ma Dane at last. "I had not realized that she had grown so much."

"Babies have a tendency to grow, Ma."

Ma Dane ignored this impertinence.

"Has there been anything . . . I mean, have you noticed . . . "

"Magic Blood?"

Ma Dane shivered.

"No, Ma. I believe she is just a quirk of nature."

"Sometimes it is slow to come," Ma Dane whispered, but the wet nurse did not hear her.

"I will inquire into a nanny immediately and you may leave when she arrives."

The wet nurse nodded before pressing her left hand to her chest in the sign of respect. She scooped the child into her arms and walked out of the room.

The little girl peeped over her shoulder, watching the large woman behind the desk stare at her before they disappeared down the hall.

───◈───

A few weeks later, a nanny was hired and the wet nurse was permitted to leave. She had managed to secure a good place in a wealthy household, discovering that families were tripping over themselves to hire the ex-wet nurse of Ma Dane Herm-se-Hollis. Still, she knew that she would miss her amethyst-eyed baby.

The morning before she left, the wet nurse brought the child onto her lap and stared hard into its violet-colored eyes.

"I am confused," she admitted. "I thought you would have dropped your strange looks by now."

The child said nothing, but continued to chew on her thumb. The wet nurse had been looking for signs of Magic Blood for the last sixteen seasons, but there had been no troublesome dreams, no twitching objects, and no wind tunnels. The child was as quiet and self-controlled as ever, playing with her hand-me-down toys, but otherwise doing little else.

"Perhaps it will come later . . . "

She said her tearful goodbyes to the child and then left Rose Herm. In the seasons to come, she would always listen for gossip and news of her amethyst-eyed baby, though for a long time there would be none.

CHAPTER FOUR

The Nanny

As a baby and toddler, the nameless little girl was shy and sweet, but this changed with the arrival of the nanny.

Ma Dane had been struck by the glimpse of the eerie being in her study that day with the wet nurse. She had not expected the child to look so much like Asha. The resemblance was uncanny despite the freakish, silver coloring, and it led her to assume that her temperament would be similar—difficult. She decided that the child would need a firm hand or else her fate would also be the same. What would become of Ma Dane's reputation then? The standing she had bought, fought for, and dreamt of. The child would need a firm hand or else she would ruin everything.

And so the nanny arrived. Her résumé promised harsh discipline and her last place was in the house of one of the State Leaders who had five young, jostling boys, which made her seem the perfect person to control the child. Ma Dane sent for her immediately and the woman arrived two days after the wet nurse departed and perhaps if it had been just a day, or if there had been a crossover period, then things might have been different. But it was not and it could not be helped.

The amethyst-eyed baby had not spent a night away from her wet nurse since she could remember. The sudden separation upset and confused her and she cried to herself all the dark, warm night, curled in a corner of the lonely nursery. A long, solitary day followed in which she was visited at mealtimes by a maid evidently petrified to be in her presence, and then passed another gloomy night. By the time the nanny arrived, the amethyst-eyed toddler was weak with neglect and loneliness. She had not stopped whimpering since dawn and that was how the nanny found her: cowering under the wet nurse's empty rocking chair.

"The child is down here?" the nanny had asked, following Ma Dane down a long corridor on the third floor.

"Yes, that is correct. We keep her in Master Eli's old nursery. I had a suite of rooms prepared for his birth, but they were not finished in time and he had to spend a few days in here after he was born. The room is sufficient for the needs of this child."

They stopped before a plain door and Ma Dane took a key from a pouch about her waist. Her fingers were trembling although she was trying hard not to show it. When she met new staff, she liked to be as imposing and haughty as possible to terrify them into submission right away, but this was proving to be difficult. Anything that concerned the amethyst-eyed child caused her nerves to jitter. She felt like a girl again, dressed in the ancient tatters of a fashion long gone, who was laughed at in the street.

"Does the child need to be locked in?"

"She has a tendency to roam about the house if left to her own devices and it upsets the servants."

"All unruly ways shall be punished."

But Ma Dane scarcely heard what the nanny said. She unlocked the door and marched inside, and at first she did not see it, but then she caught sight of a wary little face beneath the rocking chair, and she sucked in her breath. The thing was biting the nail of its thumb in that achingly familiar way.

"I will leave you to become acquainted," Ma Dane barked, sweeping out of the room and shutting the door hastily behind her. In the empty corridor outside, she leaned against the wall for a moment to regain her composure, the back of her neck slick with sweat.

In the nursery, the nanny squared up to the thing trembling beneath the rocking chair.

"I am Nan and I want you to come out immediately."

If the baby had been wary, she was now petrified and could not have moved if she had wanted to. She hoped desperately that her wet nurse would return and stared hard at the dark wooden slates of the floor, wishing to awake from this nightmare.

"Come out. This is the last time I will tell you."

A moment later, a clawed hand swiped beneath the rocking chair, grasping the doughy arm of the toddler and wrenching her out in one yank. She did not have time to cry or even take a breath before she was confronted with a cratered, thick face hissing into her own.

Nan smelled of crumpled tissues and floor polish. Her limp gray hair was raked into a twist on the top of her dome-shaped head and her sagging skin resembled dribbled wax. Ma Dane had been pleased to note her horrific presence, thinking that she was just the sort of woman who could have controlled Asha, if indeed anyone could have.

"From now on, you shall do as I instruct. You are lower than a servant here. You are a dependent, is that clear?"

The child gazed back at her in mute shock.

Taking silence for disobedience, Nan thwacked her across the thigh in a sharp, cutting slap.

Tears sprang to her violet eyes.

"When I am speaking to you, you will give me the sign of respect."

Grabbing the child's left hand, she shoved it against her chest.

"Is that clear?"

<hr />

The amethyst-eyed child did share the same temperament as Asha—Ma Dane had guessed that much correctly. But had she been cared for and shown tender affection, the child would have been merely headstrong. In fact, her initial shyness would have worked in her favor and she could perhaps have been single-minded but sensitive. As it was, this would not be the case.

Cruelty soured her. Nan was used to treating spoiled little darlings who were lavished with adoration from their parents and sorely in need of a commanding presence. The amethyst-eyed child had no one else in the whole realm and Nan's savageness squashed her. She was shown no mercy.

There was not one striking incident that did it. There was no sense that she had been pushed past her limit. Rather, it was a slow burn of brutality that could only head in one direction. It started with the sign of respect—the child would press her left hand to her chest and stab the nails into her skin, creating tiny mauve crescents while inwardly hating Nan and clenching her teeth to bite back screams of rage. This progressed to snubbing her nose whenever Nan was not looking, which filled her with secret glee. Then she began moving Nan's things around the nursery. Not hiding them, because that would be too obvious, but rearranging items enough to make it difficult.

Emboldened, she went further: not answering right away, not signing respect until told to, not brushing her hair, and so on. Eventually the child rebelled altogether and began sneaking out of the nursery whenever the opportunity arrived.

And every smarting slap that she received as punishment, every strict reprimand and nasty insult, was worth it. She would not stop misbehaving, for she could not bear it otherwise. Having escaped, she would scurry through the corridors of Rose Herm unnoticed, spying on the servants and, in particularly bold moments, on Ma Dane. At first this was enough to satisfy her rebellious urges, but soon she craved more. She began venturing into the grounds of the mansion and it was around this time that she first met Owaine.

Owaine had heard of the strange child, as all of the servants had, but he had never seen it. The maids often liked to whisper at mealtimes in the lower quarters of curses and demons and bad luck, but he took little heed of them. In fact, he barely spoke to anyone except to command his stable lads and to exchange a few polite observations with the gardeners. He found the outside servants easier to mix with than the house servants if he needed company, and the feeling was mutual. The house servants thought his lilting accent comical and difficult to understand. They found his manners rough and peculiar, but they did not expect much else from a Hillander.

Owaine's homeland was many miles away, in the opposite corner of Pervorocco—a long distance from any city and different in feel, smell, and taste from Sago. In spare moments he dreamt of moist, green hills, cool fog, and the smell of drenched earth. He longed to return to his homeland, but grief and poverty had brought him to Sago to seek work and he feared returning. As stable manager at Rose Herm, he could send a wedge of sticks home each moon-cycle to his daughter, who was cared for by a relation in his village. He missed her dearly, but he told himself that he was better off staying at Rose Herm.

His job kept him occupied and his rooms in the stable loft meant that he was rarely away from it. Owaine was a skilled horseman and the tang of horse sweat and the scent of hay were his constant companions. They were also what brought the amethyst-eyed child to him.

One morning he was grooming the carriage horses as usual when he saw something flickering in the shadows of the opposite stall. Comrade, Pa Hamish's riding horse, was whickering softly and he could hear the soft swish of straw being shuffled.

Frowning, Owaine clicked his tongue and whistled, wondering if one of the hunting dogs had gotten in there again. Comrade adored petting and would let anyone and any animal into his stall. He had not exactly turned out to be the show horse Pa Hamish had hoped for.

Owaine approached the stall and peered over the half door, expecting to see a dog or one of Sago's street cats that often prowled the grounds for pickings. Instead, two violet eyes stared back at him.

"Urgh!"

He jumped, causing Comrade to flinch and stamp his hoof in frustration.

Owaine pressed his thumb and index finger together firmly and tried to calm his beating chest. The maids' stories flew into his mind and he swallowed hard. Gathering his courage, he peered over the half door once again.

The child had buried her face against Comrade's lean ebony leg, wrapping her silvery arms around his knee. She looked so vulnerable that any misgivings Owaine harbored ebbed. She was wearing a pair of slacks that did not fit and a frilled boy's shirt with deep creases.

"Don't be frightened," he said in the soothing lilt he reserved for skittish colts.

She peeked at him with one curious violet eye.

"I won't hurt yur."

She stared at him.

Owaine wandered back over to the carriage horses and began muttering a Hilland folk song. He picked up a currycomb and started working the knots out of the first horse's tail.

> *Winds of blight that tear the earth,*
> *Rain that spills the rights of birth.*
> *Gods that weave our spells divine,*
> *Protect these ancient hills of mine.*

He heard a shuffle of straw and glanced over to see the child standing on the other side of Comrade's stall. He had not even heard her slide the bolt and open the half door.

"You remind me of Ma, girly," he said. "She were yur size when I left, but I 'spose she's bigger now."

The child stared at him and bit on her thumb.

He turned his attention back to the knots and waited. From the corner of his eye he saw a pale shadow creep closer. A moment later, he looked over his shoulder and saw her standing a yard or so away, watching him closely. She had a dark purple bruise on her temple that looked tender and sore.

"What happened there?"

She recoiled from him with a whimper.

"Hush, yur. Hush."

He moved back over to the carriage horse and carried on brushing. After a while he turned his head and saw her standing beside Comrade's stall again, cradling the horse's head in her arms and hugging his muzzle to her chest.

"He'll take any amount of that. Yur could stay there all day if yur please."

And she did. After that she came back whenever she could escape the nursery, keeping the horseman company while he worked.

CHAPTER FIVE

The Circus

In the spring of her twenty-fourth season, the amethyst-eyed child learned how to escape Rose Herm's grounds. Hitherto she had started to bolt the nursery on a daily basis, spending her time in the company of Owaine or prowling the vast, ornamented grounds of the mansion, climbing trees and playing solitary games in the punishing heat. Nan kept the child's escapes a secret from the rest of the household, since her pride could not stand the tarnish of failure. Her place among the house servants was high; they feared her for her appearance and her reputation. They respected her for keeping that freakish being in check, and she enjoyed her elevated rank.

But Nan had run out of punishments for the child. Smacking her no longer worked and neither did shouting or cursing. The child's silver skin was riddled with deep, plum bruises from pinches and punches and kicks. Nan had told her that she was the scum of the realm so many times that it no longer had any effect. The child would stand and take it all with the most infuriating blank expression, and then the next day she would find some way of escaping again. She climbed out of windows, created distractions and slipped through the door, stole keys, and hid. Nan was beginning to crack.

The child took pains to avoid everyone except Owaine when she wandered about the grounds. She was old enough to realize that her appearance caused others shock and horror, so she snuck around like a pale shadow. For a while, her favorite pastime was to find a way into the drawing room and crouch under an armchair, watching the visitors Ma Dane had over for tea. This was how she learned words other than "wretch," "monster," and "demon."

She would crouch until her whole body was numb with inertia and stare at the exotic creatures that inhabited that room. They flew in with puffs of potent scent that clogged the warm air and made her drowsy. Their olive décolletages were powdered with sweet talcum like delicate frosting and their swollen, extravagant dresses pooled in folds about their slippered feet. They would enter the room stiff and cool and slowly wilt in the sticky Sago day. The child, too, would be damp with sweat by evening and then she would creep out as she had crept in, find a fountain in the grounds, and wallow in its soothing chill before Nan eventually found her and dragged her back inside.

It was in the drawing room that the child heard about the circus and decided to escape Rose Herm's grounds for the first time. The Coo-se-Nutoes were visiting as they often did, before the Shap-se-George and after the Crit-se-Prom, and the child was squatting in her place under the armchair beside the cavernous fireplace that was never lit. This was the best spot because no one ever sat in the creaky antique chair and it gave a full view of the visitors and Ma Dane.

The child had always known instinctively who the round, bloated woman was. Though she had seen her but a few times, Ma Dane's small brown eyes, thin lips, and dark hair were familiar. The child watched her with interest, but mostly she liked to watch the ladies and particularly the Coo-se-Nutoes, who were the loveliest of all.

Ma Usa Coo-se-Nutoes was almost the same age as Ma Dane and as tiny as the latter was large. Ma Usa had two beautiful daughters, Peony and Bow, with unusual black hair, soft features, and graceful airs. Often, if she could not escape the nursery, the child would stalk about the dank room, trying to imitate their gliding walk.

Listening to their chatter and gossip over syrupy tea and sweetmeats, the child would hear about dances and fashions and marriages. On this particular humid morning, she learned of the circus.

"You must have heard of it," said Ma Usa. "Did you not feel the spells? They caused havoc in our kitchens."

Ma Dane sipped from her tea and the bone china looked strange in her thick fingers. "We have already had the usual ones for this time of year," she replied.

"But that is just it!" burst out Peony. "The usual circuses have not come this year, they have been put off by—"

Ma Usa cleared her throat and Peony quieted.

"The rouge spells you have felt are all from one circus," explained Ma Usa. "*The Beautiful Spectacular* has created havoc on its own. They say it is a phenomenon: magic that has never been seen before."

Ma Dane shifted in her seat. "I had not heard of this," she said. "And I assumed that few circuses would try crossing the borders in the current political climate. They are a rather tired tradition, I think."

"But the circuses are part of our history!" squeaked Bow.

"They are an import from The Neighbor," replied Ma Dane coolly. "And especially dangerous considering the guerrilla warfare surfacing in their capital."

"You cannot think that is serious?" said Ma Usa, setting down her cup. "It is a group of anti-Magical extremists and The Neighbor has seen and squashed hundreds before."

"Sago cannot risk appearing to sympathize with Magical immigrants, whatever happens in The Neighbor."

"Then, you do think it serious?"

"I dined with a few State members three days past and they certainly are considering the matter of great importance. If I had known of *The Beautiful Spectacular,* I would have said something."

"But the Houses have welcomed circuses every summer for thousands of seasons!" cried Peony. "It is just a glorious show!"

Ma Dane turned her bulk on the girl. "*We* Houses do not welcome political turmoil. We have more sense than that." Her eyes pointed to the golden amulet hung proudly on the opposite wall.

"But—" began Bow.

"In fact, the State is so set against breaking peace with The Neighbor that I doubt they will look kindly upon magically sympathetic leaders that intend to appeal in the forthcoming poll . . . "

All three visitors blushed and shuffled their slippers.

"Ma Dane, you know we are always very grateful for the support you have given my husband over the years."

"Good. I'm sure Pa Coo-se-Nutoes would not want to support the . . . the . . . "

"*The Beautiful Spectacular,*" muttered Peony.

"Yes. I'm sure he would not want to support something that endangered his position. In fact, I shall ask to visit it with him today to be sure. The whole thing seems very suspect to me. We do not want a repeat of the Red Wars."

Ma Usa flinched.

"Has it—is it that bad?"

"It's critical. The Neighbor has played a dangerous game," Ma Dane spat the words. "It has gone too far with its University of Magic and military force. The backlash was inevitable."

A silence ensued in which Ma Dane slurped her tea.

"Did you see that new House of Shell girl at the Crit-se-Prom ball?"

With visible effort, Ma Usa replied, "Why yes, it was shocking— her hem was practically above her ankles."

⸺∞⸺

Later, with her cheek shoved against the wooden floorboards of the nursery, the child could not forget what she had heard of the circus. She had disregarded most of the chat, not understanding it, but the circus with the magnetic ring of *The Beautiful Spectacular* had stayed foremost in her mind.

"Don't twitch!" screeched Nan, pushing her heel further into the child's back as she lay face down. "Nasty, vile creature!"

The child had been caught escaping the drawing room and was now receiving her punishment. Rather than mull over her blatant disregard for rules, as she had been instructed, the child was musing the possibility of running off again this very afternoon. She had been contemplating escaping the grounds of Rose Herm for a while, having grown bored of its constraints. She desired fresh lands to explore and had already plotted her escape: a large zouba tree that stood beside a pond and leaned toward the high iron fence. She had just been waiting for a reason to flee.

There was a knock at the door and Nan hissed irritably.

"Come in, then!"

The maid fumbled with the lock and as she swung the door open Nan released the child and tried to look as though she had been giving a school lesson.

" . . . that is how Pervorocco won the Red Wars and restored order after years of savage bloodshed. The Neighbor then repaired its State and a lenient attitude was taken toward Magics thereafter . . . "

The maid was trembling so much that the tea set rattled as she placed it on a table. The child had not seen this maid before and suspected she was new. The new house staff—fed with gruesome tales of a silver, wild being—were always the most afraid of her.

"This tea is cold!"

The maid wrung her hands on her apron and tried not to look at the child.

"But I—but I just boiled it, Nan. It's scalding!"

"You must have dawdled on the stairs. Get away and don't make the same mistake in the future."

The maid scurried from the room so hastily that she forgot to lock the door.

"Don't you even think of touching that food! You will miss dinner again for your wickedness."

While Nan fell upon the meal and began tearing into the bread and butter, the child crept slowly past her.

"If you continue to disobey me, then you will starve!"

Nan turned and in that moment, the child ran for the door. Nan was well past middle age and too slow to catch her. As the child dashed away, she was followed by an agonized howl.

Switching between the rambling, grand corridors of the main house and the twisting passages of the servants' quarters, the child expertly snaked her way to the gardens, stopping only to catch her breath before she continued. With the sun beating upon her back, she climbed the zouba tree and slithered down its long vines to the ground on the other side. There she paused, the thrill of the chase beginning to wane.

She was standing on a dusty track between two grand houses. She could see the glistening roof of Rose Herm on her right over the high iron fence and a vulgar mansion on her left, its second story peeking over another iron fence. Ahead was a flat expanse of sapphire and she headed toward it slowly, dragging her feet a little in the dust. With freedom finally in her grasp, she did not know what to do first.

The gentle crash of waves grew louder and she found herself standing on a wide, paved road before the sea. The road was deserted and the air was soft and still. The horizon rippled with heat and each rumple in the water winked silver as it bobbed in the distance. Having been used to the ornamented ponds and delicate fountains of Rose Herm, this expanse of blue amazed her. The child had a sudden urge to touch it.

Crossing the road, she climbed down a sandy slope punctured with craggy boulders and stood at the water's edge. There she watched it for a moment, lapping the ground with foaming lips that sucked the shore. In the distance she could see the shadows of boats and farther along the coast were the famous docks of Sago.

Checking that she was still alone, she pulled off her buckled shoes and rolled up the legs of her trousers. Then, tentatively, she dipped her feet into the balmy water. She giggled as it swelled about her silver ankles and then bent and splashed it with her hands. Discovering that this was fun, she splashed it some more, laughing louder. The droplets glittered in the fierce sunshine and soaked the edges of her shirt.

Suddenly, a carriage thundered past on the road above, startling the child so that she almost toppled into the water. As the hoof beats died away, she remembered the circus. Pulling her shoes back on, she climbed the slope to the road and hurried onward.

As she followed the straight boulevard, the buildings began to inch closer together, their size diminishing and their facades crumbling. The road narrowed and the azure stretch of sea was lost behind a shamble of overbearing houses. An ominous hum replaced the gentle surge of the waves and the paving slabs beneath her shoes became cracked and hard.

At first she walked alone, padding softly on the burning road, but people soon began to appear. They leaned out of windows, shaking out carpets, lay snoring on front steps, and rushed past in rickety carts that creaked and sprayed the air with thick dust. She shrank from them, and suddenly she longed for the grounds of Rose Herm and their safe enclosure. She wanted the smell of hot earth and the squawk of seagulls and the high iron fences to box her in. The circus forgotten, she was filled with the desperate urge to turn back, and she made the mistake of stopping.

A man towing a cart full of soft fruit stumbled into the back of her, cursing loudly and pushing her into the gutter.

"Move over!" he shouted.

She clambered to her feet, her senses overwhelmed with the drench of sweat, animals, and filth.

Catching sight of her, the man yelped.

"Cursed thing! Get away with you, under-realm monster!"

People began to stare. Before, she had passed unnoticed in the blank crowds that hustled and bustled through the tight roads, but now she felt eyes boring into her and widening in disgust and astonishment. All she could see were crumbling houses, hoards of people, and a haze of smut that seemed to float through the clammy air.

"There's no begging on this road!" a voice shouted. "Go to the squares!"

"What is it?"

"Must be from the circus . . . "

"The circus is that way!"

This last remark came from a stout man who stood proudly before a collapsing tumble of bricks and holes. He jerked his thumb in the direction of a road to his left and the child ran.

Roads turned to uneven streets, which became alleyways, growing ever narrower and busier. She found that the faster she ran, the less notice people took of her, and so she sprinted. Everyone was pushing and shoving and rushing, and as she became one of them they left her alone. But she could not keep it up for long; exhausted, she knew that she must stop if only to lessen the excruciating burn of her chest. Her legs began to slow and she paused, clinging to a dirty brick wall.

There were people everywhere—even more than before, although she could scarcely believe that possible. Monstrous constructions of patched brick, wood, and cardboard loomed about her, riddled with tears and soaked with muck. The paving stones of the road had been removed to build huts that bodies huddled in, turning the ground to a foul bog that swallowed feet. The air reeked of hot urine and excrement, and was filled with shouts, screams, and wails. It pressed against her, forcing her down into the churned grime of the rotting ground and she wished that she had not come.

"What's this?"

She jumped and turned to see a family of six kneeling in a circle around a bowl of black water. They watched her with hungry eyes.

Something darted to her side and she saw a child not much older than herself. It was difficult to know whether it was a boy or a girl with the dirt smeared across its face. There were layers of crud dried on its cheeks, hands, and lips that split and flaked off as it moved. She stared at it for a moment, wondering what it wanted from her. Its eyes were rolled skywards and it had a broken sack slung over its shoulder. It pushed its open hand toward her, a grunt issuing from its scabbed lips.

"What . . . what do you want?" she whispered.

The creature stank and lice crawled on its face. It pushed its hands against her harder, its face pleading.

"Spare some sticks!"

A mottled face loomed from the flow of bodies surging down the street and a hunched figure sidled up to her, limbs bent and crooked.

"Spare some sticks!"

The girl cowered against the brick wall, wishing that she had never left the confines of Rose Herm. Bile bit the back of her throat and her legs trembled.

"Spare some sticks! The circus can spare some sticks!"

A toothless, gaunt face bore into hers and a second, slimy hand reached out to her.

"No!" she gasped.

Pushing past them, she plunged back into the crowd and dodged men with greasy omelets and women selling rags. The streets curled left and right and the air grew hotter and the crowds increased. Unable to go on, she paused in a heaving square, bumped and knocked by the flow of bodies rushing past her.

"Spare some sticks!"

They had followed her and multiplied on the journey. A buzz of beggars surrounded her like flies—children and adults and things in between. Hands grasped at her and ragged nails scratched her silvery skin.

"Spare some sticks!"

"My children die for lack of food!"

"Sticks from the circus!"

Terrified tears coursed down the child's face. "I have nothing!" she cried. "No, I have nothing!"

But they would not stop. They tugged at her shirt and pulled at her trousers, trying to pat her pockets for sticks. She never thought that she would ever wish herself back in the nursery with Nan, but just then she would face seasons of abuse to be free of them.

"Get back!" a voice boomed.

With reluctant scratching and scurrying, the beggars moved aside.

A shadow fell over the child and she looked up from where she cowered in a boggy puddle of grime to see a bizarre creature. Its eyes were slanted and its nose pointed like that of the head gardener's dog, but it had the body of a human and a bushy copper tail.

"The circus has been looking for you," it said.

The child blinked at it, unsure. All around them, people stopped to watch and the beggars lingered, still hoping for sticks.

The creature offered her a clawed hand.

"Come, little beauty," it whispered.

It wore a loose, gold tunic of silk and its limbs were abnormally long and lithe.

The child hesitated.

"Spare some sticks!" one beggar started up, then suddenly they were all chattering once more, their hands grasping.

"Spare some sticks!"

"Spare sticks from the circus!"

The creature took a bundle of lead sticks from its pocket and scattered them on the ground. All at once the beggars went grabbing for them, throwing others aside in their haste. While they were distracted, the child hurriedly took the hand of the creature and it picked her up, cradling her in its arms.

"Gold stick?" a beggar cried as they began to move away. "One gold stick?"

"Lead sticks are all I can spare."

The child buried her head into the creature's chest and did not look up again until they had arrived at the circus.

CHAPTER SIX

The Little Beauty

The circus occupied Sago's only pier, its tent encasing all in a dazzling white tunnel. In seasons past, the space would have been shared by several traveling circuses, which crossed into the bordered towns of Pervorocco and then embarked upon the capital. But this year there was only *The Beautiful Spectacular*.

"I think they suspect us."

The troll looked up from his juggling battens at the old man before him. "What makes you say that?" he asked.

"The largest circus ever seen and it happens to be the *only* circus as well. It looks suspicious."

Both the old man and the troll were sitting at the entrance to the circus tent, a mixture of props and baggage gathered around them. In the recesses of the tent, Magic Beings and Magic Bloods were resting or practicing their acts.

"We didn't have trouble crossing the borders," said the troll.

"That was thanks to me."

"Just keep on doing them spells, then."

"It is not so easy. I do not know how much longer I can last . . . the Wild Lands are a long way away yet."

The curtains of the tent parted, letting in a lyan and a slice of hot, muggy air.

"Where've you been?" grunted the troll. "We're not supposed to go out. You heard . . . " he trailed off as he caught sight of a child clinging to the lyan's neck.

"The beggars thought she was one of us and she was being set upon. I could not leave her there," explained the lyan. "Hush, little beauty," he whispered as she whined into his shoulder.

The troll looked for support, but the old man was staring at the floor.

"It's not one of ours and you know we can't take on any more," he muttered.

"Come on, little beauty, come on," soothed the lyan, unlocking the child's arms from around his neck. He set her gently on the ground before him and patted her white hair.

"She must be one of us," he said. "Look at her coloring."

The girl stared into his strange cat eyes and her terror subsided. She felt his hands petting her hair and face, but she did not understand what it meant, for she had not felt a caring touch in a long time.

"Do you not know what she is?" the lyan asked the old man.

But he was wearily rubbing his face, wanting no part in the matter.

The girl watched in awe as the troll flicked juggling batons between his fingers. She had never seen such a being, with shell-like skin and a squat, dense build, except in the pages of a nursery book.

"You truly are a strange beast," the lyan whispered, studying her amethyst eyes. Turning to the old man, he added, "Not many seasons since, you yourself would have been fascinated by such a little beauty as this."

"I have seen enough of Magic Beings to last a lifetime," he muttered.

"Well, perhaps I have seen enough of Magic Bloods to last a lifetime."

The old man's lips twisted in a wry smile, and he tugged at his worn robes.

"Besides, I do not think she is a Magic Being," said the lyan. "Perhaps a Magic Blood? I am not sure—that sort of thing is your specialty."

With a sigh, the old man looked at the child and he froze.

"Asha!"

The lyan glanced at him.

"What did you say?" he asked.

The old man clasped his face and stared at the child.

"Asha," he breathed. "Asha . . . what have you done?"

Suddenly there were footsteps on the planks outside: the steady march of soldiers and the commanding tone of State officials. The circus creatures did not have time to react before the curtains of the tent were pulled roughly aside and the bright sun blazed into its shadowed depths.

"Pa Coo-se-Nutoes here to have a look around," said a tall, slight man with a dark moustache. Behind him stood two soldiers in gray uniforms, and to his side was a large, overbearing lady who, upon seeing the amethyst-eyed child, screamed loudly.

"Ma Dane, do not be alarmed," said Pa Coo-se-Nutoes, thinking her afraid. "These are but Magic Beings. Surely you have been to a circus before? It is just a troll and a lyan."

Ma Dane ignored him. "What are you doing here?" she shrieked at the child who was recoiling against the lyan's legs.

"You know that child?"

"Are you all right, little beauty?" asked the lyan.

"*Little Beauty?*" spat Ma Dane. "How did you get here?" She reeled around to the lyan. "You stole her from me!"

Pa Coo-se-Nutoes looked at the strange child and his face contorted with disgust. She was not looking her best, with shanty slime coating her legs and her shirt ripped.

"This is your child?" he asked Ma Dane.

Ma Dane fought to control herself. Her fan fluttered manically around her face and beads of sweat trickled across her forehead.

"She is my—my ward. She is in my care. Do you not remember my cause some seasons past to take in the beggar children of prostitutes?"

"Vaguely," said Pa Coo-se-Nutoes. "How found you this child?" he asked the lyan as the soldiers behind him put their hands to their sabers.

"She was being set upon by beggars in the Haz shantytown. And you are mistaken, she cannot be the child of a prostitute. She has something altogether—"

"Thank you for saving her!" cried Ma Dane, reaching across and snatching the child to her side. "She runs off and gets lost. I am indebted to you!"

The child whimpered as she felt Ma Dane's nails digging into her silvery skin.

"Asha . . . " whispered the old man, still staring at the child and oblivious to all else.

Ma Dane's blood rushed to her head.

"What do you say?" asked Pa Coo-se-Nutoes. "What is that of which— Wait! I know you, Pa! You are a professor at the University of Magic. I saw a talk of yours while I was traveling in The Neighbor. I believe it was about diversity in Magic Beings in the Eastern Realm and—" he glanced quickly at Ma Dane—"and we have heard some rumors of magical immigrants. May we check this circus, Professor?"

The troll nudged the old man with his boot.

"That is a child of Asha, I know it, for she told me once that—"

"I believe there is nothing for us to check here, Pa Coo-se-Nutoes," said Ma Dane. "It is just a circus like any other. The rumors I have heard were incorrect."

Pa Coo-se-Nutoes noticed the rouge slipping from Ma Dane's face in sweaty rivulets and the deep red of her neck.

"Ma, you look unwell. Is it the heat? I find it is often too stuffy to bear being this far into the city."

Ma Dane looked at the group in turn with wild dark eyes. "You are right, Pa, I am not feeling well. Let us go from here and leave these men to practice their acts."

"You no longer suspect them?"

"I was wrong!"

"Pardon us bursting in on you like this, Professor." Pa Coo-se-Nutoes leaned forward and shook the limp hand of the old man. "We will leave and let you prepare for tonight. My family and I will be watching."

"But Asha—"

"Thank you again for finding my ward!" Ma Dane cried to the lyan before whisking away the child.

The lyan made as if to follow, but the troll pulled him back.

"Good bye, little beauty!"

Outside the tent Ma Dane heard him and her face puckered with revolt.

"Little beauty?" she hissed. "*Beauty?*"

The soldiers followed her, and after a moment Pa Coo-se-Nutoes also appeared.

"So, I take it that you will retract your statement about *The Beautiful Spectacular?*"

"Yes."

"And I may return to State now?"

"Yes."

They were standing in a nicer part of Sago. The houses here were rickety and close, but nothing like the infested huts of the shantytowns.

"Would you like me to take you to Rose Herm?"

Ma Dane nodded.

The party made its way to a carriage nearby that was drawn by two horses the child knew well. They snorted at her as she passed, but she had no time to pet or feed them with Ma Dane dragging her along.

The child had never sat in a carriage before—only cleaned them with Owaine—and the leather seats felt foreign beneath her legs. The journey was strained and quiet, with Ma Dane sitting in a silent, fuming rage, and Pa Coo-se-Nutoes trying to make awkward chitchat.

"So, what is your ward's name?"

Ma Dane glanced down at the child.

"Little Beauty," she said with curled lips.

"Ah . . . unusual. Good day to you, Beauty."

The child hesitated before putting her left hand to her chest.

⁂

The name stuck. The child became Beauty, though for a long time she did not realize that it was said in cruel jest.

When they returned to Rose Herm that day, Ma Dane hauled Beauty through the house screaming, "Beauty? Beauty! Little Beauty!"

She towed Beauty from one side of the mansion to the other, finally flinging them both into her study. She was angry and terrified of what could have been. Maids had left a selection of omelets on a side table and she threw them to the floor in her rage, ruining the fur rug.

"What were you doing there?" she shrieked.

Terrified, Beauty curled into a tight ball on the carpet.

"What did you tell them? How did they know about Asha?"

Beauty began to snivel and cry.

"Answer me!"

Ma Dane stalked across her study to the servants' bell and pulled it so hard that the cord snapped. There was a clanging through the house followed by a long pause, no doubt while the servants pulled straws for who should answer their mistress in this rage.

After a moment the scuffling of feet could be heard and a meek head peered around the door. It was the new maid who had brought Beauty's lunch that morning.

"You rang for me, Ma?"

"Bring me Nan!"

"Right away, Ma."

The maid disappeared and Ma Dane strode across the room, knocking papers off of tables and kicking books. She heard the sobbing of the child and it enraged her further. Marching over to Beauty's side, she yanked her up by her arm and stared into her amethyst eyes.

"So, *Beauty*," she spat. "What grieves you so? You are trouble just as I knew you would be, you are so like—"

Suddenly there was the sound of a wave crashing. The windows of Ma Dane's study were always open and you could usually hear the soft sucking of the sea, but this was different. It instantly took Ma Dane back to seasons past, to a promise that she had made while she stood at twilight on Sago's docks, bidding farewell to a loved one.

The memory took her by surprise and she staggered slightly.

"Asha," she said, one tear escaping her eye. "Asha, why must it be like this?"

Beauty blinked back at her with innocent eyes and bit on her thumb.

Ma Dane gently let her go.

"It is hard for me," she said, reaching out a tentative hand and slowly brushing a lock of white hair from Beauty's eyes.

The door opened and Nan entered, her shriveled face set in a hard expression.

"You rang for me, Ma."

"I wish to dismiss you."

Nan's mouth dropped open.

"I charged you to look after my ward, and you have not fulfilled your duty."

"No one can tame that fallen creature! It bewitches me!"

Ma Dane's vast chest puffed up to double its size. "Be wary of what you suggest," she growled. "This child is not a Magic Blood."

"No . . ."

Ma Dane looked visibly relieved, as if she had actually feared saying those words.

"But she is evil all the same! I will hand in my notice, for I cannot look after such a damned creature."

"Leave—it is all the same to me."

Nan glared at Beauty, her sharp pupils needling into the clear violet of her eyes.

"You are damned," she whispered, and she swept herself from the room, never to be seen by the girl again—except in the fetid darkness of her nightmares.

Chapter Seven

The Child with Amethyst Eyes

S o Beauty became Beauty and her life dramatically changed.

In her study that day, Ma Dane realized that she could no longer pretend that Asha's child did not exist. Shutting her away did not fulfill her promise, and she had a new sense that it might be dangerous to avoid her duty. The professor had recognized something in the child and Ma Dane was wary.

Nan left that evening, muttering curses to the family—although Pa Hamish paid her highly to ensure that she kept her time at Rose Herm to herself—and Ma Dane introduced Beauty to the rest of the Herm-se-Hollis family over dinner. Pa Hamish coughed and looked the other way as Beauty entered, hoping that the thing would disappear back to wherever it came from soon. Eli was far more interested in her. He was now in his thirty-third season and spoiled to the point of no return.

"It is true what the servants say then!" he exclaimed after Ma Dane had stiffly introduced Beauty as her ward.

He stared at her long and hard. "We can play together," he said decisively.

"You shall not play together," grunted Pa Hamish.

"We shall!"

A silence ensued, and Beauty's legs trembled.

Ma Dane called for a maid and instructed that Beauty be bathed and put to bed. "Brush out the knots in her hair," she added. "Be gentle, for she has had a difficult day."

The maid glanced at the silvery being in horror.

"*Do it*," Ma Dane added.

The maid pressed her left hand to her chest and did as she was ordered.

In the days and seasons that followed, Beauty lived a dual existence. Sometimes tolerated by Ma Dane, sometimes detested by her, and sometimes ignored—but never loved. Riddled with guilt, Ma Dane would occasionally send presents of sweetmeats to Beauty's room, only to cast her from the dinner table later that evening. She did not want Beauty to have to wear her son's old clothes anymore, but neither did she want her to have the formal, lavish dresses of a young lady. Instead, Beauty wore plain peasant clothing of expensive cloth. She was given the smallest grand room in the mansion and told that she should make herself useful rather than have lessons. As a result, Beauty spent most of her time in the stables.

Having met Beauty in the carriage that day, Pa Coo-se-Nutoes promptly told the rest of Sago high society about the strange girl and gossip spread, fogging drawing rooms all over the city with its scandalous news. Keen to avoid all the rumors, Ma Dane decided to introduce Beauty openly. In the weeks following Nan's dismissal, curious families arrived at Rose Herm in droves, and after they were seated and sipping syrupy tea, Beauty would be marched down to stand before them.

"Her skin is just as lustrous as Peony said!"

"Yes, she is of a curious coloring."

"You are so good to look after her, Ma Dane."

"Quite an angel."

While they stared and talked of her, Beauty would stand quietly, her eyes downcast and her cheeks flushed. It felt so very strange to be standing before these people who she had once peeked at from various hiding places.

One time, a fat State Leader ogled her silently for five long minutes before breaking out in a snort of laughter, "Oh, Beauty? I get it!"

The truth was that Beauty did not look as strange as she once had. Her shiny skin and white hair were still as bizarre as ever, but they did not seem threatening anymore. Looking upon her, humans no longer felt that she might suddenly attack.

"Is she some kind of Magic Being?" a gentleman asked at one particular soiree once Beauty had been called into the room.

Pa Hamish, as usual, did not like to deal with questions about the strange child. He had some sense that his wife was not telling the whole truth about her, but he did not care to be enlightened. Ignorance was bliss.

"Ma Dane . . . this gentleman . . . " he motioned to his wife and the gentleman repeated his question.

"I only ask because collectors in The Neighbor would be very interested," he added. "They are trying to document new species at the University of Magic."

Ma Dane gave a high, trilled laugh.

"I can assure you that there is nothing Magic about this child. She is human through and through."

"Magic Blood, then?"

"Certainly not, Pa! You think that I would allow that in my house? I'm afraid to say that she is the child of a common prostitute."

And that always appeared to settle matters.

Circumstances had changed greatly for Beauty and it was some time before she was able to adjust to her new life. At first she lived in fear of Nan returning and the formidable punishment that would ensue, but as her purple bruises faded, she began to find strength. Her new life did not demand her to sneak and hide and escape. In fact, she was almost afraid of the freedom that she now commanded. She soon realized that Ma Dane wished nothing more of her than that she would stay quiet and out of the way, so she lived by these unsaid rules. When she was called upon she came, but otherwise she could be found with Owaine in the stables.

"May I groom Comrade?" Beauty asked one autumn afternoon.

It was the rainy season and outside thick, fat droplets were drumming against the roof.

Owaine glanced up from a stall he was cleaning, pushing a damp strand of his gray hair from his eyes. Unlike the middle-aged men of Sago, he kept his hair long in the Hillands custom.

"All right, then," he said, though Comrade had already been groomed by one of the lads that morning. Beauty had been talking lately and he wished to encourage her. Besides, Comrade was her favorite.

With a wide smile, Beauty slid the bolt of the black stallion's half door and led him out. Though she had grown recently, Beauty only reached the horse's belly in height.

"How old're yur now?"

"Twenty-six seasons."

She found her stool in the store cupboard and took a body brush from the pile.

"Where were yur this morn?"

Climbing onto the stool, she began strong, long strokes across Comrade's flank, delighted as he bent his head and tried to lip her elbow in response. He always went soft on anyone that petted him, but he became as sweet as a lap dog whenever Beauty was around.

"The Coo-se-Nutoes were visiting and they wanted to see me."

Peony and Bow were entranced by Beauty. She was disappointed now that she had ever thought so highly of them. They treated her like a spectacle, begging Ma Dane to command her to the drawing room and then asking her pointless questions for hours on end, thinking her answers quite hilarious.

"Hmm," grunted Owaine. "Yur not some circus performer."

Beauty started at his words, thoughts of *The Beautiful Spectacular* flooding her mind. It was two seasons since she had escaped Rose Herm's iron fence, but she had not forgotten the lyan, the troll, or the Sago slums. At night she was troubled by odd dreams about them.

"All right?"

She looked up to see Owaine gazing at her with concern.

She nodded, but the back of her neck was suddenly slick with sweat.

Keeping an eye on her, Owaine went back to raking straw and he began to sing one of her favorite Hilland songs:

Hills of Magic,
Lakes of Gold,
Keep your truths and secrets untold.

His lilting voice echoed around the wooden stable, soothing the horses and enchanting the air. Beauty found her nerves calming and she began to hum along:

When the realm,
Was fresh and young,
Spells and myths were born and sung.

In the hills,
Where they belong,
The wind will sing them seasons long.

She found her brush moving to the beat of the words, and as the song petered to an end she switched to a currycomb and began working on Comrade's tail. By this time, the stallion was standing with his nose resting on the ground and his eyes closed, completely relaxed.

"I'm taking the horses to town to buy feed. Should yur like to come?"

Beauty thought of the slime and the lice and the beggars and shook her head. She had been happy to retreat to the safety of Rose Herm's ornamented grounds and she did not wish to leave them again. She had not forgotten what lay out there.

Sensing her tension, Comrade snorted.

"I should a' thought yur might be getting bored."

Owaine watched her closely. He was vaguely aware of what had happened the day Ma Dane burst into the mansion, dragging Beauty behind her. The kitchens had been rife with gossip that evening as one maid complained of how she had been instructed to bathe and look after the silver thing. She spoke of how it had snapped at her fingers and spoken in tongue, at which point Owaine shouted at them all not to tell such lies. As he had stomped out, he had heard them all furiously whisper behind him. It had not gone unnoticed that he spent a lot of time with the silver being.

"Are yur happy?" he pressed.

The child looked confused.

"I should like to learn to ride," she said after a pause.

He laughed. "Yur so good around them horses that I forgets yur can't ride. I'll teach yur, but yur'll need to ask the Ma."

Beauty nodded. She suspected that if she chose the right time, Ma Dane would not object. It was always better to ask her questions after dinner, when Ma Dane was feeling her most placid.

"Yur get taught books by that teacher that comes in for Master Eli?"

Beauty shook her head.

"Well, maybe I teaches yur to ride and yur can be a stable hand like me?"

She blinked at him. She had never considered her future.

"I do not know what will become of me," she whispered.

Owaine said nothing for he did not know what would become of her, either.

CHAPTER EIGHT

The Incident with Eli

As the seasons passed, Beauty grew restless. She became tired of Ma Dane's flitting attitudes, which could have her seated on the veranda with the Herm-se-Hollis family in the morning, but banished to her room for dinner. She was tired of Pa Hamish ignoring her from across the table and sick of entering the drawing room on visitor's whims.

The servants barely said a word to her, serving her at the table with pursed lips and passing her in the corridors with their eyes fixed on the carpets. Her own dress-maid treated her like a dumb animal, and she could pass days speaking to no one but Owaine. Beauty was increasingly tempted to be troublesome. In the same way that she had fought Nan to bring life to her dismal existence, she began to rebel against Rose Herm.

She moved around her hairbrushes to confuse her dress-maid and left boots by the door that would trip Pa Hamish up as he hurried to his gentlemen's club. She tested Ma Dane's temper as frequently as possible: purposely clanging silverware as she ate, wearing her hair free instead of pinning it up, and—worst of all—staring straight back at the visitors who called her down to the drawing room.

"She looks . . . she looks fierce today," said Peony one morning when the Coo-se-Nutoes ladies came for syrupy tea.

"Yes, different," agreed Bow.

They glanced warily at the violet eyes that bore into them. Once Beauty had looked meekly at the floor as they surveyed her; now she locked them with a bright, challenging stare.

"Ha, not at all!" cried Ma Dane. "She is just a little . . . stubborn, like any child."

Beauty paid highly for her impertinence later.

"How dare you act so!" Ma Dane boomed at dinner. A glass flew through the air and narrowly missed Beauty's head.

Beauty drew herself up and took a deep breath. "I will not be looked at anymore."

"Get out! Get out!"

Ma Dane was still screeching long after Beauty had left the room. As her temper finally began to cool, Ma Dane growled, "Just like Asha," clenching her fingers into fists under the table.

Beauty spent the rest of that evening and the next day cooped up in her room, but she was not called down to the drawing room again.

Beauty despised her lowly status at Rose Herm, but there was one person who she would rather see even less of. Eli watched her constantly with undisguised fascination. He had been forbidden to play with her, which made her all the more intriguing to him. So he lurked and lingered whenever she was about.

In the house she found him following her from room to room, never speaking and always appearing to be looking the other way at some painting or ornament. In the gardens Beauty would be splashing in a fountain, only to feel a presence suddenly near and turn to see him whittling a stick or catching a frog. Where Eli was concerned, she would have preferred to be ignored.

"Mayhap yur could play with Master Eli?"

It was a clammy summer's afternoon and Beauty was sitting astride Comrade, her thin, silver legs squeezing his ebony sides. For three seasons, Owaine had diligently been teaching her to ride and today Eli had disturbed their solitary lesson, wandering onto their practice lawn to swipe the air with his saber.

"I am not allowed to play with him."

"Seems he don't care."

"I care. I wish he would leave me be."

They both looked at the boy who was surprisingly fine despite his parentage. Even at thirty-five seasons he had strong, square shoulders and a broad chest. He was as tall as his father, without Pa Hamish's awkwardness, and his brown eyes held the same intensity as Ma Dane's, but they were larger and softer.

"He bother yur often?"

"If he is not at lessons or with friends then he is somehow near me."

"Beauty, he wants to be yur friend."

Owaine had finally adopted her name, but she knew that from his lips it was not an intended insult.

"I do not think so," she said, and they did not mention it again.

<hr>

When Ma Dane caught her son near her ward it was always Beauty's fault.

"How many times have I told you?" she would hiss, dragging Beauty from the room and pushing her down the corridor.

Beauty would find another quiet lounge in the mansion and settle down, but a few hours later Eli would be near again.

"What do you want?" she had cried once.

But Eli carried on counting the tassels on the curtain and did not reply.

In fact, he did not speak directly to her until one warm winter's night when she awoke to the sound of a scream.

Her room was at the end of the guest quarters, far from the family apartments and the servants' rooms, but still she had heard the scream. It seemed to vibrate through the darkness, jostling her body so that splashes of color burst across her vision. She slid from the bed and stumbled to the door, her head foggy and her skin sticky with sweat. Staggering into the corridor, she blinked in the harsh light of the oil lamps that were kept burning all night.

Another scream sounded, this one ending in a low groan of pain.

She ran along the corridors, following the sound and knocking into walls as she passed, her vision still lilting before her eyes. To her surprise, there was no one else about.

She came to Ma Dane's suite, which she had not ventured into since her younger years, when she would escape the nursery and prowl the corridors. Surprising herself, she lurched into the lounge without stopping, running farther into the bedchamber. There she saw Ma Dane's inflated mahogany bed and Eli lying upon it in a hot sweat with sheets twisted wildly about his limbs.

"There is a war!" he cried. "There is a war!"

Ma Dane ran in from an adjoining room, a jug of water in her hands. Out of her huge jeweled gowns she looked vulnerable and tired. She almost fell when she caught sight of Beauty.

"What are you—"

"I heard screams."

Eli sat up in bed, his eyes the filmy blankness of a dreamer.

"I cannot do it! I will not fight!" he gasped.

Ma Dane ran to his side and splattered his head with the water.

"Get away from here!" she hissed over her shoulder at Beauty.

Eli's body bowed and quaked. Suddenly, he cried out loudly and snapped to life, looking about the room with terrified eyes. He saw Beauty and whispered, "You cannot say no."

"What do you mean?" she whispered.

"You cannot say no, for there is no choice," he replied. "You will come with me."

"I said get away from here!" Ma Dane spat.

Beauty scurried from the room, but lurked in the shadows by the door.

"Mother, was that Beauty?" Eli whimpered.

"She is gone now, my sweet."

"I saw her again. I saw death and fire and—"

"Do as I have always taught you."

Beauty peeked around the doorframe to see Eli squeeze his eyes shut, clench his jaw, and clutch at the bed sheets.

"It hurts!"

"You must do it, Eli. I had to."

<hr>

The next morning, as she sat beneath a zouba tree in the gardens, Beauty saw four small figures marching toward her. Eli was leading the group, and behind him trailed Pernet Shap-se-George and her twin brothers, Nez and Gilly. As Beauty scrambled to her feet, she wondered what they were doing so far from the house. Eli usually played on the veranda by the back windows where Ma Dane could watch him.

"There she is!" he cried.

Nez and Gilly ran over to her, then stopped short.

"We've seen it before! Why have you brought us all this way?"

"I wanted to see it again," snapped Pernet. "I heard Mother say that it spoke last time she came and I never heard it speak before."

Pernet straightened out her frilled skirts, patting their fine beading and woven ribbons. Beauty looked down at her own plain brown smock.

"She does not always speak," warned Eli, sidling closer to Beauty than he had ever dared to venture before. "Most of the time she just talks to the smelly horseman."

"Make it speak now," said Pernet, tossing her dark hair.

"I command you to speak."

Beauty clenched her teeth.

"This is boring! Can we play a game?"

"I want her to speak!" snapped Pernet.

Eli glanced at his divided audience.

"We can play a game with Beauty."

"A speaking game?"

"Exactly."

"Magic Cleansing!" squealed Nez and Gilly. "We have to play Magic Cleansing."

Beauty picked up her picture book and turned to leave.

"What's that?" said Pernet, snatching it from her hands. "This is for babies! It's a nursery book. There are no words!" She flipped to an illustration of a troll.

"You have to play with us," said Eli. "I command it."

"I will not."

"She spoke!"

"Sounds just like a normal person," retorted Nez. "Let's play Magic Cleansing. She's boring."

"Give me back my book."

"Actually it's my book," said Eli with a satisfied smile. "And I'll give it back to you if you play with us."

"No!"

"Then no book."

"Hurry up, I want to play *now*," insisted Gilly. "I'll be Pa Coo-se-Nutoes and Eli can be that other State Leader. The rest of you are Magic Bloods and Magic Beings."

He grabbed a nearby branch and waved it in the air.

"No," said Eli. "We have to be State Leaders from The Neighbor. There is no Magical Cleansing here."

"There's gonna be, my father says so."

"Be any kind of State Leader," sighed Pernet. "It does not matter." She looked down at the book in her hands. "I will be one of them," she said, pointing at a sprite.

"Get back, scum!" screamed Gilly, running at her with the stick. "And you!" he cried, turning on Beauty.

"I am not playing. Give me back my book."

"You are an evil being! A wicked under-realm monster!"

Beauty yanked the branch from his hands and swung it around, smacking him hard across the head. Gilly stood dazed for a moment before breaking into a loud cry.

The other children gasped.

"It hurts!" he sobbed, fat tears dribbling down his face, and he ran yelling back to the mansion.

Pernet and Nez glanced at each other before running after him, Pernet dropping the nursery book on the ground as she fled.

"We had better go too," said Eli.

Beauty stormed past him, refusing to speak. As the two of them approached the mansion, they could see a fussing party of people waiting. Gilly was bawling into Ma Shap-se-George's skirts, Pernet and Nez were denying all responsibility, and Ma Dane was standing with her hands planted on her hips, her face a purple contortion of rage.

"You!" she roared.

Beauty gulped, trying to ignore her buckling knees.

"It was me, Mother. I did it."

Ma Dane looked at her son in astonishment.

"I just wanted to play a game. I did not mean to hurt anyone."

The children exchanged fervent glances.

"I am sorry," Eli added.

Ma Dane's gaze slid to Beauty and she stared at her long and hard for a moment.

"Go to your room," she muttered before turning back to her son. "As for you, Master, I believe that I should take away your saber . . . "

As Beauty walked toward the house, she could feel a pair of eyes watching her, but she would not turn and look back at him.

After that, she stayed away from Eli more than ever.

CHAPTER NINE

The Threat in Sago

When Eli reached his fortieth season, Ma Dane announced that Rose Herm would hold a ball.

"You may invite all your friends, my sweet," she said over dinner one evening.

As the maids cleared away the soup bowls and brought in the second course of fruit bread, Ma Dane described the plush, ritzy affair she was planning.

"Are you sure that this is wise?" asked Pa Hamish, in an unusual bout of clear thinking. "Talk has been different in the club of late. People are shaken by the Magical Cleansing in The Neighbor and—"

"What does that have to do with my son's fortieth season?"

Pa Hamish looked back at his plate.

"You will want the Shap-se-Georges there, of course," Ma Dane continued. "For I know how you like that girl Pernet."

"I think her rather stupid."

"Hush, Eli! You do not!"

"The dark haired girl with the silly father?" grunted Pa Hamish

"Pa Shap-se-George is running for a State Leadership next season, and I have heard that he is favored."

Pa Hamish pulled a face.

"Mother, I should like to invite Beauty."

Ma Dane dropped her knife and the maid carrying out the dishes stumbled.

"What . . . what ever made you think that she would not be there?"

"She has never been to a ball with us before."

Ma Dane took a large swig of wine. "This is different. We will be holding it at Rose Herm so she will be present whether she likes it or not."

Beauty staunchly avoided Eli's gaze.

"But—"

"Eat up your bread, Eli. A boy in his fortieth season must be big and strong."

Later that evening, Beauty was sitting in bed humming Hillands songs and plaiting her white hair when there was a rap at the door.

"Come in," she called, wondering if her dress-maid had forgotten something.

Ma Dane entered with a sweep of her bejeweled dressing gown and glanced about the room. It was the barest that she could find without casting the child to the servants quarters.

"I have come to speak to you about the ball."

Seeing the child in her white nightshirt, Ma Dane could not help but think that she was gaining ethereal beauty as she aged. Her hair shimmered in the lamplight and her violet eyes were warmed to a deep indigo.

"I wish you to be on your best behavior."

Beauty stared at her.

"The ball is a moon-cycle from now, and you will have a dress made specially for the occasion."

Ma Dane stepped forward suddenly and brushed a strand of hair back from Beauty's face. The child shuddered and Ma Dane snatched her hand away, wondering what had come over her.

"I want no trouble."

Ma Dane turned as if to leave, but stopped abruptly and licked her thin lips.

"Beauty . . . do you dream?"

Beauty's chest fluttered.

"Sometimes."

"Have you ever dreamt something that came true?"

She shook her head and Ma Dane looked as though she wished that she had never asked.

"Very well."

<hr />

Beauty had a dress made for the ball, as Ma Dane promised, and she thought it very fine until the other girls entered with gowns of velvet, silk, and gauze hung with fat rubies and diamonds that they could scarcely carry on their dainty, slippered feet. In comparison, Beauty's white cotton dress and purple sash did not appear quite so dazzling.

Unlike these girls from prominent families, Beauty was not introduced at the top of the staircase to descend to the ballroom floor with a flurry of applause. Instead, as the guests began to arrive at the mansion in carriages, her dress-maid guided her to a side door and left her to enter alone.

No one flinched as she appeared. By now, she was well known in Sago high society and of little interest. The curious pet that evening was a tame moorey, captured from the edges of the Wild Lands by a famous explorer who touted it about the ballroom all evening on a chain.

Beauty wandered across the mosaic floor, weaving between gaggles of rich women in yards of embroidered, beaded, silken, shimmering skirts. The men were in the libraries, waiting until the dancing began, and while they were away, the women took the opportunity to assess each other's outfits.

"Have you seen Ma Dane's gown?" Beauty heard someone whisper as she paused beside a fountain.

"I do not need to see it! That pink taffeta is as stiff as a board. I would not be surprised if they could hear her rustling in the shantytowns."

They laughed.

"Yes, it is a good deal grander and uglier than her last."

"And that amulet again. Pa House of Rose may have been a House, but he was a gambler and a lout all the same. Does she think we do not remember?"

Beauty glanced over her shoulder to see Ma House of Glass, her own amulet nestled proudly on her bosom. She had met her in the drawing room a few times, and it was clear that neither she nor Ma Dane liked each other.

"The desperate must cling to something. After helping Pa Coose-Nutoes to Leadership, she has fallen out of his favor."

"Yes, perhaps she wishes to remind him of her *heritage*."

Another lady joined them and they began discussing the latest fashion for high, boned collars instead, so Beauty moved on.

After a dozen more stricken girls had trodden the staircase to be limply greeted by Eli below, Ma Dane called the men in and the orchestra started up. Dancing began at the far end of the ballroom and food was brought out on heaped platters. Servants came to open the long windows that ran the length of the ballroom and were already steamed with the heat of the crowds. The warm night's air did little to alleviate anyone.

As Beauty ambled about the room, drinking in the sights of her first ball, she noticed Eli standing alone. His forehead glistened with sweat and he looked uncomfortable in his grand, frilled clothes. Pernet Shap-se-George was lingering by his side in a pretty gown, but he took little notice of her. His eyes met Beauty's. He stepped forward, as if to make his way toward her, but a throng of people swept past on their way to the food tables and Beauty slipped away. She did not wish to be near him.

As the evening wore on, the air inside the ballroom grew hotter. Ladies fervently fanned themselves and couples dribbled onto the moonlit veranda, tugging at their heavy clothes. For the first time, Beauty was glad that her dress was so light.

The dancing stopped and the orchestra played a soft melody to accompany the loud chatter that had broken out. Groups stood in wide circles, tumblers trembling in their hands as they gossiped and discussed politics.

"Well, we should stop trading with them!" a shout echoed about the ballroom and caught the attention of most of the guests.

Beauty peered around bodies to the largest of the groups in the middle of the ballroom, where Ma Dane was nodding her head vigorously.

"And what gives you the right to make such statements?" said Pa Coo-se-Nutoes, exchanging glances with a fat State Leader next to him.

"The Neighbor has been building its Magical defense for seasons," replied Ma Dane. "Do the rebels not think that they will rise up? This Magic Cleansing is only infuriating the Magic Bloods and Magic Beings. They will triumph in the end, and then where will we be? We cannot afford to take the rebels' side!"

Pa Coo-se-Nutoes smoothed his dark moustache. "What makes you so sure that the rebels will not win? They have taken the capital and its surrounding cities. They are driving out the Magical beasts."

"This is just like the Red Wars! The Magics won then, and they will win now. We cannot afford to get involved again."

There was an audible intake of breath among the onlookers.

"If I remember correctly, you wished us to side with the rebels," said Pa Coo-se-Nutoes in a low voice. "It seems you have changed your mind rather quickly!"

"It was right then, but now—"

"I think you are nothing more than a Magic sympathizer!"

The women around Beauty gasped.

"How dare you!"

"Just look at the Magic thing you house." Pa Coo-se-Nutoes pointed across the ballroom and Beauty felt all eyes turn to her. In the sea of faces, she saw Peony and Bow, their expressions hard.

"My ward? She is not Magic! She is—"

"I have always been suspicious." Pa Coo-se-Nutoes leaned toward Ma Dane's red, damp face. "I remember the circus," he whispered.

Ma Dane visibly trembled.

"I think that I should like to dance with my husband," said Ma Usa Coo-se-Nutoes, appearing from the crowd. She had not forgotten how Pa Coo-se-Nutoes had forged a place in State and it did not do to make enemies of one of the largest, richest families in Sago. Not yet.

"Yes!" cried Ma Dane. "More dancing!"

She signaled to the orchestra and they began to play a boisterous tune.

"Mark my words, the rebels will be here soon," said Pa Coo-se-Nutoes. "They are stronger than you think."

Couples flooded to the end of the room, anxious to dance away such thoughts.

That night, Beauty dreamt of fire, swords, and death.

CHAPTER TEN

The Danger

Three seasons later, the rebels marched into the Border Cities of Pervorocco. News of it rippled to Sago in hysterical waves. It was said that the rebels came in the night, towing canons and brandishing sabers and rifles. They called for Magical Cleansing and took all of the Magic Beings and Magic Bloods they could find and gathered them in pens like cattle. It is not known what happened to them after that. Some reports said that they were tortured; others that they were killed immediately. Either way, they were never seen or heard of again.

In Sago, the shantytowns rioted. Anyone suspected of Magic was hauled into the streets and beaten and kicked. Those that had not already fled to the Wild Lands now left in droves. People were surprised to find friends and families disappear overnight—there were more Magics in Pervorocco than anyone had initially thought.

The State Leaders gathered for emergency meetings to feverishly discuss what should be done. The rebels wanted alliance and if Pervorocco refused, they would invade. They had taken the whole of

The Neighbor by force, and all were uncertain whether Pervorocco could withstand their guerrilla warfare. They had already barricaded most of the Border Cities, driving the residents from their homes and leaving bodies in the streets. Their only demand was an end to Magic.

The Herm-se-Hollis dining table conversation was strained in these days. Pa Hamish and Ma Dane barely spoke, their fear tangible. Pa Hamish had often suspected his wife of Magic but he had always pushed such troublesome thoughts to the back of his mind. However, he could no longer ignore the impending threat.

"Should we leave?" he said one afternoon as the family sat quietly in one of the mansion's lounges.

There were few guests visiting these days and Beauty was permitted to spend more time with the family, though she would rather be in the stables with Owaine. Ma Dane made her sew handkerchiefs since she did not like to see her sitting and staring into the distance.

"Leave?" whispered Ma Dane, smoothing down her baggy dress. Since news of the rebels hit Sago, she had been deflating at an alarming rate.

"We could shut up the house and stay in the Forest Villages for a while. It would only be until things have blown over," Pa Hamish said.

Eli looked up from his book.

"I will not be driven out," hissed Ma Dane. "We have nothing to hide."

Her eyes fell on Beauty and she quickly looked away.

The following morning, the State announced that Pervorocco's Magical Cleansing would begin in the next moon-cycle.

Beauty was with Owaine at the time, tending to a skittish colt by the barn. They had just managed to calm it when a stable lad ran toward them.

"Owaine, have you heard the news?"

"What news?"

Beauty tried to steady the bucking colt, whispering soothing words as she had seen Owaine do.

"State has announced Magical Cleansing," said the stable lad. "Anyone that needs to should leave the city now."

Owaine's brow furrowed.

"Thank yur, boy. But yur should go back to cleaning stalls."

The stable lad slouched off.

"What is the matter?" Beauty asked.

Owaine stared at the ground, and the colt, sensing his unease, bucked even more.

"I feel I should go home."

"Leave?"

"Yes. I never meant to stay, and if this is the way that Sago is turning, I should be in my hills. I worry for my daughter."

"Please . . . please do not go."

Beauty's purple eyes begged and her lips trembled.

"Hush my child, yur shall see how things go."

———⊗⊗⊗———

Over the next few days, Rose Herm was filled with an aching silence. Dread clogged the air and no visitors came, not even Eli's teacher. The members of the house heard that there were more riots in the streets of Sago—as well as petitions and marches. People were indignant, frightened, and angry. But the State would not change its mind. One evening, a Leader was attacked while leaving the Chambers and his body was paraded through the squares. The next day, State officials were sent out into the streets to batter and slay anyone who stood in their way.

And the Magical Cleansing loomed closer. The State sent out leaflets asking citizens to give the names of those they suspected to be Magics, and it released a statement informing all that the State would send out Magical Hunters to seek those that tried to hide. There would be no escape.

The evening this news broke, Beauty's dress-maid led her to Ma Dane's office. Entering, Beauty was shocked to see Owaine standing uncomfortably on a fur rug, his hands deep in the pockets of his trousers. There were boxes everywhere and Ma Dane was rushing about the room, her loose dress sliding from her gaunt shoulders. When she saw Beauty, she stopped short.

"You are sure?" she asked Owaine.

"My hills are almost a separate country in themselves, Ma. The rebels won't go there. What would they want with hill folk?"

Ma Dane nodded, but her fingers trembled.

"We, too, are leaving," she said. "So when you take her, you will not be able to bring her back."

"That's fine, Ma."

"She is dangerous."

Owaine turned to look at Beauty and he shook his head.

"She isn't, Ma."

"Her looks raise suspicion."

"Everyone in the hills is suspicious."

Ma Dane swallowed.

"I will give you sticks."

"I have saved enough." Owaine turned to Beauty. "Are yur happy to come with me to the Hillands, child? It's a long journey."

Beauty scarcely dared to believe what she was hearing.

"Yes," she whispered.

"Yur'll become my daughter. Are you happy with that?"

"Yes . . . *yes*."

Owaine smiled.

"She is more than she seems," said Ma Dane, but he was not listening.

"I want to take Comrade," said Beauty.

Ma Dane glanced at Beauty and she felt the bonds of a promise breaking.

"Pa Hamish's riding horse? You may take him if you wish."

Owaine did not have the heart to say that such a fine animal would be no use on the journey or in the Hillands. Beauty loved that horse and it would hurt her to leave it.

"You must go and pack now," Ma Dane added in a voice that was breaking, "for the Magic Cleansing begins tomorrow and you must be out of Sago. We all must go."

Owaine pressed his left hand to his chest and told Beauty that he would meet her by the stables once she had gathered her things.

A tense silence followed his exit from the room. Finally, Ma Dane turned to her ward.

"Beauty, I have something of yours that you must take with you."

Ma Dane took a golden amulet from her desk and it caught the edge of a book, making a loud *chink* that vibrated around the room. Carefully, she carried it to the girl as though it pained her to hold it.

"The House of Rose?"

"Yes."

Beauty touched the engraved rose and felt her fingertips crackle. Ma Dane placed the red sash around her neck and the amulet dropped to her chest, thumping against her beating heart.

"But what—"

"It was your mother's . . . my sister's, and it arrived with you when you came here. I will give Eli my amulet when I die. Do you understand?"

Beauty's eyes widened. She had always believed that she came from a paupers' hospital, the child of a fallen woman, as Ma Dane told everyone.

"You lied to me about my birth!"

"There is no time for that—"

"I am a House of Rose! I am your kin!"

"No, you are the daughter of a Hillander now."

Beauty's eyes flashed. "Who is my father? Where did I come from?"

"That, I do not know."

"More lies!" she screamed.

Ma Dane took her by the shoulders and shook her hard. "There is no time now. But you must answer me this, for it is important. What do you dream, Beauty?"

Beauty hesitated.

"Do your dreams come true?"

"No."

Ma Dane held her for one moment longer.

"Then you are lucky," she whispered, turning away. "You must get ready to leave now. You most likely will not see me again."

Beauty glared at her, seasons of abuse spurring her bitter anger.

"Why did you treat me so?" she cried, tears prickling her eyes. "Why did I have to suffer?"

Ma Dane paused, her face flushing.

"I was protecting you," she said. "I was protecting all of us. You do not know what you are—"

"You are cruel! You are evil!"

"No! You do not understand . . . but you must leave now. You are not my responsibility anymore."

Ma Dane went back to packing her books and Beauty wiped away a stray tear with her fist.

"You will die!" she screamed. "For I have dreamt it!"

Ma Dane gasped as Beauty fled the room.

Part Two

A girl stood on the docks of Sago at twilight in the balmy heat. Her dress was plain and old fashioned, but she held her chin high, as if she were a true lady with great riches.

Sailors passed, offering her winks and whistles, but she stoutly ignored them. The general bustle of the city was beginning to ebb at this time of evening, and all were flowing into the squares to savor the very best that Sago's nightlife had to offer. Cargo ships were tethered and stocks were locked away. The tide was in and the water was high. The girl stood amongst it all alone, waiting.

A smoldering dash of amber ripped the horizon against the oncoming darkness and the sea glinted in the fading light. It was muggy and warm and the water slapped sleepily against the docks, beating a dull rhythm. The girl touched an amulet around her neck out of habit, feeling the hard undulations of the engraved rose at its center.

"Dane!"

She turned to see her elder sister, Asha, running toward her, skirts tangled around her ankles. Asha wore the tattiest and oldest of their shared dresses but never seemed to care.

"Where have you been? Mother is worried."

Asha waved away her suspicions and stopped to catch her breath.

"Mother knows where I have been."

Dane's eyes darkened.

"Asha, you did not mean what you said last night—you cannot leave!"

"I cannot learn any more here."

"But what will happen—"

"Mother knows and she gives me her blessing."

The sea rippled and waves crashed against the docks in bursts of white froth.

"Dane, why must you fight it? Why did you stop your lessons? It can be more than dreams, visions, and premonitions. I have learned spells and I can—"

"I do not wish to hear what you can do."

The waves crashed louder and water splashed onto the edges of the docks. Seagulls squealed and squawked and in the distance the temple bells pealed.

"Come with me. Do you not get tired of holding it in, Dane? Does it not drain you?"

"I can control it and no one need ever know."

"You sound just like Father and look what happened to him."

Dane shoved her sister hard. "Do not speak like that! How dare you leave us—what will everyone say?"

Asha looked at the ground. "No one will remember me," she whispered. "I can do that, you see."

"But Mother—"

"I have told her what I will do and she has accepted. It is the only way."

Dane's brown eyes glistened with tears.

"Even . . . even me, Asha?"

"No, you must never forget. I dreamt that seasons from now I will have a child—an important child—and you must look after her for me."

She paused and touched the amulet around her own neck. It had been given to her when their father died. Dane had received hers when their great-aunt passed away and left no heir.

"The baby will come with this."

Dane gasped.

"But that does not necessarily mean—" Asha paused.

"So, this will be the last time that I ever see you?"

"Perhaps."

The sisters looked at one another as the last rays of light disappeared over the horizon.

"Promise me that you will care for my child."

The waves crashed.

"Promise!"

"Yes. I promise."

CHAPTER ELEVEN

The Journey

On a warm Sago evening, Beauty followed Owaine out of the city. All that she owned in the realm could fit into a small saddlebag and she had packed it before Owaine had even readied the horses. As they went on their way, he gave her a thick cloak to cover her white hair, which made her sweat in the heat, and a pair of large gloves.

"We don't want no trouble leaving and they'll be useful on the journey," he said, hoisting her into Comrade's saddle. "We're going somewhere that ain't so hot."

Beauty did not need to bid farewells, but as they rode through the iron gates of Rose Herm, she looked over her shoulder. In a far window of the mansion, she thought she saw a figure watching, his eyes following her as she disappeared. But when the house slipped away, she felt nothing.

The streets of Sago were dangerous in the current turmoil and would be worse still at night. Beauty remembered her last trip into the shantytowns, and her hands trembled as they held the reins.

Comrade tossed his head in response, used to trotting down the boulevard and not understanding why it troubled her so.

As they rode into a busier area, Owaine slowed his horse to a walk. He had chosen a bay named Sable from the carriage horses on account of her stocky build and sweet nature, in the hope that she would make a good field horse.

"Ride briskly," Owaine whispered, pulling up beside her.

Comrade was so tall that Beauty had to look down on Owaine.

"It should take us a few hours to get out of the city. Make sure you stay close."

They pressed on, traveling into the heart of the shantytowns. Shadows ran past them in alleyways and they cantered through a brawl in a square, the sound of State officials blowing shrill whistles echoing after them. Bodies slept on corners and under rubble while night-women prowled the streets. The darkness was thick—the moonlight could not penetrate the deep bowels of the slums, and the air reeked of feted slime and fear.

"Spare some sticks?" the pair would occasionally hear a voice murmur from the gloom.

At one point, two patrolling State officials came upon them and glanced at Beauty's cloaked figure suspiciously, but at the same time there was a scream from another street and a cry for mercy. The officials ran in the opposite direction and Beauty and Owaine hurried on.

As the tense hours passed, Beauty found herself growing tired. She began to sit limply in the saddle, her hands resting on the pommel and her chin bumping on her chest. Comrade, too, was lagging, his hooves dragging against the roads, for he was not a young horse, nor was he used to such thorough exercise.

"We'll stop at an inn soon. Yur look fit to drop."

Beauty jumped at the sound of Owaine's voice and her eyes snapped open. She had not noticed him fall in step beside her and she looked around, realizing that they were no longer passing alleyways and huts.

"We're in the Sago suburbs now. Made good time, Beauty. I'm a proud of yur."

She smiled weakly at him.

"But we can't stop for long. No one knows what will be happening here."

They rode on for another hour before Owaine finally halted at an inn. Comrade snorted loudly, stretching his neck, and Beauty stumbled to the ground, her legs buckling as she fell from his saddle.

"Steady, Beauty, steady 'em," muttered Owaine, going to help her.

She waited in a haze of exhaustion as he booked a room and stalls and tended to the horses. Despite it being so late, other travelers passed on the roads, some stopping at the inn and some continuing on. They had a haunted look about their faces, as if they, too, were fleeing.

"Come on now, Beauty."

Owaine led her toward the inn door. It was smoky inside, but he guided her swiftly past a raucous group of men and up a set of rickety stairs to a dark room. She fell on the bed and was immediately asleep.

<hr />

She was awoken at dawn.

"We must go on."

Owaine's cot had already been folded away and Beauty blinked at the dim, muggy room. Her limbs ached from the long ride and she groaned softly. She was still dressed in her cloak and gloves and she felt stiff and sore.

"We can't stop, Beauty. It's dangerous."

She forced herself up and climbed out of bed, wincing. The room looked different in the harsh light seeping through the window. The walls were patched with dew, the floor riddled with lice, and the bed sheets yellow. She suddenly wished to leave.

In a matter of moments they were riding on the roads once more, Beauty flinching at every jolt in the saddle and Comrade tossing his head in frustration. They stopped for omelets at a market at mid-morning and then pressed on, heading away from Sago and the Magic Cleansing.

And it continued like that for the next moon-cycle. Beauty's days became an endless rotation of waking at dawn and riding till night. They stopped briefly at inns and taverns along the way and she ached every waking hour. When her saddle sores became too much to bear, Owaine tried to buy ointment, but every herb dealer and healer had disappeared with the threat of the Magic Cleansing and he could find nothing more than a balm that helped little.

Comrade suffered too. He was a fine riding horse, not a sturdy animal. Had Beauty not been so attached to him, Owaine would have sold him already. Instead, he did everything in his power to ease the old stallion.

"What are you doing?" Beauty asked one evening in the stables of a saloon.

Owaine was rubbing Comrade's legs in circular motions while the stallion sighed.

"I'm worried he's gonna go lame."

Beauty hugged the horse's face to her chest and kissed his forelock.

"I knows lots of stuff like this that I never showed yur," said Owaine, trying to distract her. "In Sago, there were always ointments and the like that could do the same, so I never bothered with my Hilland skills. They calls us Hill folk horse whispers, did yur know that?"

Beauty shook her head.

"That's where horses come from—the Hillands. Some still make sticks rustling the wild ones. I used to do a bit of that in me young days. I got my place at Rose Herm for being a Hillander—Ma always wanted the best."

At the thought of Ma Dane, Beauty shuddered.

Beyond the suburbs of Sago lay the Strap Cities, which were smaller, paler imitations of the capital. Traveling through them, Owaine bared left so as to remain as far from the Border Cities as possible, as he was concerned with how deeply the rebels had leaked into Pervorocco after the Magic Cleansing.

They received little national news on their journey, preferring to remain anonymous and speak to no one, but occasionally they would hear snippets of conversation.

" . . . the torturing of Magic Bloods last week in Sago."

" . . . they were hunting them all night."

" . . . said that they could hear the screams from the boulevards to the shantytowns."

Beauty glanced at Owaine as they led their horses through a busy part of one Strap City, but his head was turned firmly the other way.

After they had been on the road for three moon-cycles, the cities began to thin and turn to towns and villages. The temperature cooled although it was still summer, and the paved, wide roads became graveled paths. They were entering the fringes of the Forest Villages and stretches of green rolled before them.

"Have you seen the like of that before?" Owaine asked gleefully, pointing at fields of sloping jade.

The lawns at Rose Herm were watered three times a day to keep them from drying out and yet Beauty did not think that they were half as moist.

"The Hillands are greener still," said Owaine. "Ain't never seen their match."

Beauty pulled her cloak closer around her. She wore it always, at first to hide her appearance, but as they moved farther north, it provided much needed warmth. At times she still drew stares if passersby caught sight of her bright violet eyes beneath the hood, but so far they had not been stopped. Neither the Magic Cleansing nor the rebels had reached this far, or so they thought.

One evening, they were booking a room at a lodge house when the landlord pushed a parchment toward them.

Owaine glanced at its contents, the blood draining from his head.

"The State is on the lookout for Magics," said the landlord, glaring at Beauty. "And the rebels are sending out hunters."

Beauty instinctively slid her hand beneath her cloak and touched her golden amulet. She kept it hidden always for fear of attracting more unwanted attention, and at this moment the heavy hexagonal disk was scratching her skin.

"I thank yur for this news," said Owaine in a husky voice. "But this means nothing to us."

The landlord did not stop looking at Beauty.

"We must go on," she said, scratching her chest harder. The itch was stinging and it would not abate.

Owaine was taken aback. Just a moment earlier, he had helped Beauty stumble into the lodge house as she was so tired from the day's hard travel.

"We must go on," she said.

The landlord nodded and turned away.

"We must go from here," Beauty whispered, and Owaine did not ask further questions.

They saddled up the disgruntled horses and rode into the night. When they were well away from the town, they stopped in a bare shepherd's hut in a valley. It was the first time that Beauty did not have a bed to lie on and she did not sleep well.

"At least it's summer," said Owaine.

But Beauty had only ever known the humid Sago nights and could not adjust to the cool change in temperature. She did not find the greenness beautiful as Owaine did, or the cows and sheep comforting. It was all faintly unsettling to her.

"We would have to have started sleeping rough soon anyways," said Owaine. "Once we get past the towns of the Forest Villages then there'll be nothing but hamlets and then the hills."

Beauty could not fathom these great undulations of which Owaine always spoke.

"Good job we got these here bedrolls," he muttered before rolling over and falling asleep.

Beauty did not find them as comfortable as her companion. Her body ached from the days of travel and she could feel every lump and rock beneath her. But at last, as she heard the gentle snorting of Comrade outside, she slipped into slumber.

That night she dreamt of State officials in gray uniforms, prowling the roads and paths for Magics. One came to a lodge house and drew his sword asking for information, and the landlord tried to explain that he had seen something, but he could not remember what it was.

CHAPTER TWELVE

The Hillands

From then on they slept in shepherds' huts, under rocks, and often, if they could not find a suitable spot, under the stars. As the days passed it grew colder, the paths turned to overgrown tracks, and the ground bogged with damp. There were more fields and fewer people. Then came more stretches of green scrubland and fewer fields.

Summer turned into autumn and the trees yellowed. In Sago, the rainy season would just be beginning and Beauty found its absence distressing. Instead, the leaves about her dried to red, orange, and amber, becoming crisp before falling and crunching beneath Comrade's hooves. Fogs billowed in the mornings and gusts of cold wind blew, chilling Beauty. They entered dark forests that smelled spicy and made her sneeze, and they passed gushing streams, then rivers, then lakes.

Owaine's smile widened the farther north they traveled. He had spent too long wallowing in the hot stickiness of Sago and now he longed for his hills with a passion. In the evenings, as he made a fire to cook the little meat they brought on their journey from passing villages and hamlets, he would speak of nothing else but his Hill folk.

"They has been in the realm the longest, so it has always been said. The first race made by the gods when Magic weren't contained."

"How do you know?"

"It's written in our scripture."

They had been on the road so long that Beauty could not remember when her life had not begun at dawn, with hours of hard riding ahead, and ended on a bedroll with the darkness all around her, dreaming of strange things like colors in the sky and a man with a scar over one eye. In fear of the Magic Cleansing, they did not speak to anyone except when buying food, and even then it was Owaine who dealt with such matters. But both were craving the company of others.

"This be the last town," said Owaine one cold morning.

"We are almost there?"

The town was typical of the places they had recently passed, with its wide, cobbled square lined with stores and a maze of houses spreading in opposite directions.

"No," laughed Owaine. "It's two days ride till we reach the edge of the Hillands and then farther to the Hill villages."

Beauty's shoulders sagged.

"Hill folk come here to trade horses in the summer."

Beauty was beginning to grow tired of hearing about the Hillanders and she had not even met them yet.

"How much farther do you think we can go before nightfall?"

"We should be close enough to see the hills properly tomorrow. But while we're here, I'll send word to my family. I'd like them to ready a house for us." He paused and grinned. "They'll be so surprised to hear I'm back. We left Sago in such a rush that I weren't able to warn them I were returning."

Beauty minded the horses in the square while Owaine went to the local messengers, and for the first time she thought of the new land that she would call home. She realized she did not like the idea of Owaine having a family—she did not want to be forgotten again.

❈❈❈

The first time she saw the hills, they emerged from the mist like ships. It was noon and Beauty's bones ached with chill as a light drizzle began to fall. Owaine said that they were lucky they would reach their destination before the harsh Hilland winter, but she could not imagine it being any colder. She never thought that she would long for the dry, hot Sago summers.

Dark shadows loomed from the silver haze and the ground jerked sharply upward. Faint outlines towered over the horizon like bruises in the sky, and the air tasted moist and dense. Comrade snorted at the sudden incline and Beauty leaned forward in the saddle to help him climb.

The mist swirled, leaking into the hood of her cloak and biting the back of her neck. Her clothes felt damp and heavy and she could barely see Sable and Owaine in front of her. The ground rose forever upward and the path turned rocky. Suddenly, she heard a shrill neigh that echoed all around them.

Both Sable and Comrade answered and Beauty peered into the milky mist, but she could see nothing.

"That were a wild stallion," said Owaine. "I used to chase them as a lad."

They continued upward, the horses' flanks dark with sweat and rain. Beauty's legs throbbed from leaning forward in the saddle, her head was dizzy, and she was out of breath. She clung to Comrade's mane and closed her eyes, trusting him to carry her onward.

Suddenly, he halted and she felt a hand gently pat her back.

"The altitude is getting me too, Beauty," said Owaine, panting. "It'll give yur headache and sickness for a while, but yur'll get used to it in the end."

Beauty sat up, her head spinning.

The mist was gone and before her were miles and miles of hills and valleys. The hills were tall, stout, and green. Some dipped below where they stood and some stretched higher, their peaks clouded in white fog. There were bundles of forests and sheets of lakes and wave upon wave of hills.

"How long before I feel better?" Beauty murmured.

"A few days at least."

Owaine glanced at the horses.

"We'll need to take it a bit slower for the animals."

Comrade's sides were heaving and Sable was snorting into the cool air.

"My hills," he muttered, taking deep, moist breaths.

They moved on, picking their way down the other side of the hill and heading for a deep valley that would lead them toward Owaine's home. They traveled through the Hillands for two more days, passing no one along the way.

"Are there not other villages around?" asked Beauty on the second day, as they stopped to drink from a surging river.

"Yes, but they ain't on this main track."

Beauty scooped a palm full of water into her mouth. She felt a long way from the grand dining table of Rose Herm now.

"But could we not stop at a village?"

They had run out of meat and only had a small piece of cheese and a hunk of stale bread left.

"Hill folk don't . . . mix. We have our villages and we stay in them."

Beauty gulped down the chilling, clear water that made her teeth sting.

"How did you come to Sago, then?"

The muscles around Owaine's jaw clenched.

"That were unusual," was all he said, and they mounted the horses and moved on.

Beauty saw her first waterfall later that day. She heard its swishing crash before she saw it spouting from a boulder high above them. It splashed against rocks, tumbled down in a thread of blue glitter, then gushed into a pool at the bottom, spraying her with flecks of foamy white as she passed.

She giggled, brushing the lather from her cheek, and felt sad when the waterfall's rumble faded to silence as they moved on. Seeing her forlorn look, Owaine assured her that waterfalls were plentiful in the hills.

Later that afternoon they came upon the village of Imwane.

"What is that?" she asked, noticing a golden structure ahead.

They were scaling a broad, steep hill, and peeking over the edge of its crest, Beauty could see a golden wall. This was the highest that they had climbed yet and the horses were puffing and snorting.

"That's Imwane's temple," said Owaine, the joy bursting from his voice. "That's my temple."

As they reached the peak of the hill, Owaine reined Sable in and pressed his thumb and index finger together, lifting his arm and holding his hand up to the sky. Beauty had always known that Owaine went to the temples in Sago, but she had never understood why.

"All Imwane Hill folk go to this temple," he explained, seeing her expression. "In Sago they are mostly forgotten, and that's why the preachers there build them bells that ring across the city to try to remind the peoples. Ain't no bells needed in the Hillands—we go to the temples for as long as we remembers. My great-grandfather helped build this one when the last fell down in a storm."

Beauty looked at the golden barn with its peeling paint. It would be another new thing for her to get used to.

"Why is it here alone?" she asked. "Where is the village?"

Owaine nodded at a deep valley below them.

"All our temples are as close to the gods as we can make them. We build them from the biggest, strongest trees."

"Like those?"

Beauty pointed across the gulf to a dark, tangled forest that smothered the opposite hill in a carpet of dark green all the way to its peak.

"That's the mountain. We don't go there."

The valley below them was deep and lush. Pale, square cottages with flaxen thatched roofs climbed its sides and huddled in a pack at the base. Animals were left to roam the hillside freely and the land looked wild and untouched.

"Do yur like it?" asked Owaine, trying unsuccessfully to keep the hopefulness from his voice.

"Yes," said Beauty, but her eyes slid to the forest—she could not help but feel its heavy presence.

"Why do you not go to the forest?" she asked, as Comrade and Sable picked their way down the hillside.

She thought that she noticed Owaine's shoulders stiffen.

"No one ever goes there. I have heard strange things."

"But—"

"Yur will love Imwane, Beauty. I know yur will."

She nodded and fell silent, hoping that he was right.

They were only halfway down the track when someone spotted them. A man with gray, unruly hair who had been leaning against a rock sat up as he caught sight of them. He was wearing a crushed leather hat and a jerkin.

"Owaine!" he cried. "Owaine, is that yur?"

The sheep that he had been tending scattered at his shout.

Owaine jumped down from Sable and ran to his side. They embraced and slapped each other heartily on the back.

"Cousin!" Owaine laughed. "I don't know how long it's been since I saw yur face."

"Too long! We thought we'd lost yur to them cities. Isole didn't believe it when yur message came—none of us could have guessed after all this time."

"There's trouble in Pervorocco and we fled the city, but I'm more than happy to return to my hills."

"We've heard of no peril here. You are always safe in these hills, Owaine. But just listen to that city twang of yurs! Yur have been away too long!"

Owaine turned back to where Beauty sat on Comrade, her head bowed shyly.

"Papa!" a screech echoed through the valley.

In the cottages below, a crowd was gathering, led by a tall figure who began to run toward them.

"Papa!" she cried.

Beauty was the only one who saw the shock on Owaine's face upon seeing his daughter, who was now a young woman.

"Isole?"

She charged him, persistent despite the awkwardness portrayed in her brown eyes. Like Owaine, she was stocky with rough, olive skin and straggly brown hair, which was stuffed under a white headdress.

Behind her, men, women, and children rushed up the hill to greet their returned friend. Beauty noticed that the women of the village were all wearing tall, lace headdress and the men donned crushed leather hats and jerkins.

"Papa! I can't believe yur home!"

Isole wrapped her arms around Owaine's neck, and he carefully patted her shoulder.

"We've a house ready, all like yur asked," she went on, reluctant to release her father. "It ain't the best of houses, but it was what we could do at short notice."

"Thank yur, my child," said Owaine. "I'll be happy to see it, but first I should like yur to meet a sister. This is Beauty."

Heads turned her way and Beauty pushed her hood back from her face. She was roughened and scrawny from living on the road for so long, but she was silvery nonetheless. There were gasps and mutterings and cries of surprise.

"A sister?" whispered Isole, her hands falling by her sides.

"Yes, she were entrusted to me, and she's now my child."

There was an awed silence and the villagers pressed their thumbs and index fingers together in turn.

"What is it?" whispered Isole, and Beauty understood that things would not be any different here than back in Sago.

CHAPTER THIRTEEN

The Sister

Owaine would not explain where Beauty had come from, which did not help matters. He had known that his hill folk would be suspicious, but he had ambitiously thought that they would accept her. Besides, to him, Beauty was as sweet as she was silvery, and he thought her shimmering looks pretty. How could anyone see malice in her clear, violet eyes?

As the villagers welcomed him home that first evening in Imwane, they asked questions about the strange girl.

"Where did you find it?"

"Is it sent from the gods?"

"Will it hurt us?"

But he would only answer that her name was Beauty and that she was his child. The more questions they asked, the angrier Owaine grew, and it was Isole who had to settle things.

"My papa is hungry," she said. "We mustn't hassle him."

There were murmurs of agreement before the travelers were told that there was a feast planned in their honor and they were then led to a barn at the bottom of the valley.

"Yur must tell us yur tales someday, Owaine," said the man who had first met them, who was named Hally. "But first, let us put a belly on yur!"

The barn doors were pulled back to reveal a long trestle table waiting to be filled, and women disappeared in a buzzing cloud of chatter to fetch the food.

"We been keeping it ready for when yur came," added Hally.

Villagers began to carry out plates of meat, bread, and cheese, all the while keeping a wide berth of Beauty. The travelers' bags were taken from them, and Comrade and Sable were untacked and allowed to wander about the hillside like the other animals.

"Are yur all right?" Owaine whispered to Beauty, but Isole ran over and pulled him away.

"Papa, I made this pie for yur."

They were ushered to their seats and Beauty found herself alone at one end of the table, open space on either side of her. A young boy sat opposite and stared with half terrified, half fascinated eyes.

"Thanks be to the gods," called out Hally, pressing his thumb and index finger together and raising his hand to the ceiling. "Thanks be to the gods for returning our Owaine to us."

"Thanks be to the gods," the other villagers muttered, doing the same.

Beauty caught Owaine's eye and she copied their gestures.

"Thanks be to the gods," she whispered, and those around her flinched for it was the first thing that they had heard her say.

The meal began with much chattering and shouting. It was nothing like the dinners at Rose Herm, which were stately, regimented affairs. Instead, hands grabbed at chicken legs and slices of bread. Broth was sloshed into bowls and ale and cider were passed around the table. There were no omelets to be seen and everyone spoke at once. Beauty had thought Owaine's accent strong, but she could barely understand the talk at the table, which was lilting and deep. She was relieved when they began to sing songs.

Winds of blight that tear the earth,
Rain that spills the rights of birth.
Gods that weave our spells divine,
Protect these ancient hills of mine.

Keep your people safe and strong,
Save us from the tempt of wrong.
Use us to defend your lore,
When we must fight for you once more.

She joined in, her voice mingling with the lulling harmony that seeped through the walls of the barn and into the oncoming dusk. They sang until their voices grew hoarse, a sleepy enchantment having fallen over all.

"I thank yur for this feast, Cousin," said Owaine after they had sung one more song. "And I thank yur also for caring for my Isole in my absence. Yur've made her a fine daughter for me."

Isole beamed.

"Say nothing of it," replied Hally, slapping him on the back. "I've become prosperous with the generous sticks yur sent from the capital. I owe yur this meal. Besides, it is time to fatten up before the winters—yur have not forgot our white winters here, have yur, Cousin?"

Owaine laughed and Beauty wondered what Hally meant.

"Thank the gods!" cried Hally, signing with his fingers.

"Yes, thank them for bringing me and my child home," added Owaine, and everyone turned to look at Beauty, having forgotten that the silvery creature was among them.

"Thank the gods," they all murmured.

When the last drop of the ale was gone, the villagers took the travelers to see their new home. A long procession of women in white headdresses and men in jerkins wound their way across the valley in the fading light. The travelers' scanty possessions were carried by the lads and the children scampered all about, silly from their first sips of cider at the table. Beauty followed in the shadows.

"It's not much, Papa," Isole was saying. "At such short notice, we did what we could."

They made their way to a cottage apart from all the others, perched on the hillside nearest the forest.

"It were that widower's cottage, do yur remember, Papa? I cleaned it all myself, scrubbing it from top to bottom." She wrung her hands in the white apron about her waist.

"It's perfect," said Owaine. "Thank yur, my child."

But his eyes wandered to the forest—a black block in the evening light—and Beauty noticed him shiver.

"Go and look inside!" said one woman, her tall lace headdress bobbing on her head as she spoke. "Isole's done it all up real nice."

Taking her father's arm, Isole led him into the cottage, and Beauty meekly followed. It had only two rooms: the downstairs and the attic. On the far wall were three pens with various livestock in them and a wooden table set before a fireplace in the corner. A ladder near the door led to the attic and there were two large chests with fasten doors.

"I been saving the sticks yur sent me," said Isole. "And I bought them animals myself. I hoped yur'd come home."

Owaine clumsily embraced her.

"Thank yur, my child. I can't thank yur enough."

Beauty stared at the goat, calf, and chickens in horror. Owaine noticed and hid a wry smile.

"Winters are hard here, Beauty," he said quietly. "And we live simple lives. Yur'll learn to love Imwane, yur will."

Isole frowned. "These be the best animals about. I got Hally to buy them from town."

"They're just right, my child. But this's a different life for Beauty. . . . And speaking of, there's only two sleeping chests."

"Well I didn't know yur were bringing a . . . child."

"Mayhap I could buy another? But I scarce have sticks left after the journey."

Beauty did not like the idea of sleeping locked in such a thing.

"No, I can sleep on a bedroll." She glanced at the pens. "In the attic," she added.

"I'll do that, child. Yur can sleep in my closet."

"No. I insist."

"Yur sure?"

Beauty nodded and Isole fixed her with a hard stare.

———◦∞∞◦———

After they were sure that the travelers were settled, the villagers of Imwane brought in the luggage and then left for the evening.

"We'll give yur a few days to straighten out before we speak of work," said Hally, shaking Owaine's hand as they left. "It's good to have yur back among us, Cousin. I know Isole has prayed to the gods for yur return."

Owaine glanced over his shoulder at his daughter, already sewing before the fire, and he smiled.

"I thank yur, Cousin."

When they were finally alone, Owaine began unpacking the saddlebags and setting things to rights.

"What yur doing?" he asked Beauty, noticing her lingering by the door. "Yur should be resting, gods know yur deserve a rest after that journey."

"I am worried for Comrade," she muttered.

"All Hilland animals roam around the village. He'll be safe, Beauty, don't fret."

"But he is not a Hilland animal."

Owaine sighed. "I'll check him for yur, but yur stay here. Isole? Why not measure Beauty for an anth and dress? Then she'll look like a proper Hill girl."

Owaine left and Isole motioned Beauty to her side.

"Get here, then."

Up close, Beauty noticed Isole's ruddy cheeks and thick jaw. The lines about the edges of her eyes gave away her age, for she was older than she acted.

"Don't stare at me so!"

Beauty squeaked as Isole pinched her hard on the arm. A deep, plum bruise rose to her silvery skin.

"Let's measure yur then!"

She shoved Beauty to the side and roughly pulled a tape measure around her.

"Yur might wear the clothes, but yur'll never be a Hillander," she snarled. "Remember that."

Beauty stumbled away from Isole in surprise.

"I said don't stare so!"

Isole jumped up, looking as if she might slap her, and Beauty quickly grabbed her bedroll and climbed the attic ladder to safety.

"Yur stay up there! Yur beast!"

Owaine entered some moments later and looked about the room.

"Where be Beauty?"

Isole glanced up from her sewing. "She went to the attic. She were tired."

"I don't doubt it. Beauty?"

She peered over the edge of the ladder and Owaine smiled at her.

"Comrade be fine, I checked him myself. Thought I should tell yur before yur went to sleep."

Beauty nodded.

"Papa, come and sit by the fire. I want to tell yur stories."

Owaine obeyed his daughter and Beauty went about laying down her bedroll. She had thought that in the Hillands she would at least have a real bed. She had not realized how different it would be among these people.

Downstairs she could hear Isole chattering away and she tried to block the noise. Beauty did not understand why Owaine's daughter hated her so—she did not understand why anyone hated her so.

She pulled her cover over her, trying not to notice the uneven floorboards or the sacks of grain in the corner that saturated the air with the scent of maize. The thatched roof above her had cobwebs in it and she thought that she could hear a mouse scuffling, not to mention the various sounds of the animals in the room below.

Beauty shivered. It was the first night that she had spent under cover in a long time, but she was still cold and she could not get comfortable on the hard floor. Wriggling around, she decided to take off her amulet, for it was pressing into the skin of her chest. As she pulled it over her head, she looked at its glinting disk and touched its engraved surface. She realized that she was a long way from Houses and ballrooms and syrupy tea. There was a beam above her head with a loose nail and she hung the amulet on it. There would be no point wearing it any longer, for it meant nothing in a place like this.

CHAPTER FOURTEEN

The Temple

Beauty tried to adjust to her new life in the hills, but whenever she left the house, the villagers ran from her. They whispered as she explored the valley, pointed as she passed on the paths, and mothers called children to their sides whenever she was near.

Beauty felt even lonelier than she had at Rose Herm and were it not for Comrade she would have no one to speak to. Owaine was busy sorting out work with Hally and she did not like to stay in the house with Isole around, ready to snap and smack her when her father was away. One time, Isole heard Beauty call Owaine "Papa" and it threw her into a rage.

"How dare yur! He isn't yur papa! He's nothing to yur!"

"But . . . but he told me to call him that," Beauty cried, cowering.

Isole slapped her hard, leaving a burning sting across her face.

"Never call him that again! Do yur hear? Never!"

With nowhere else to go, Beauty spent long hours sitting on the hillside with Comrade grazing beside her. She would speak to the old black stallion, and sometimes she would weep on his shoulder, breathing in the sweet, dusty smell of his coat.

She did not regret leaving Sago, for she was old enough to realize that she had escaped mortal danger, but she was beginning to resent the Hillanders. When Owaine came to find her one evening to tell her the "good" news that Isole had finished making her an anth and Hilland dress, Beauty could not muster much enthusiasm. She had spent the day sitting on the hillside with Comrade again, watching the rest of Imwane go about their business.

"Yur'll come to the temple tomorrow?"

Beauty had not attended a ceremony at the temple on the hill yet, since Owaine had wanted her to settle first.

"Yur'll be able to go dressed like a proper Hilland girl now."

Beauty nodded glumly. The thought of sitting among those who despised her did not fill her with joy.

"I am worried about Comrade," she said.

Owaine looked at the black stallion who was standing nearby, and panic flashed across his face. Beauty saw it and her heart sank.

"Tell me the truth," she added quietly.

"He's old and the journey were hard."

"Can you not do something? Can you not help him?"

"There ain't no cure for old age, but he ain't in pain either. Don't be sad, my child—"

"Do not call me that! I am not your child!"

Owaine glanced at her bowed, white head.

"I won't call you so if you don't want to be."

"I do not."

He nodded and quietly walked away.

Once he was gone, Beauty ran to Comrade's side and wrapped her arms around his neck. He snorted softly and nosed her back as she sobbed. "Please do not go," she whispered. "Please do not leave me."

But she knew that he must, because she had dreamt it.

⸺∘∘∘∘∘⸺

The next evening, Isole came to fetch Beauty.

"Yur should make yurself more useful!" she snapped, hauling Beauty from the rock she had been sitting on and propelling her down the hillside. "I been making dinner and sewing yur dress, and what yur been doing? Talking to that horse! Troublesome, bad creature. The temple's no place for yur."

Isole dragged Beauty to the cottage and pushed her inside.

"Put on them clothes I made!"

Beauty peeled off her dress and climbed into the blue smock that all the Hilland women wore. It had a high neck and long sleeves and its skirt came to her ankles. It itched and chaffed her shoulders, and she looked longingly at her old peasant dress. She had brought all her clothes from Sago with her, though there were few of them and they were looking tatty and worn from the hard journey.

"Yur still look strange," hissed Isole, tying a white apron around Beauty's waist.

The cottage door opened and Owaine entered, startling the chickens in the pen.

"Look at yur, Beauty!" he cried. "Don't yur look a pretty girl!"

She smiled weakly at him.

"Yur did a great job, Isole."

"Thank yur, Papa. It weren't easy, and I hope she appreciates it."

"Yur does, don't yur, Beauty?"

She turned to Isole and slowly placed her left hand to her chest. Isole's lip curled.

"Now put on her anth and we can head to the temple. I suspect Beauty wants to show off her pretty new clothes to all them other girls."

Isole took a white headdress from a stand. She had ironed the lace into intricate folds all day and then set it with starch to create a stiff, coned hat.

"It . . . it won't go," she muttered, trying to fix it to Beauty's silky, white hair.

Beauty winced as a pin stabbed her scalp.

"Careful, Isole, you gotta be gentle," said Owaine.

"It won't go!"

The anth kept sliding off of Beauty's head.

"It's Magic!" screamed Isole, throwing the anth to the floor.

"It ain't! And I will never hear you say such a thing!" said Owaine.

Isole blinked at her father in surprise.

"I'll try it again," she whispered.

In the end, Isole fixed it with a row of tight pins that looked as if they might slip away at any moment. The anth sat lopsided on Beauty's head and wobbled precariously whenever she moved.

"It'll do," Isole growled, her brow damp.

They left their cottage and climbed the steep hillside with the other villagers. A steady stream of families was making its way to the temple and congregating outside its doors. When Beauty appeared there was much muttering and shifting among the crowd, and one by one, everyone made a sign to the gods.

Feeling their damning eyes on her, Beauty bowed her head.

"Good evening to yur Imwane brothers and sisters," said a booming voice.

It was the preacher. Dressed in the rags of a peasant he traveled the hills giving sermons in the village temples. He had a strong, muscular body and a clean, clear face despite his nomadic lifestyle.

"I have much to speak to yur of," he said, patting his satchel of scrolls about his shoulder. "Enter and we may begin."

Following him, the villagers crowded into the temple, chattering. There was nothing inside except the bare, hard floor, and Owaine guided Beauty to a corner where they knelt, pressing their hands against the earth. She glanced up at the high, wooden ceiling, painted gold like the rest of the temple and coming away in places.

"Settle, all of yur," cried the preacher. "We have much to speak of—"

"There is an evil one among us!"

Gasps of surprise echoed around the temple, and a woman stood and pointed at Beauty.

"I can't be silent no longer! Not in the gods' house! Owaine, yur my kin by marriage, but I can't let yur bring that under-realm thing here!"

Hally pulled at the elbow of his wife, Duna.

"No, Hally!" she gasped. "The women be scared! We can't let this happen."

"I fear for my children!" another voice cried.

"It'll tempt us!"

"It'll poison us all!"

"No!" cried Owaine. "No, Beauty ain't like—"

But tears of shame and rage were prickling Beauty's eyes. Through a watery gaze, she saw Isole smiling triumphantly as the preacher tried to control his crowd. Then Beauty jumped to her feet and fled.

"See how it runs!" someone yelled as Beauty burst through the doors of the temple. "See how it flees from the good of the gods!"

Beauty ran down the hillside, away from the temple, away from the valley of Imwane, and away from the accusing faces of the villagers. Winter was almost upon the hills and she slid and tripped in the muddy ground. The drizzle that forever fell mingled with the tears on her cheeks and wilted her anth so that it lost its folds. She continued running blindly through the green growth until she heard a familiar rumble. She followed it to a waterfall, panting for breath as she skidded to a halt in front of its splashing pool.

There she knelt, sobbing. It was not fair that wherever she went people were afraid of her. They thought her evil and wicked before they had even asked her name. She was tired of persecution and abuse. It just was not fair.

She buried her fists into the muddy ground and cried harder. Sniffing, she caught sight of her reflection in the pool—silvery and pale—and it made her angry. She grabbed handfuls of mud and slathered it across her face and hair. Before long, she was completely covered and she looked in the pool again, seeing a dark shadow.

But that did not please her, either.

Dried of tears, she sat on the cold ground. She wondered why she had come here. Why had her mother left her in the care of Ma Dane? Why did she look different from everyone else? And why at night did she dream of a man with a scar over his eye?

She caught sight of her anth lying in the mud beside her and she snatched at it, suddenly angry. She tore it in half and then in half again, deliberately savoring the feeling. Then she threw it back in the mud.

She leaned over the pool and took a palm full of water, splashing it across her face. And then another and then another. It was deathly cold and her teeth chattered, but she did not stop until she had completely washed the mud away. Then she stared at herself, silvery once again, and she knew that she was not evil.

She closed her eyes and, listening to the sound of the waterfall, she began to sing softly.

The gods did build the hills for those,
That does good deeds for one they chose.

They shelter with old spells and might,
For one who comes to them to fight.

They know not what—

She heard a sound and jumped.

The preacher was standing before her, smiling.

"What is yur name, child?" he asked over the roar of the waterfall.

"Beauty."

"That's a fine name."

The water rippled before her.

"What made yur sing that song, Beauty?"

She shrugged. "The sound of the waterfall."

"Did yur know that's scripture?"

"No."

"All Hilland songs be scripture. We transfers some of it into songs to remember it easier. Better than carrying this thing around." He patted his pack of scrolls. "And we preach in temples because it's easier to gather people, but it'd be better to sing to waterfalls."

Beauty frowned.

"I ain't making fun of yur, child. For yur understand what it means when all them others don't."

"I was just singing. It does not mean that I understand anything."

He smiled.

"But it does, child. Everyone does something for a reason, even the gods."

Beauty glanced at her reflection in the pool.

"Yur are different for a reason."

"How do you know that?"

"I've faith."

The preacher glanced at the anth in the mud and tried to hide a smile.

"I see that yur are strong willed too," he said. "That is good, for I wish to see yur in the temple tomorrow evening. We've postponed service tonight till them lot calm down."

"I suppose I am strong willed for a reason too?"

He laughed. "See," he said. "Yur do understand."

He turned from her and began walking away. "I'd say may the gods be with yur, but I know that they are. Instead, I'll say that I'll see yur tomorrow, child."

Beauty watched him disappear.

When she entered the cottage that night, Beauty was worried that Owaine would be angry, but instead he wrapped her in a tight hug.

"My chi—Beauty, where have yur been?"

"I am sorry," she muttered.

"Don't be sorry. The villagers don't mean it, yur mustn't be put off by them, yur—"

"I will go to the temple tomorrow."

Owaine released her in surprise.

"Yur will?"

"Yes."

"I'm glad to hear it, Beauty. So glad. But come and let us give yur dinner. Yur soaked and cold."

Owaine hurriedly spooned broth into a bowl and set it at the table. Meanwhile, Isole moved to Beauty's side.

"Where be that anth?"

"Gone!" Beauty hissed, her violet eyes flashing, and Isole jumped back in surprise.

She kept away from Beauty for the rest of the evening as they sat by the fire, and the next day also as they carried out household chores together. When evening came, Beauty walked to the temple with the rest of the villagers and wore one of her old peasant dresses with her hair loose.

The villagers muttered and whispered, but when the preacher came, Beauty marched into the temple straight after him and knelt right at the front before his feet. Owaine took the place beside her, but the others kept a distance.

"Hello, child," said the preacher, and he touched her head.

The villagers watched, mouths open.

"We'll begin with a song," he added. "It's a prophecy, but we know not for who."

The gods did build the hills for those,
That does good deeds for one they chose.

They shelter with old spells and might,
For one who comes to them to fight.

The villagers sang and their voices charged the air with a hum that made the temple walls shake. It echoed around the hills and was carried to the mountains by the wind.

Beauty shivered, suddenly cold, for she saw a gray shadow and then a castle in the forest. *They will find me here*, she thought. *He will trace me here.*

Her vision disappeared and she gasped, Owaine grabbing her arm in support. Those around them thankfully did not notice, but Beauty looked up and saw the preacher smiling.

CHAPTER FIFTEEN

The Winter

C omrade died and Beauty cried for days. It was winter and bitterly cold, and she awoke in the night knowing that he was almost gone. She ran out of the cottage to be with him in his last moments, as the dull light spread over the hills. Owaine found her later, sobbing with Comrade's large, dark head cradled in her lap.

"Oh, Beauty," he whispered, stroking her shoulder.

But she would not be consoled and continued to weep.

"She's fit for nothing," Isole complained. "Ain't no chores getting done unless I do them myself with her sniveling. That horse were a drain on us and we couldn't afford it anyways."

"It were her friend," said Owaine, but his daughter was not listening.

Snow came, coating the hills in a thick slather of white and hardening the waterfalls into icy fingers. Though it was the first time that she had ever seen snow, Beauty was not interested in what winter had to bring.

"The other children be playing in the snow, Beauty," said Owaine. "Do yur want to go out and play too?"

She was seated in front of the fire, sewing badly. She now stoutly refused to wear the Hilland dress and instead was endeavoring to make her own clothes.

"I wish to stay in here," she said quietly.

"Yur sure?"

"Yes."

Beauty's first Hilland winter was long and cold. She awoke with frost upon her pillow each dark morning and spent the day shivering despite the heavy furs she fastened over her uneven homemade dresses. Trudging through snow, she would collect firewood and then argue with Isole over the chores to be done in the cottage.

They would sweep, scrub, and clean, muttering curses at each other all the while, and Beauty's fingers would ache. Her hands were calloused and blistered now—her knuckles split and peeling. She did not much mind the appearance of them, for she was not vain, but they throbbed incessantly. She dared not mention it to Isole who would delight in the fact, and so she suffered silently all day long until Owaine came home and she could stop her work for dinner.

Hally had appointed Owaine the first Imwane horse trainer. Owiane had been worried that they would send him to work the fields in the next valley or to herd livestock on the hillside, but it was decided that his skills honed from his seasons in Sago were to be put to good use instead. He could no longer hunt and catch wild mares and stallions, but he could breed the right sire and dame to make the perfect filly and turn a skittish colt into a dignified riding horse in a matter of moon-cycles. The villagers were hopeful that he could bring much needed prosperity to Imwane, for among all the Hill villages, they were one of the poorest.

<hr />

Finally, the Hilland winter came to an end and the snow melted and the rivers flowed freely once more. Beauty had forgotten what it was like to be warm, but flashes of sunshine began to fall on the hills between bouts of rain, and the villagers grew more cheerful with each passing day.

Beauty was still regarded as an oddity by the people of Imwane, but after the incident at the temple, they were wary not to treat her too unkindly. They were suspicious but obedient folk, and if the preacher felt that Beauty was to be trusted, they would not go against him. There were still whispers and frowns wherever she went, so mostly Beauty preferred to be alone.

Beauty still mourned the loss of her friend. Owaine had burned Comrade's body on a hillside, as was the Hilland custom, and she walked to the spot daily to sit on the ground and murmur to him. He had taught her to ride, helped her forage a friendship with Owaine, carried her from Sago—and she missed him dearly.

One afternoon, as he rode Sable back from a day spent training a young mare, Owaine found her on the hillside.

"Beauty, would yur ride home with me?"

She was in the middle of telling Comrade how Isole had given her the hardest house chores again today. She did not want to be disturbed, but Owaine's expression was pleading, so she let him hoist her into the saddle and they trotted to the cottage.

"Why don't yur ever play with the other village children, Beauty?"

"They have all been told not to speak to me."

Owaine grunted. If he were not so aware of how precarious their position was in the hierarchy of Imwane, he would have taken the village to task for their treatment of Beauty long ago.

"It is all right. I do not want to play with them either."

"I feel . . . I feel that yur ain't happy here, Beauty."

She bowed her head but could not find a suitable reply.

The coming of spring altered the daily routine in Imwane. Villagers left their doors open in order to step out into the sunshine between chores. The penned animals were moved outside the homes. Families ate their dinners on grassy banks, and cottages were turned inside out as they were aired after the long winter.

"We're washing at the river today," said Isole one bright morning.

Washing clothes was normally a difficult affair that involved future planning and a whole day heating water and hanging wet garments over the fire, but in the spring and summer, the Hilland women met regularly to wash together at the river.

"Carry this." Isole shoved a huge basket of clothes into Beauty's arms and they trudged to the river together. The water gushed on the far side of the valley, and as they reached it, Beauty was surprised to see so many women lined on its bank.

"Isole!" cried Duna, motioning to a spot that she had saved next to her.

Beauty carried the basket over, but Isole pushed her back.

"That's my place! Yur'll be at the end of the line."

Beauty stumbled downstream, where the youngest Hill girls were working. When they saw her approach, they moved over, leaving a large gap, and she knelt down, pretending not to notice.

The water there was soapy and difficult to wash out of the garments. Fumbling with clothes, Beauty looked upstream, past the row of white anths to the top of the river, where Isole was sitting at Duna's side, surrounded by the older, respected Hill women. They spoke loudly enough for all to hear.

"How yur finding things now, Isole?" asked Duna. "Are yur settled? Hally and I misses yur much. Yur were our last young one."

"It ain't been easy, Auntie."

A glare was shot downstream.

"My papa were gone so many seasons. He's almost a stranger and we've not a lot of sticks for he spent much on his journey."

A few of the older Hill women flinched. Beauty had noticed that Hillanders did not like to speak of sticks. They found it distasteful, unlike in Sago where it would be a common topic to discuss over syrupy tea.

"If yur needs anything, my child, yur come to me and Hally. Yurs a daughter to us."

Isole beamed. "My apron is almost worn through. I spent so much time making our dress for that *thing*. Did I tell yur she ruined it? Completely tore it to shreds."

"Yur said, my child. It were a nasty, evil thing for it to do to yur."

This was said loudly, in case Beauty was not aware that they were speaking of her.

"Of course Papa won't say a word against her."

"He's probably scared of it, my child."

"She's completely spoiled!"

Beauty stood and picked up her basket.

"I told yur that yur have to stay down there," said Isole as Beauty approached her.

Beauty slammed the basket down in front of her.

"What do yur think yur doing?"

"Giving you washing to do," she replied. "I am not going to do it listening to you speak of me so. Do it yourself."

Isole gasped. "Did yur hear that? I swear she never helps me, Duna. I've gotta keep that cottage all on my own."

"Don't yur fret, my child," Duna soothed, before turning to Beauty. "Yur go and do that washing!"

Beauty bent close to her face. "No."

Duna made the sign of the gods and Beauty marched away.

"Yur bad creature!" she shouted after her. "Yur bad, bad creature!"

At first, Beauty thought that she might go to Comrade and tell him the whole sorry tale, but instead she turned in the opposite direction. Climbing up the hillside, she headed for the next valley, where the men were tending the crops. Owaine, too, would be working nearby, training horses to be sold in town.

"What yur doing, Beauty?" he panted as he spotted her approaching.

The men in the fields caught sight of her and watched, open-mouthed.

"I thought yur were washing today? Yur should go back. This ain't the place for women and girls."

She stopped beside him and he saw her sad, pale expression.

"I cannot spend my days with Isole," she whispered.

"Things are hard between yur, ain't they?"

Beauty nodded.

"Owaine! Owaine!" shouted Hally, jogging over. "Things all right here?" He pushed his crushed leather hat back from his eyes.

The men in the fields behind him were still watching.

"Cousin, I wish to ask yur another favor, though yur've done enough for me."

Hally glanced at Beauty. "We're happy to have yur back and for the work yur have done. What's it to be?"

"I'd like Beauty to help me in my work."

"Owaine—"

"She's good with horses."

"Hill women don't get—"

"She ain't a Hill girl, as everyone keeps reminding her."

Hally tugged his beard. "They won't like it, Owaine."

"She'll stay by my side always, yur'll see. And with her helping me, we'll have double the horses to take to town come autumn."

"Double?"

"Double."

Hally counted the mares running loose in a field behind him.

"I count three wild horses. Yur tamed one since yur got here and yur did a good job. If yur can tame all them three, plus three more before autumn, and make 'em good riding horses, then she can help yur if yur so please."

Owaine ducked his head. "I thank yur, Cousin. We can do that and more."

Hally sighed before striding away.

"I can really help you train the horses?" Beauty asked quietly.

"Yur can, yes. But we better keep that wager. Hally's my cousin, but he's Imwane's Head Man and can't give me too much special treatment."

Beauty looked over at the wild horses, bucking and cantering in the field nearby.

"How did he get to be Head Man?"

"The villagers voted him in after the last one left."

"Who was the last Head Man?"

"Me."

Chapter Sixteen

The Girl with Amethyst Eyes

Beauty and Owaine worked hard together training horses. Every day they awoke at dawn, walked with the other men to the next valley, and then backed and disciplined horses until the sun began to set.

Though Beauty had helped at the stables at Rose Herm, she had never handled a wild horse before, and it was not as easy as she had anticipated. In her first few days, she fell off more times than she could count, was bitten continuously, and had purple hoof-shaped bruises covering her body. This gave Isole some satisfaction. She saw Beauty hobbling home in the evenings and she would smile.

"Good day?" she would ask. "I been working my fingers to the bone cleaning this house while yur been out. Make yurself useful and chop some wood."

When Isole was told that Beauty would now be working with Owaine every day, she had kicked up a huge fuss. She accused her father of not caring for her and, afraid that it was the truth, Owaine agreed that when Beauty returned from working the horses, she would perform odd chores to help Isole.

"I'm sorry," he had muttered to Beauty, after the agreement was made.

"It is all right. I would rather that than spend the whole day working with her."

So all through the bright springtime and the hazy summer, Beauty worked hard. As the days passed, she grew stronger and she finally settled into her Hilland life. She enjoyed the ceremonies at the temple, having never learned anything about the gods in Sago, and she liked training the horses. She was still ignored by the vast majority of Imwane villagers, but she cared little about that now.

When the faint drizzle that always pervaded the Hilland air began to thicken to fat rain and the trees began to shed their leaves, Owaine and Beauty made plans to travel to town. They had backed and trained seven horses, overreaching Hally's bargain, and they were keen to see what their steeds could raise at the market.

"Imwane ain't never tried to sell riding horses before, just wild ones," said Owaine proudly one evening over dinner. "I think they gonna fetch even more than Hally's been thinking."

He grinned at Beauty and slurped a mouthful of ale.

"That's all very nice, Papa," said Isole. "But I got some stuff I want yur to get from town for me. I need new cloth for a dress and more lace for an anth."

"But Duna and Hally gave yur a new apron only a season ago."

"That ain't a dress! And I need ribbons—like the kind Pia were wearing at the temple yesterday."

"Whatever for?"

"I ain't ever had nothing fine and if yur horses is gonna make as much as yur say then I want my share."

Owaine looked like he might refuse.

"If yur must know, I want to look nice for Mama's remembrance," she added.

Owaine froze and Beauty looked up from her bowl.

"I want yur to come, Papa," said Isole. "I ask Hally to hold it every year and this's the first year yur gonna be around to attend."

Owaine's face turned ashen and he looked as though he might be sick. There was a long silence.

"Well?" said Isole, shifting in her seat. "Yur gonna come, ain't yur? It's important to me."

Beauty watched Owaine worriedly; she had never seen him look so pale.

"Yes," he said at last, as though it gave him great pain. "Yes."

Isole glanced at Beauty.

"Yur not to come," she hissed.

Owaine slammed his hand against the table.

"I say who attends my wife's remembrance!" he roared.

Beauty had never seen him so angry and Isole trembled.

"I knew yur would do this!" she screeched. "Yur care for that *thing* more than yur own daughter! What would my mama say if she were alive?"

Isole ran from the table and out of the cottage, banging the door behind her. The chickens, which were now inside the cottage waiting for the colder seasons, squawked at the noise. Then there was silence.

Owaine rubbed his eyes.

"I do not have to attend if it causes you so much trouble," said Beauty.

"But I'd like yur there."

"Then I will come."

He pushed his half eaten dinner aside.

129

"Do you think . . . do you think that your wife would have liked me?"

Owaine smiled. "I know so, Beauty. My wife were sweet but strong. She were pretty and so young. So very young."

He bit his lip.

"Is that why you came to Sago? Because she—"

"Yes 'em. We were young, but I loved her much and we were doing so well in Imwane. I were Head Man and we lived where Hally does now."

"The big house?"

Owaine nodded.

"She come from a village on the other side of the Hillands—a prosperous village. She married beneath herself with me, but I were gonna make it up to her. I worked so hard, but then she died. She caught a sickness after Isole were born."

"Did Isole know her?"

"She were but a few seasons old. I couldn't stay when she were gone. I had to leave and Hally were so good to take Isole in and be Head Man. I used to sometimes think I were never gonna come back."

"But you did."

"Yes 'em. Don't think I could've managed it without yur, Beauty. I misses my wife everyday, but I'm gonna see her again in the end. That's what the scriptures say."

Beauty smiled.

<hr />

When the first great gusts of autumn wind started to whistle through the hills, Owaine and Beauty set out for the nearest town. They tethered their horses in a long line and all the villagers of Imwane came out to wave them on their way.

"It is the first time that they have smiled at me," said Beauty as they passed the temple and looked down on the crowd of crushed leather hats and white anths.

"They're hoping we return with many sticks," replied Owaine.

The nearest town was two days' ride and they made the journey easily. Owaine took the lead with Sable, who was still as calm and trusty as ever, and Beauty followed at the rear on a dapple-gray mare—the first horse that she had tamed.

They entered the town market, drawing many curious glances, for trained Hilland horses were rare and quite valuable. It was said that horses from the hills were wilder than any other and the most difficult to break, but they outlived, outran, and outperformed all others. Owaine and Beauty were expecting to make many sticks.

And the town market did not disappoint. All seven horses were sold for at least double the expected amount at auction.

"Hally'll be blessing the day he saw yur, Beauty," said Owaine, grinning broadly. "There's a bundle of sticks here even after we've given our third share to Imwane."

"Can we watch the rest of the auction?" Beauty asked, sad to see all the horses go.

"Of course. We got the rest of the day—I can't believe we sold 'em all before noon."

With Owaine laughing and smiling to himself, they made their way back to the auction ring and stood in front of the fence to watch the animals being led in.

Having become accustomed to the solitude of the Hillands, Beauty found leaving them strange. This flat, cultivated land now seemed dull to her. The paths felt too narrow and the people too loud. She was surprised to find that she missed the hills and was looking forward to her return.

Suddenly she stilled, all thoughts of Imwane vanishing from her mind and the hair on her arms rising. A colt was led into the ring and she fixed her eyes upon it. It was dragged and slapped, its terrified eyes rolling in its head. There were cuts on its bedraggled, thin flanks and knotted clumps in its mane and tail. It was covered in muck and diminished in size, and she knew right away that she must have it.

"I need that horse," she whispered. She saw a forest and a castle and gray shadows chasing her. "I need that horse."

"What yur say?"

Beauty's fingers clenched the wooden bars of the fence.

"I must have that horse, Owaine. I must have it!"

"That sorry thing? Beauty, it's owned by an Edywnson rustler. They don't treat their horses right. That poor animal is no use to anyone except for meat."

"No!" she cried.

The people around them looked over in surprise and when they saw the silver girl, they quickly moved away.

"I must have it! Owaine, please."

In the ring, the animal was whinnying and trembling, its whipped body too weak to fight back. The man leading it whacked it hard on its rump and its legs buckled. A few members of the crowd laughed.

"What can we get for this piece of meat?" cried the auctioneer.

"Please!" gasped Beauty, her violet eyes begging.

Owaine could do nothing but nod.

"Sold!" she screamed. "Sold for anything!"

———⌘———

They arrived at Imwane two days later than expected, for the bay colt could not travel far or fast. Owaine rode Sable and Beauty followed on foot, leading the sickly creature. Many times Owaine would halt and look back to see Beauty whispering and coaxing the petrified animal. She walked as slowly as it needed to, her hand always pressed against its trembling flank, and whenever they stopped, she stroked and petted it, paying no heed to her own aching legs.

She called it Champ, and though it had bucked and shied from its handler, when Beauty walked into the pen to retrieve it, it had let her lead it away without any fuss. The unusual sale had caused whispers and everyone had stared suspiciously at the silver girl. Realizing how besotted with the sickly creature she was, the Edywnson rustler had raised his price and Owaine had begrudgingly paid five times the amount the colt was worth. So keen was he to get Beauty and their new addition away from the market and the questioning gaze of the town citizens that Owaine had also forgotten to buy Isole's fabric and ribbons.

"What be that?" Isole cried when the pair finally returned to Imwane.

Having spotted them making slow progress down the hillside, one of the young lads had gathered the village out to greet them.

"That's Champ," said Owaine while handing Hally a fistful of sticks.

Hally took the bundle and spluttered. "Them horses made this much?" he gasped.

"Yes 'em, they did!"

A few men nearby patted Owaine excitedly on the back.

"There's enough here to plant four more fields of grain!"

"Where're my ribbons?" interrupted Isole. "Yur must have gotten some nice ones if yur made so much."

Beauty and Champ approached the crowd, both looking the worse for wear. Beauty's boots and cloak were coated in thick mud and her colt was panting and shaking more than ever.

"I didn't get no ribbons," muttered Owaine. "I brought the colt."

"Yur . . . yur didn't get no ribbons?" Isole's brown eyes darkened. "What about my fabric?"

"No."

"What yur gone and brought a horse for? That creature's as good as dead! We can't afford no other horse and we don't need one! What be the point of this?"

The shouting attracted a few more villagers, eager to take part in the unfolding drama.

"We can talk about this later, Isole. Beauty and me are tired. We—"

"I'm tired of yur treating her like a daughter!"

"Hush, my child!"

"Don't hush me!"

Hally took Isole's arm. "Don't fret, child. Duna's got some fabric left over and she'll help yur make a new dress."

Isole glared at her father. "That horse'll be dead soon, by gods, I know it!"

With that she stormed off to the cottage, the villagers muttering and whispering after her.

Beauty stood with her arms protectively wrapped about Champ's skinny neck.

"I thank yur for trying to help, Cousin," muttered Owaine.

"This ain't a time for quarrels, this is time for a celebration," said Hally. "Imwane ain't never brought in so many sticks from a market sale before. Yur've done us proud."

"And Beauty?"

Hally nodded and turned to the silver child. "I thank yur, Beauty," he said and pressed his left hand to his chest.

She stared at him in surprise.

"As payment for yur work, I offer yur my stable for the next moon-cycle. Isole is right—that colt don't look good. Yur can nurse him there, if you please. He stands more chance undercover."

"I thank you," she whispered so fervently that Hally found himself warming to her. "I thank you heartily."

All excepting Beauty celebrated the great prosperity that the market had brought to the village that evening. The villagers filled the barn and ate and rejoiced at the trestle table—even Isole stopped sulking to celebrate and be merry with her fellow Hillanders. Pies and bread and crumbles were laid out for the feast and a barrel of cider was opened for the occasion.

From a stall in Hally's tiny stable, Beauty heard them singing songs and she quietly joined in. She stroked Champ's head as she murmured the verses, tracing his white blaze and counting his four white socks hidden beneath the grime. He was weak—she knew it—but he would get better. She cleaned and tended to his wounds and combed the knots from his matted hair—and all the while she sang to him.

When night fell, she curled up in the straw by his side, warming his trembling body with her own.

"You will carry me many places," she whispered, and she saw his ears flicker. "You will be a great strong horse—I have seen it. And all those that hurt and doubted you will be proven wrong."

CHAPTER SEVENTEEN

The Dreams

Isole made much of the fact that she had no ribbons the day of her mother's remembrance ceremony. She wore her hair unadorned and without an anth to show that they were missing, and she put on her shabbiest dress. But if she hoped that Owaine would notice and feel remorse, then she was mistaken, for he scarcely registered her presence.

For the first time in his life, Owaine was late rising. Normally he would be eating sticky porridge when Beauty climbed down from the attic and it was Isole that needed prompting from her sleeping closet, but that morning Beauty was forced to tap lightly on his fastened door.

"I'll be a moment," came the muffled reply, and half an hour later a rough, weary old man climbed out. Owaine's eyes were red-rimmed and the lines across his face were deep—he did not look as though he had slept at all.

"How's the colt?" he asked as if he had nothing else to say.

"He is a little stronger." But she was not sure that Owaine even heard.

"Do I look presentable?" prompted Isole. "Sadly, I've no pretty things to wear for this occasion. This's the best I could do."

"Fine," muttered Owaine, and she looked disappointed.

"Yur know, Pia had a ceremony for her papa not so long ago and she had pink and blue ribbons," Isole tried again, as they climbed the hillside to the temple.

But Owaine did not say a word.

"I really wish that I'd had something nice to wear for this special day."

The preacher was waiting for them outside the temple. He nodded a greeting to all as they approached, and he even smiled at Beauty.

"Hally and Duna be already inside?" asked Isole.

"Yes 'em, but yur take as long as yur need before yur enter," said the preacher.

Isole looked puzzled, for she had not even noticed her father's pale, damp face as they approached the temple.

"I'll go in and join them," she said, leaving Beauty, Owaine, and the preacher outside.

Then there was silence except for the high whine of the wind through the hills. It fluttered golden leaves across the ground and ruffled the edges of the dark forest.

"We were married in this temple," Owaine muttered. His eyes were glassy and his head bowed.

"I were but a boy, but I remember it," said the preacher. "The ceremony were handsome and the bride the prettiest I've ever seen. She wore fresh daisies in her hair."

Owaine nodded, some of the color coming back to his cheeks. "That's right. I had almost forgotten. She were beautiful."

He straightened his shoulders, brushed down his jerkin, and nodded to the preacher. With a deep breath he walked boldly into the temple without looking behind him.

Beauty watched him go and the preacher smiled at her.

"We can try to run," he said. "But one day we must all face our past."

———∞———

The seasons passed and Champ grew. He did not die that first winter, as everyone predicted, nor the next winter as Owaine feared, nor the winter after that as Isole hoped. Instead, his thin ribs were gradually covered with a thick layer of muscle and fat, his dull coat shone to a deep bay, and his legs grew and grew until he was an astounding twenty hands high. He followed Beauty around like a faithful dog and nudged and nosed her if he felt that she had neglected him for too long. A few times he even tried to follow her into the cottage, but Isole shooed him out. After that, he would wait patiently outside the door as Beauty slept each night, greeting her warmly when she appeared in the morning.

"About time yur tried to back him," said Owaine one summer afternoon. "He must be older than twelve seasons now."

Beauty turned to look at her horse, who was grazing nearby. She and Owaine were working in the valley next to Imwane, training wild horses as they always did. They had grown popular in the Hillands and the town for producing excellent steeds, and they had brought much wealth to the village over the past seasons.

"I already ride him."

"I never seen yur put a saddle on him!"

Champ raised his head and flicked his ears. He liked to watch his mistress and Owaine train the other horses and he was never a bother. When all the workers stopped for lunch he would sometimes trot off to visit the men in the fields, who would feed him crumbs and odd crusts, receiving a good-natured neigh in return.

"I do not ride him with a saddle yet. I just sit on him and he carries me around."

"When?"

"Oh, just sometimes in the evenings."

Beauty bent down to pick out the hoof of the horse they were grooming. It was a fine palomino mare that an Imwane rustler had captured a moon-cycle ago. She would make an excellent riding horse for a pretty lady, and they were hoping that she would fetch a good price come autumn. Occasionally, the mare would whicker coquettishly at Champ, but he ignored her.

"Beauty, where do yur ride him?"

"Around."

Bored with Imwane, Beauty and Champ had begun venturing farther afield. He was fast and she was a good rider, and they could cover a great distance without being missed for long.

"Yur know it ain't right to stray from Imwane."

"But I am not a Hillander."

"Only because yur choose not to be one. The villagers know all the work yur do though they'd never admit it. They respect yur, Beauty. Yur'd be surprised."

"They hate me and I know it, so you cannot pretend otherwise."

Owaine made a face and began gently sponging the palomino mare's muzzle.

"Besides, I will not stay here forever." She looked up and met his worried gaze.

"How do yur know?"

She swallowed hard. "I have dreamt it."

"Dreams don't mean yur—"

"I have dreamt it many times."

"Beauty . . ."

"I must tell you! It is getting stronger—first it was dreams, and then visions, but I know that it is growing. Do you see what I mean? I am—"

"No!"

The palomino mare shied away as Owaine grabbed her hand. Sensing his mistress's distress, Champ whinnied and trotted over, his tail high.

"Yur mustn't say it, Beauty, it's too dangerous."

"But—"

"One day I'll not be able to protect yur, but till then I'll always do my best to keep yur safe. I brought yur here, but I don't know if that'll be enough."

"So, you always knew?"

He reached out and squeezed her shoulder.

"Ain't every day yur see a child with violet eyes."

She squeezed his hand back.

"I always wish to obey you," she said. "But I cannot stay in this valley, and I am safe with Champ. Please trust me."

Owaine nodded and tried to push away the large head that was coming between them, nudging for affection.

"All right, yur daft beast," he muttered. "Yur best take care of my Beauty."

Champ snorted.

"He will, I promise."

It was a dream that she had had many times before. The rose began hard and golden like the engraving on her amulet, and then it melted. Its petals burned scarlet red and they shivered and curled as though it were a beating heart. Its head was full and heavy, bent slightly on a slim green stem with purple thorns, and it seemed dark and dangerous. She saw it always on its own, with nothing surrounding it but blackness, and she did not know what it meant.

She woke suddenly to the roar of a beast. Sitting bolt upright on her bedroll, she panted into the spring air and felt droplets of sweat trickle down her spine. The amulet above her head was swinging slowly from side to side. Since her first night in Imwane she had not removed it from its place on the rusty nail. She sensed that it made her dreams stronger—these strange dreams that had visited her since she could remember.

She reached up and touched the amulet. Her ears still rang with the rumble of a howl and her body was trembling.

"It is a deal," she whispered, although she did not know to whom.

She took her cloak, wrapped it around her, and then she quietly climbed down from the attic and slipped out of the cottage.

Outside, the sun was just appearing over the swelling land and the valley was dim and cold. Taking in a deep lungful of moist air, Beauty tried to calm herself. No dream had ever troubled her as much as this one.

She felt warm breath on her shoulders and a muzzle nudged her back.

"Morning, Champ."

He rubbed his face against her and sniffed at her pockets. He had grown even taller lately and the villagers were muttering about his pedigree. There were rumors that he was descended from the great warhorses of ancient times, when the gods first created all and placed fantastical beings in the Hillands to run to the four corners of the realm as they pleased. He was an unusually handsome creature with a shinning conker-bay coat and dark mane and tail, but Beauty thought that there was nothing mythical about a horse that would still try to steal an apple from your hands as you ate it.

"What yur doing, Beauty?"

She turned to see Owaine standing in the doorway, rubbing his chin.

"I woke early."

"Yur all right?"

"Yes, but . . . Owaine, are their any roses in the Hillands?"

"I ain't never seen a rose except on Ma Dane's amulet. They're not a Pervoroccian flower, I don't think. I remember Ma tried to get them shipped to her once, but they died on the travels. Why'd yur ask?"

"I had a dream."

Owaine swallowed. "I see. Well, yur best come in and have some porridge. I'm hoping we'll back that young gray mare today. She's of a feisty temper."

Beauty nodded. "I will come for breakfast in a moment."

Owaine disappeared into the cottage, and Beauty was alone once more.

Champ turned his head and pricked his ears. Following his gaze, Beauty saw the dark forest. No one in Imwane walked closer to it than where the cottage stood, as if it were an unspoken law. There was plenty of game in its dark depths and a few times, when she had stopped to look at it, Beauty had been sure that she had seen movement in its trees. There must be many horses in there, too, but no rustlers would so much as enter its fringes.

She felt the forest's presence always, like a shadow in the corner of her eye.

Champ sighed.

"You feel it too, boy?" she whispered, placing her palm on his broad chest. "It's waiting for us, but I do not understand why."

CHAPTER EIGHTEEN

The Matchmaker

As seasons came and went, Beauty dreamt of the rose more and more often. Some nights, when she closed her eyes she could see nothing but its full, scarlet petals; often she awoke with a sweet, heady scent in the air, and always her amulet would be swinging above her like a metronome counting time.

She found herself looking for roses whenever she could. When work was done and she had eaten dinner with Owaine and Isole, she would scramble onto Champ's back and they would ride about the hills together, searching. Each day they traveled a little farther, exploring more of the green, lush land. They discovered nearby villages and new waterfalls and mountains. There were hillsides of daisies, buttercups, heather, and in the spring, bluebells and snowdrops, but they never found any roses.

"May I finish early this evening, Owaine?" she asked one summer's day. "I would like to train Champ."

Owaine was suspicious of her request, but he did not like to ask too much of his silver daughter. Besides, she was becoming better and better at training the wild horses they received and this autumn, they would enter town with a whole herd to sell.

"If yur wish it, but yur must be back by nightfall."

"I will."

Later that day, Beauty left the men working in the valley and whistled for Champ to follow her to the temple. When they both stood outside its golden doors, Beauty climbed on a rock and scrambled onto Champ's tall back.

Though it was summertime, there was the usual drizzle dampening the Hilland air. It made a series of rainbows that burst over the horizon in thick arches and crowded the sky with colors. A thrill in her chest, Beauty gently pressed her heels into Champ's sides and they trotted away.

Beauty had once asked Owaine what came after the Hillands and he had just stared blankly at her.

"The hills be in the far western corner of the realm, Beauty. Yur knows that."

"But there must be something at the end of them," she had persisted.

He had scratched his head. "I don't know. The sea, I suppose."

But she wanted to know definitely and she was going to find out.

Beauty urged Champ into a canter and then a full gallop. They began on a track they had followed before, rushing past a waterfall and a wide, flowing river, before skirting the edge of a nearby village and racing on over the hills. The farther they traveled, the faster Champ galloped.

When they had been riding for a full hour without pausing, Beauty slowed him to a walk, noticing that he was not even panting or sighing.

"You all right, boy?" she whispered, pressing her palm to his neck.

He had not worked up a sweat, but then neither had she. Beauty felt enlivened and excited. No other Hillander had tried to travel to the edge of the hills before and she did not know what she would find.

Beauty nudged Champ on and they galloped over the rocky green hills once more, moving ever faster than before. The wind rushed through her white hair and smarted her violet eyes so that they glistened. Champ's mane and tail rippled like ribbons, and his hooves barely made a sound on the damp turf.

Hill folk in the valleys paused in their afternoon work and looked up to see a shadow flying across the land above them. They blinked, not trusting what they had seen, for they thought that it was a silver girl astride a warhorse.

Beauty and Champ galloped on. She hugged her silver legs around his broad, bay sides and buried her hands in his black mane. They hurried on and the land grew rockier and the lush green growth turned to scrub. Then before them, Beauty caught sight of a thick, blue horizon. She tugged on Champ's mane and he gradually slowed his pace. He jogged up a steep hill covered with blue slate and then skidded to a halt.

They stood on the tip of a cliff before a dark sea. The cliff was white and chalky and it made the water appear that much darker. There was a strong, salty breeze that blew tendrils of Beauty's long white hair from her back and brought chilly bumps to her arms. It was not like the sea of Sago, which was calm and sleepy. The heavy crash of the waves here was wild and ominous, and it stretched for as far as the eye could see.

Beauty felt faintly disappointed.

"We will follow the cliffs around," she said, and Champ flicked his ears. "I want to see if there is anything more."

She turned the horse and they galloped along the cliff's edge, a chalky spray rising from Champ's hooves. They moved faster than she thought possible, outlining the Hillands like a silver line as the sun slowly sank from the sky and disappeared.

Beauty and Champ galloped all the way across the coast of the Hillands, but they saw nothing and no one except the blue choppy sea. When the stars began to glow in the sky, they turned for home, arriving at Imwane in the early morning hours.

It should have taken a moon-cycle to cross the Hillands, yet Beauty and Champ had ridden it in a night.

⸙

Two days later, Duna knocked on the door of the cottage to say that the matchmaker was coming. Beauty had seen the matchmaker a handful of times before. Though she spent most of her time in the next valley training horses, it was difficult not to notice him as he paraded about the village demanding favors of the people. He traveled the hills from village to village in the summertime, matching couples, and women would primp and fawn over him, hopeful that he would find their daughters suitable husbands.

"I just thought yur should like to know," finished Duna, winking at Isole. "We all be very excited when the matchmaker calls."

Isole gave a delighted, hopeful smile, and Owaine blushed. He was well aware that his daughter was too old to be matched with anyone, but she was ever optimistic and would giggle like a silly Hill girl whenever the matchmaker was around. In the messages he had sent home while in Sago, he had never urged her to marry and now he regretted it. Hally and Duna, although good to her, had indulged Isole like a child long after she had stopped being one, and they had failed to think of offering her name to the matchmaker. Now he knew it was too late.

"I thought yur could invite the matchmaker to sup here, Owaine," added Duna.

"Here?"

"Yes 'em," she said with a forceful smile. "Then he can't overlook no one."

"Oh, Papa, yes!" cried Isole. "We must have him here, and I'll cook him a dinner like no other!"

"If yur wishes it, my child."

"I do! I do!"

Duna and Isole began chattering about suitable dishes and Owaine turned to Beauty who was cleaning his saddle by the fire.

"I'll give yur the day off when the matchmaker comes, Beauty."

She paused and both Duna and Isole fell quiet.

"Whatever for?" she asked with a frown.

"So's yur can meet him proper."

"No one'll want her!" scoffed Isole. "She works like a man and—"

"Enough!" snapped Owaine.

Beauty stared ahead and her lip curled a little.

"Is the thought so terrible?" laughed Owaine when he saw her face, but she did not reply.

"I suggested the idea so *Isole* could impress him," began Duna. "When he sees her fine cooking he won't—"

"He can consider both my daughters, seeing as he be in my home."

Duna bit her lip and Beauty shivered.

When the afternoon came to prepare the meal for the matchmaker, Beauty was even less enthusiastic. Isole was determined to impress him with her cooking skills and nothing Beauty could do to help was good enough. Isole yelled and shouted all afternoon, and Beauty remained oddly compliant. She received criticism for an unsatisfactory short crust pastry with her head bowed meekly and her hands clasped in her lap.

When the matchmaker entered the cottage that evening, Beauty was as pale as silver snow. Isole had laid out a truly spectacular feast with an army of pies and dripping beef and steaming broth that could have fed the whole village twice over. The potent scent of the food made Beauty feel nauseated, but it had the desired effect on the matchmaker, who rubbed his barrel belly in anticipation and smiled broadly.

"This be a Hill woman that can cook," he said, taking off his crushed leather hat to reveal a mop of brown hair.

"That be all me!" squealed Isole, helping him off with his cloak. "I loves to cook."

In his shirt and slacks, the matchmaker looked fatter than it seemed possible a man could be. Beauty had seen him every summer season, of course, but always at a distance and never with a thought that she would ever be under his assessing eye.

"I assume yur are the Hill woman I am considering today?"

"Yes 'em, I be Isole—"

"And Beauty."

Owaine gestured to the silvery woman hiding in a corner and the matchmaker turned.

"My, my, I'd heard the rumors, but I'd never seen it with my own eyes."

Beauty nodded a welcome to him and placed her left hand to her chest.

"Sit down," said Isole quickly. "Try some salt bread, it be my specialty."

The family sat at the table and made the sign of the gods before they began digging into the food.

"What're the matches like this season?" asked Owaine.

The matchmaker crammed in great mouthfuls of beef. "It be good. There're more than usual."

"Have some more pie," said Isole, loading a second colossal helping onto his plate.

"Oh, I thank yur, woman."

Beauty picked and pushed her food about her plate.

"Be that a crumble I spot for dessert?" asked the matchmaker after a loud belch. He had somehow managed to devour most of the food laid before him.

Isole nodded and hurriedly filled up his mug of ale. "And a trifle and sugared custard."

The matchmaker licked his slack lips and Owaine looked worried. This meal had cost him sticks, and though they were making more than ever before, he did not wish to needlessly waste them.

Beauty declined a dessert.

"This be superb," announced the matchmaker after his third helping of crumble. "Do yur have more sugared custard?"

"Of course!" said Isole.

The meal finally came to an end, and Isole swept away the mountain of plates and bowls. Beauty was sure that she would have to clean them later.

"I wonder . . ." muttered Isole, coming to sit nervously back at the table.

The matchmaker raised an eyebrow.

"Yur wonder?" he asked.

Owaine prayed that his daughter would not be disgraced by her question.

"Yes 'em, I wonder if yur . . . "

"Yur wonder if I can find yur a match? Well, Isole, yur cooking has swayed me, and I happen to have the right Hill man. He be a widower in a village northwest called Dousal, would yur take him?"

Isole gasped and Owaine smiled in amazed relief.

"He has two children, but they be young and well behaved," added the matchmaker.

But Isole seemed barely to hear him; she looked absolutely delighted.

"I'll take him," she cried, her cheeks flushed.

"Would yur wish for me to arrange a meet?"

151

"No, I'll take him!" She clapped her hands.

"I'm happy to settle it then. And for yur other daughter, I've many matches to choose."

Beauty jumped and Isole's smile fell from her face.

"For Beauty?" asked Owaine.

"Yes 'em. A young, pretty Hill woman is easy to match but a beautiful one is easier. Begging yur pardon, Isole, what be yur young sister's name?"

Owaine and Isole both turned to look at Beauty, and they no longer saw a peculiar, frightening child, but a radiant, graceful woman. Her violet eyes were like two jewels placed in a pearly soft face. Her long white hair hung in a shimmering sheet to her waist, and though her baggy, poorly made clothes tried, they could not conceal her fine figure.

"No, yur don't understand," said Isole. "She be strange."

"Some men are collectors," replied the matchmaker. "She be a prize."

Owaine saw Beauty's deep shudder and he said, "There be no matches for Beauty." He had wanted both his daughters to be treated equally, but if Beauty did not wish it, he would not make her marry.

She looked at him gratefully.

"Ah, *Beauty*," said the matchmaker. "That be a fitting name."

"I said there be no matches for her. Yur found my Isole happiness and I thank yur kindly for it, but none needed for Beauty."

"Yur sure? She be such a fine match . . . "

"I said none."

The matchmaker stared into Beauty's amethyst eyes. "So be it," he said.

He left that evening, agreeing to arrange the marriage of Isole and the widower from Dousal, but he also spread the tale of Beauty throughout the hills. And all the Hilland villages and all the nearest towns had soon heard of a beautiful silver woman that lived in Imwane.

Chapter Nineteen

The Woman with Amethyst Eyes

Isole's marriage happened quickly. Though she would never admit it, Isole knew that she was old and she wished to have the greatest chance of conceiving a child. She and her match, Manwelly, were wed on the last day of summer in the temple in Dousal, and Owaine forked out enough sticks to ensure that his daughter had the wedding of her dreams. She must have been the only Hilland bride to ever wear so many ribbons in her hair.

Manwelly was a tall, weak-looking man with two weak-looking children that had a tendency to hang off his arms. Upon setting eyes on him, Isole resolved to fill him out with pies, and after they were married she promptly began working to her goal. She moved out of the cottage and over to the village of Dousal despite many tears wept on Duna and Hally's shoulders. But if Imwane thought that they would not see Isole again, they were sorely mistaken.

She stayed away for the first winter, resolving to run her own family, but come springtime, she began creeping back to Imwane. Over the hills she would walk briskly with the weak-looking children trailing behind her. Manwelly was not a bad husband, but he was not a good husband, either. He was prone to ailments, and if it was not his stomach giving him trouble, then his back was out of joint or his head was full of cold. Whatever it was, he said he could not work, and often Isole would be forced to ask her father for sticks. Of course, Owaine could not refuse his daughter.

"Everyone speaks of that horse of Beauty's," she said one day. "Papa, why don't yur sell it? Yur'd get a bundle."

"Champ isn't mine to sell."

"But—"

"If you want more sticks from me then yur better hush up!"

Isole pursed her lips and did not mention it again.

Though they no longer lived together, Isole still hated Beauty. Having heard rumors of a silver woman, villagers at Dousal would hassle her with questions of her mysterious sister. She tried to spread lies about an evil, violet-eyed creature, but they preferred the circulating whispers of a gods-sent being, brought to save them from something, though they knew not what. It had begun with the matchmaker's gossip and grown into a thriving rumor. The Hillanders saw Beauty galloping about the hills astride a great bay stallion and they made the sign of the gods to her as she passed.

Without Isole around, Beauty ran the cottage in Imwane. She was no great cook, but she had learned a little from Isole's lessons and she and Owaine managed well. Beauty decided to keep her bedroll in the attic though there was now an unoccupied sleeping closet downstairs. She could not imagine closing her eyes to any sight other than the yellow thatch above her with the tang of maize in the air. She swept and scrubbed the cottage to the best of her ability, fitting the chores around her work with the horses, and if it was not exactly as pristine as they were accustomed to, they thought it good enough to be free of Isole.

"Ain't yur husband gonna be wondering where you are?" Owaine asked her wearily after she had arrived yet again on their doorstep.

"Manwelly's ill."

Beauty patted the heads of the weak-looking children who were playing on the floor and went back to preparing dinner.

"Yur ain't doing that right—yur shouldn't knead the dough so. Let me do it."

"I can manage fine."

Isole settled back in her seat, her lips bared in a snarl.

"Shouldn't yur both be working?"

"Beauty and me trained as many horses as we can travel to town with next moon-cycle. Don't need to break no more."

"Yur be making bundles of sticks then?"

"Yes 'em, I suppose we will."

"I been meaning to ask if yur could spare me some for the children, see."

Owaine sighed.

———⊙⊙⊙———

A few days later, Beauty and Owaine were exercising the horses in the next valley. Beauty was riding a gray gelding in smooth circles, teaching him to arch his neck as he cantered and pick up his dainty feet.

"What d'yur think?" called Owaine.

"Perfect!" she yelled back. "He has better strides than the bay mare. He is a dream to ride."

Champ was watching nearby as always. Someone had once suggested that he be trained as a carthorse to work in the fields. His huge build would lend itself to the job, there was no denying it, but the suggestion had been quickly hushed up by others. Beauty and her stallion had become something of a charm in the Hillands and the superstitious Hill folk did not disturb their charms.

"Shall we work the black stallion next?" called Owaine.

"I will be over."

As Beauty was dismounting the gray gelding and petting and untacking him, Hally approached. He greeted his cousin warmly with his usual backslapping, but then he pulled him into a tight hug.

"What be the meaning of this?" laughed Owaine.

"Yur've brought much to Imwane since yur been back, Cousin, make no mistake!"

Hally waved a folded piece of paper in front of him as Beauty approached.

"What be that, then?"

"This be from a horse dealer in the Forest Villages. They wants to have first pickings of yur herd this autumn. News of yur quality steeds has traveled far!"

"They be more Beauty's than mine, Cousin."

Hally was grinning so much that he barely heard what Owaine said.

"Yur must travel first to the Forest Villages and let this man pick from yur herd, then sell the rest at town. This be an honor for us, Owaine, a true honor."

He passed the message to Owaine, who opened it and read for himself.

"Look here, Beauty! This man says he's already bought some of our horses from other sellers and they be the best he's ever seen!"

Owaine showed her the dots and lines on the page and she nodded vaguely, for she had never learned to read and never told him that she could not.

"I wonders how many he'll buy?" said Hally, looking over the various horses they kept grazing in pens.

"I thank yur for this news, Cousin."

Hally nodded and he went back to overseeing the men working in the fields.

"We must prepare for a longer journey," said Beauty once he was gone. "We will need to shut up the cottage, and perhaps we should start out sooner, while the weather is good?"

She looked to the drizzly, teal sky.

"Beauty, I'm not sure that yur should accompany me."

"But I must. Why would I not?"

"I brought yur to the Hillands for safety. I feel the Forest Villages are too far and unsafe."

Beauty frowned. "We would only travel to the outskirts of them," she insisted. "If this dealer is so keen to have our horses then he can surely meet us halfway?"

"I'm worried. We hear no news in these hills, but Pervorocco's a dangerous place."

This was true and Beauty knew it. The Hillands were cut off from all news of the cities, but everyone was aware of the Magic Cleansing that was still raging; the Hill folk just did not believe that it concerned them.

"I am not so sure that *you* should be making the journey, though. You are not a young Hill man."

"Yur charming," Owaine laughed. "But yur must listen to me in this, Beauty. I want nothing but yur safety, you knows that."

"I must stay if you wish it."

"Come now," said Owaine, patting her shoulder. "Don't be that way."

"I suppose I shall keep the cottage nice while you are gone."

"Don't be sad, child. There be nothing yur miss out on and yur knows I'm right."

She did, but she jutted out her chin all the same.

"I will train more horses while you are away. It will not make a difference that you are not here."

"I knows it. Yur the one that trains them all these days. Don't worry, I knows it."

"I will miss you," she added quietly.

"I'll miss yur too, child."

Owaine patted her shoulder again and they went back to work, trying not to think of it anymore.

Over the next few days they began preparing for Owaine's departure, gathering supplies and plotting a suitable route. Hally spread news among Imwane of the great honor Owaine and Beauty had brought and the villagers turned up at the cottage often to congratulate Owaine and nod shyly at Beauty. They wished him luck and said that they would pray for high sales in the temple.

"Dousal all heard bout yur going to the Forest Village too," said Isole.

It was the day Owaine was to leave, and she had turned up that morning for a surprise visit that acutally surprised no one. Sitting by the fire in the cottage, she had been chattering to her father about nothing all afternoon, waylaying his packing.

"Yur be famous around all the Hillands soon, Papa. Imwane used to be a tiny, unknown village. Yur made it known to all."

"It be Beauty that's done that."

The fire spat and Isole poked at it.

"I should remind yur to be careful on yur travels, Papa. Manwelly tells me it be dangerous outside the Hillands. Be sure to remember yur grandchildren while yur be gone also."

The weak-looking children blinked at him from where they were crouching by the fire.

"I can never forget them," muttered Owaine, gathering together his saddlebags.

Beauty was outside readying Sable and Owaine carried his luggage to her. She had been very quiet all morning, performing her chores with a solemn demeanor that she hoped he had not noticed.

"Everything is set," she said, stepping away and biting on her thumb.

Champ was loitering behind her, his ears turned back.

"Yur be upset, Beauty. Champ tells me so."

"Well, of course."

The horses to be sold were waiting in a long line by the temple, already tethered together and minded by Hally until Owaine was packed and ready to leave.

"I wishes yur could come with me, child. Yur knows that, don't yur?"

She nodded.

"Beauty . . . be there anything that I can buy you from the Forest Villages?"

"I suspect that Isole has already asked you for ribbons."

"Yes 'em."

"I only ask that you come back soon."

He smiled at her and stroked the top of her smooth hair.

"Would yur like dresses or ribbons or pearls?"

Beauty laughed. "I want nothing."

But Owaine did not look satisfied. "I'll find yur something, child. Those sticks be yurs anyway, not mine."

Isole and the weak-looking children came out to say their goodbyes, while Owaine heaved himself into Sable's saddle and pointed the mare in the direction of the temple.

"Take care, Beauty. I be back with yur soon."

She nodded; she could not speak, and then he was gone.

She had not been without Owaine for seasons and seasons, and she surprised herself with how deeply she felt the loss. As soon as he was gone, Isole promptly left, towing the children behind her, without even a parting word; and then Beauty was very alone.

"Champ," she whispered that evening, stepping out of the cottage after a long, solitary dinner.

He was waiting for her and trotted over as she appeared, placing his large head in her open arms. She traced the outline of his white blaze with her forefinger, tickling the whorl in the middle of his forehead. He sighed, pushing his soft muzzle against her silver chest.

She looked up at the autumn sky smattered with stars that clustered about a full moon. She had always noticed how wide and clear the sky was in the Hillands compared to the foggy narrowness of Sago. She thought of Owaine somewhere on the road, camping in a shepherd's hut or under the shelter of a tree.

She kissed Champ's nose and reluctantly went back inside the cottage.

That night she dreamt of the red rose, and gray shadows crowded her mind. She awoke in the early hours of the morning and she was fearful.

CHAPTER TWENTY

The Gray Shadow

A moon-cycle passed, and Beauty spent the chilly days tending horses and keeping the cottage clean. She spoke little to anyone and felt painfully lonely. Champ, at least, was able to offer her some comfort, but she could not shake off a sense of dread that grew steadily darker within her. Her dreams were worsening each night and the forest felt as if it were creeping nearer. She caught herself staring at it sometimes and had to quickly look away.

One morning, Hally brought her a message as she worked with a wild dun mare in the valley. The mare was newly caught by Imwane rustlers and in the early stages of training. Beauty was trying to get her used to human company and she was sitting in front of her pen, cleaning tack and singing Hilland songs quietly. The mare's dull golden sides had once heaved with terrified, hurried breaths, but listening to Beauty's soft voice had helped her to gradually calm down. She no longer cantered in agitated circles or bucked to be let out. A few days from now, Beauty planned to try grooming her and depending on how the mare received that, she would know when she could begin breaking her.

"Beauty! Beauty! Yur won't believe it!"

The mare's head shot up and she flattened her ears, bucking and shying away to the other side of her pen.

Beauty grimaced.

"I'm sorry for that, but yur have to hear this," puffed Hally, running to her side. He held out a piece of paper to her and she took it, pretending to read the writing.

"Ain't yur rejoiced?"

"Yes . . . "

"I can't barely believe that man gone and bought *all* the horses. I were hopeful for five or six, but all!"

Beauty gasped. "Owaine is on his way back?"

"Yes 'em, so he says there."

She grinned. "Thank you for this information. I truly am over-joyed."

Hally grinned back. "Sorry 'bout the mare, but yur see now why I rushed. I hope Owaine's gone and sold them for a good price. Oh, it's better than any one of us thought!"

Hally continued to babble, but something over his shoulder caught Beauty's eye. There was movement in the depths of the dark forest that bled over this side of the valley, and suddenly a bird screeched. A white-feathered thing soared into the air, disappearing into the wet sky. The dun mare whinnied shrilly and Beauty shuddered.

"It be cold and getting colder," said Hally.

"Yes, I have noticed." Beauty looked at the blank sky behind him.

"I be seeing yur, Beauty." Hally nodded a farewell before hurrying off to spread the news.

"Champ!"

The stallion trotted over to Beauty and she leaned against him, her heart beating quickly.

"Another moon-cycle and he will be back," she said, staring at the forest.

She had dreamt of strange things every night since Owaine left and she longed for his safe return. She hoped that he returned before . . . before whatever was going to happen came to be.

⬥

The harsh Hilland winter arrived early and a moon-cycle after she had received the message about Owaine, Beauty was chopping wood when snowflakes began to fall. They fluttered from the gaping sky like pearly droplets, quickly layering on the ground. She watched them, her chest heavy with foreboding, as they came thicker and faster.

It had been bitterly cold lately, and the villagers had prayed at every ceremony in the temple that the snow would hold off. In this weather the hills would be treacherous and sleeping in little shelter would be almost impossible. Beauty hoped that Owaine had not set out from town yet and could wait out the snow there. She pleaded to the sky to wait until he returned, but inside, she knew winter was here to stay.

Throwing down her axe, she ran to the next valley. It was eerily deserted and she began herding the horses to a shelter. The rest of the men must have finished already and taken refuge for the night. The snow was increasing rapidly and already coating the ground in a film of white. There were clumps in Champ's mane and tail, and she tried to put him away with the other horses but he would not let her.

"Fine," she snapped. "Freeze then!"

But she knew he would not and he waited outside for her as he always did.

163

She moved around the cottage restlessly, picking up and replacing pots and pans and anything that came within her reach. Her eyes flicked constantly to the dark windows, which were gradually becoming white. Wind grated against the walls and whistled and roared outside. The fire was low in the grate and she should have been preparing dinner, but she did not feel hungry.

Taking a candle, she opened the door and peered out, seeing snow everywhere. The blustery gale dragged at her flame before blowing it out, and a biting chill tore through her furs and hit her to the bone. She squinted through the blizzard looking for Champ and saw him standing hunched under a tree down the hillside. He would be safe there, but she worried all the same. With great effort she closed the door once more and retreated into the cottage.

She felt feverish. Her forehead burned and her hands had turned glittering silver. She thought that she must be dreaming. Grabbing an extra blanket, she stumbled up the ladder to the attic and tumbled onto her bedroll. She pulled the covers over her, her head woozy, and she thought she saw her amulet swinging above her before she was pulled into a dark sleep.

She dreamt of the red rose once again and it called to her. The blood of death. The blood of battle. She remembered hearing something long ago about a war that lasted generations and painted Pervorocco scarlet red with bloodshed. The rose in her dream was suddenly crowded with gray shadows that were drawing near. They were upon it, chasing it. She woke to the roar of a beast. She was drenched in sweat and gasping. Above her, hanging from the rusty nail, the amulet was deadly still.

Throwing off her covers, she scrambled down the ladder and threw open the cottage door once more. The cold hit her with a rush and a vision came to her clearly. At the top of the hill, outside the temple of Imwane, stood a gray shadow. The State officials had found her, and they were led by Eli.

CHAPTER TWENTY-ONE

The Proposal

Beauty knew better than to try and run, so she waited instead. The unceasing whirling of the blizzard had stopped and flakes now fell steadily. The ground was thick with snow, fresh and blistering white. It crumpled beneath her feet as she went to retrieve Champ, and it almost leaked over the top of her boots.

As golden dawn reached over the hills, she hand-fed Champ maize, as she used to when he was a sickly colt. He enjoyed it immensely and licked her fingers as they both shivered in the gnawing chill.

Beauty concentrated on tending to her horse to keep herself calm. She allowed herself one glance at the temple but that was all. She thought that she saw shadows around it, but she could not be sure.

After an hour, villagers began to emerge from their cottages and clear paths to their doors. Children wandered out to play, dogs scrambled in the whiteness barking, the men shouted to one another about a day off work, and the gray shadow traveled down the hillside.

Beauty saw it right away but it took the villagers a little longer to notice. Someone yelled and several women screamed, and then there was a mad dash in a white flurry as people ran to their cottages. The thundering of the State officials' horses echoed across the valley and their gray uniforms blazed in the icy clear.

"We claim this villages as ours!" boomed a voice. "Come out of your houses at once!"

There were more screams and cries and shouting.

The State officials charged into the center of Imwane where Hally's house stood, brandishing their sabers and rifles. There were twenty of them in all—not many to fight against, but Hillanders did not fight. They did not even own weapons.

"Come out!" she heard Eli yell.

He rode at the head of the troop, a sword raised in one hand and a rifle in the other. He wore the gray State uniform, but he had a golden sash across his shoulders and several badges on his lapel. He had grown into a handsome, terrible, man, as Beauty always knew he would.

"I said, come out!"

A shot was fired into the air, and those outside threw themselves on the ground, crying.

"What be the meaning of this?" cried Hally, striding from his cottage. He stared at the State officials in shock and Duna cowered behind him.

"Are you the leader here?" Eli asked.

"Y-yes 'em."

"I am claiming this village as my own until you hand over a young woman to me. Her name is Beauty House of Rose and I have learned that she is here."

There were gasps.

"There be no one—"

"I warn you, punishment is death." Eli pointed his rifle at Hally and Duna screeched.

"P-p-please," stammered Hally. "Have mercy on us, we be—" He paused and stared.

Everyone turned to see Beauty and Champ. She walked slowly and carefully in the snow toward them, her hand pressed to her horse's neck.

"I believe you are looking for me."

She did not feel as brave as she looked—her teeth ached she was clenching them so fiercely.

Eli smiled and let out a long, deep breath. "You have been hard to find."

"I did not want to be found."

Beauty glanced at the terrified villagers around her. "Leave these people, they have done nothing wrong."

Eli turned to his troops. "Surround the village. No one goes anywhere until I say so. I will speak with you," he pointed at Beauty. "Alone."

She turned and began walking away.

"Stop!" Eli screeched.

"If you wish to speak to me, then you shall be invited into my cottage. It is the Hilland way."

She heard him following her on his horse, and she pressed her shoulder against Champ's side. She was frightened, but she knew better than to show it. The commotion had destroyed the beautiful blanket of snow, churning it into turmoil, and she waded through muddy whiteness to the cottage. Her gaze flicked to the forest and she prayed that there would be a way out of this.

Patting Champ, she left him outside and entered the cottage. A few moments later Eli followed, and she made the sign of the gods behind her back. Silently, she called to Owaine; wherever he was, she wished that he would stay there, safe from the harm that she sensed would come.

"Beauty, Cousin, I have found you. I should have known that horseman was a Hillander, but who would think to search for you all the way up here? Not I." He looked around the room, taking in the simple furnishings and pens of animals. "Things have changed for you, Beauty. I have changed also."

"Yes, I see that clearly."

He smiled.

"How came you to be a State official?" she asked.

"Somehow you managed to escape Sago, but we did not. We were stopped on the outskirts of the city and sent right back."

"That does not explain how you came to wear that gray uniform."

"All in good time, Beauty. I am purely happy to have found you at present."

His eyes wandered over her and her knees trembled. "I always knew that you would be beautiful. I saw it before everyone else. Where they saw a terrifying child, I saw a fine woman. Last season, I was posted to the Forest Villages and we were pushed farther north, hunting out Magic Beings. That was when I heard the first whisperings of a silvery woman in the hills. I knew it was you immediately and I followed the rumors here."

"That is a long journey."

"Yes, we do extraordinary things for treasure. My men were not delighted to hunt through a desolate, forsaken place such as this, but we stopped in villages along the way. These people are remarkably welcoming with the right incentives."

Outside, the buttery light of the winter sun flashed on the snow.

"How came you to be a State official?" Beauty whispered, but Eli ignored her.

"I dream of you every night, Beauty. Do you understand what that is like?"

She shook her head and Eli's lips tightened. "I know that you dream. Am I right?"

"Everyone dreams."

"Not like we do."

He was taller than her and his powerful, lithe figure loomed above her own. He stepped forward.

"How came you to be a State official?" she asked once again.

"By killing my mother."

"Ma Dane is dead?"

"You knew that already."

She did. She had known it would happen when she was a child and it had haunted her since, but only now did it make sense. She had always seen Ma Dane tied to a stake; a tiny, thin figure dressed in rags and that was all. Now, she saw the logs at her feet and the guttering flames licking them. Now, she saw Eli standing at the front, in the crowd of State gray uniforms, his hand pressed to his chest as he watched with his fellow comrades as a Magic Blood was destroyed. He watched his mother smothered in flames and burned to black ash. His expression did not flicker.

Beauty coughed, the smoke of the vision disappearing as quickly as it came.

"Ma Dane was a Magic Blood, and she had to die. If I did not turn her over to the State, their hunters would find her," said Eli.

"They would not find you?"

"No. She taught me strong methods and I am more powerful than she ever was or could be. Only one person knows of what I have, and she stands before me now."

Beauty's fingers tingled with fear. Outside she heard a muffled thump as a pile of snow fell from the cottage roof.

"What do you want with me?"

"I wish you to marry me."

She gasped.

"You cannot say no for there is no, choice. You will come with me."

"I will not."

"You may marry me, or you may die."

CHAPTER TWENTY-TWO

The Red Rose

At noon that day, Beauty stood in the cottage, biting down on her lip to stop it from trembling. There was a State official posted outside the door to watch over her while Eli left to speak with Hally, and Champ was frantically whinnying outside, sensing something was amiss. She wished to go to him but she was paralyzed with fear.

She stared at the chickens clucking and scratching in the pen near her. She had never been particularly fond of them since they smelled the worst of all the indoor animals, but she was glad for them now. She would not have been able to endure total silence, and their familiar sounds reminded her of winter evenings sitting in front of the fireside with Owaine singing Hilland songs while Isole prepared dinner.

Champ whinnied again, rousing her from the memory, and she pulled an extra fur over her shoulders, instructing herself to be brave. She opened the door of the cottage to see that it was still snowing. Upon seeing her, the State official on guard put his hand on his rifle.

"There is no need for that. I am just going to feed and tend to my horses."

"You are not allowed to leave."

"I must, but you may follow me if you wish."

She strode away from the cottage and the State official glanced worriedly around before stumbling after her.

Champ cantered to her side, his ears flat against his head, and she tried to soothe him with gentle words, but her voice sounded strained. He followed her closely as she walked through Imwane to the next valley, almost clipping her heels with his hooves.

"If you try anything, I shall be forced to shoot," warned the State official behind her.

"There will be no need for that."

As they passed the cluster of cottages at the center of Imwane, Beauty saw worried faces at windows. The hillside was deserted of animals that—having heard the gunshot and sensing the fear of the villagers—had fled to a safer place, and the village felt eerily quiet.

The next valley was also empty. The snow there was a thick, uninterrupted sheet like a sweep of white satin, and Beauty regretted ruining its smoothness with her boots. Champ's great feathered hooves left dish-shaped tracks in the snow that followed the neat footsteps she made.

The horses were pleased to see Beauty and she petted each of them in turn, lingering on the dun mare that had recently made such progress. She considered setting them free, instinct telling her that she would not see them again, but she reasoned that they would be well looked after by the Imwane villagers once she was gone. They would not be forgotten. Perhaps Owaine would even be home soon, but where he was concerned, her premonitions drew a blank, and that frightened her.

She fed and watered the horses, breaking up the ice in their trough, all under the watchful eye of the State official who was standing hunched against the cold.

When she had finished, she began climbing the hillside.

"Where are you going?" called the State official.

"To the temple. You may follow me again if you wish."

"No. No, I order you to return to your cottage now."

"Eli will not mind. I wish to pray before I marry him. It is the Hilland way."

"W-what? Marry Pa House of Rose?"

Beauty continued on, her hand buried in Champ's mane to stop her from slipping in the snow, and the State official followed, too shocked to delay her again. Once she reached the temple, she patted Champ's side before pulling on the creaky doors.

The golden walls were flaking and peeling more than ever. Owaine had once told her that it had been an Imwane Head Man's bright idea to buy gold paint from town and adorn the temple walls with it, but the villagers thought it a ridiculous thing now.

"Yur don't need no pomp to worship the gods," he had said. "Yur don't even need a temple. It's the faith, is all."

She entered the silent temple. It was completely bare and she knelt on the cold ground at the far end, pressing her palms to the floor. Behind her she heard the State official slip inside and wait awkwardly by the door, but she paid him little heed.

She knew not how long she stayed there. With her eyes closed she fell into a trance, searching herself for answers but finding none. She had never been able to control her visions and dreams; they seemed to come to her instinctively and she wished now that this was not the case. She sought guidance and, unable to awake whatever strange powers she had, she turned instead to Hilland scripture. It was a confused and shrouded thing. The ceremonies at the temple revolved around the gathering of the village, the thanking of the gods for blessings sent, and the singing of songs. Beauty had heard many commands from the scripture spoken in ceremonies, but at that moment, she could focus on nothing. Instead, she asked the gods what they wished her to be, but before she could form an answer, she felt the barrel of a rifle prod her shoulder.

She gasped and her eyes snapped open.

"What are you doing?"

The State official was gone and Eli stood behind her, a rifle cocked in his hands.

"Praying to gods? Cousin, you have turned positively native."

Beauty tried to stumble to her feet, but her legs were numb.

"While you have been *praying*, I have been conversing with that simple leader of yours. He denies knowing anything about your powers, even after some . . . persuasion."

It was darker in the temple now.

"Have you made your choice, Cousin?" He brushed the barrel of the rifle from her collarbone to her chest.

"If I marry you, I will surely be killed," she said. "You may be able to hide your power, but they only have to look at me and they will be suspicious."

"I will protect you."

"Like you protected Ma Dane?"

Eli's eyes hardened and he jabbed her with the rifle. "That was unavoidable. I have become indispensible to the State and they would not dare harm my wife."

Beauty shuddered at the word. "Why should you even wish to marry me?"

"Because I have thought of nothing else, awake or asleep, since the moment I saw you. I must have you. It is important, although I do not yet know why."

He reached out and lightly touched the silvery smoothness of her cheek, running his finger down the curve of her neck. His touch left a smarting sting.

"No."

"Cousin, I have already warned you of the alternative."

"No!"

He grabbed her arm and thrust her toward him, pressing his face to her own, and she could smell the cleanness of his skin and feel the heat of his body. He pulled her forehead to his lips and kissed her, paying no heed to her cries.

"You will come with me."

"No!"

Suddenly there was an almighty bang and Eli fell to the floor. Beauty stood shaking over him with the rifle in her grasp. She did not remember grabbing it or firing it, but her finger was hooked around the trigger.

Eli yelped; there was blood everywhere. Red clogs of it pooled on the floor and the air reeked of a metallic tang. Sticky, scarlet liquid was spurting from the wound in Eli's right leg and he flailed wildly on the floor, choking and gasping.

Beauty watched for a second, the thump of her pulse ringing in her ears and then, suddenly, she ran. The rifle dropped from her hands, clattering on the temple floor, and she fled through the doors, slamming them shut on Eli's deathly screams.

Outside, the hills were quiet and the only sound was the whining of the wind. It was dusk and the Imwane valley was dark and deserted. Beauty had expected to see State officials running up the hillside to capture her, having heard the gunshot, but there was no one. Perhaps the temple's walls had contained the sound. She did not know.

She held out her hands in front of her and they were silvery in the fading light, though she sensed them splattered with blood.

I must leave, she told herself.

She inspected her palms and fingers, expecting to see at least a droplet of red, but there was nothing.

I have taken a life, she thought.

She whistled for Champ, but for once he was not near, and instead she climbed down the hillside alone, skidding in the snow.

As she approached the center of Imwane she heard raucous laughter. Keeping to the shadows, she crept close to the villagers' barn and saw the State officials feasting inside. Hally and Duna stood at the back beside some of the Hill women, their heads bowed. When a State official ordered it, they brought forward more food and watched with sad hearts as it was devoured.

Beauty made the sign of the gods and slipped away.

She hurried to the cottage, intending to pack a saddlebag and flee, when she saw a sight that stopped her in her tracks. Standing outside with her reins in disarray stood Sable, her ears flat against her head and her eyes rolling. Champ was nearby, nudging her with his nose and attempting to comfort her as she snorted and stamped her feet.

Beauty ran to her immediately, but Sable bucked.

"Easy, girl, easy."

She had never known Sable to be anything but sedate and steady. Manwelly's weak-looking children liked to hang off her nose and pull her ears and she was always gentle with them.

Beauty calmed and soothed Sable as if she were a newly caught mare, but still her flanks trembled and she sidestepped nervously. As soon as her saddle and bridle were off she cantered away, tossing her head as if she were running from something.

"Owaine?" she cried, carrying the tack into the house. It was not like him to leave a horse untended and she feared that he had been taken by the State officials.

"Owaine?"

"Beauty? Be that you?"

She gasped and dropped the tack, rushing to the old, withered man beside the fire. He was so frail that he could not sit on a chair, but instead lay on the floor with his traveling furs still wrapped around him.

"What—what happened to you?" she cried.

There were new wrinkles on his face and his body shook.

"I got it for you, Beauty . . . " He reached inside his fur and brought out a dark red rose that stopped her breath.

"Where did you get such a thing? Owaine, what has it cost you?"

He licked his dry, cracked lips. "I sold all our horses and made for home, but a storm were coming. I wished to be in the hills, and I thought I'd make it but it crept up on us. I gave Sable the reins and she walked, gods bless her. We were lost in a forest and then I saw . . . a castle."

Beauty could smell the red rose already. Its perfume was clogging the room with a sweet, light scent that made her senses ache.

"It were like nothing I ever seen before," Owaine continued. "The castle were huge. Sick and starved, I goes to it and it . . . welcomed me. I woke next morning to leave and then I saw a garden full of red roses. I remembered my Beauty asking me bout them once. There were so many, I never thought anyone would mind me taking just one."

"Who would mind?"

Owaine's face crumpled. "A beast—a great and terrible beast!"

Beauty clutched her head, her vision lilting before her eyes.

"He said I stole that rose. He said I must pay, but I were so afraid, I barely understood. I prayed to the gods to save me, but he said I would suffer—said that if I did not stay at the castle then I'd die."

Owaine coughed. He seemed to be getting weaker by the second. Beauty took his hands in hers.

"Owaine, you are . . . dying?" she whispered.

"Hush, Beauty. Hush."

"I must go to this castle and see to this beast."

"No!" he cried, spluttering and wheezing.

"I must. There is no time to explain, but I will not let you die, and either way, I need to flee Imwane tonight, for something terrible has happened."

"My child, I cannot let you go."

She held his withered hand. "You are my father, and you once saved my life. It is my turn to save yours."

"No, Beauty. No!"

"Do not fret, I know I will be safe, for I have dreamt it," she lied.

"My child . . . my child . . . "

She kissed his dry, papery cheek. "I am only sorry that I must leave you in this state. But lie still. I will bargain with this beast and you will feel strong again. As soon as you do, go to Hally. He will care for you."

"Beauty . . . "

A sob caught her throat, but she swallowed it. She took the terrible red rose from his fingers and felt the heaviness of it in her hands. The soft, full petals spiraled out from its tight center, interweaving in folds of scarlet, and it had one purple thorn on its stem that glittered in the firelight.

Without it in his hands, Owaine's body slumped and his head lolled against the floorboards.

"Goodbye, Papa," she whispered.

Then she heard a shout from outside. Running to the door, she saw that it was snowing again and heavy flakes were raining down. Across the hill, lights were dancing around the temple, and she guessed that the State officials had found Eli. She looked over her shoulder at the cottage once more before shutting the door and whistling Champ to her side. He came easily, as if he had been waiting for her call all along.

Straightening her fur cloak, she clambered onto his back and placed the red rose behind her ear. Burying her hands in Champ's mane, she tried to ignore the intense fear churning in her stomach.

"It is now, boy."

She barely needed to press her heels into his sides before Champ was galloping toward the forest. It loomed before them in the black night, thick and dense. She could see nothing in its depths but brambles and trunks and darkness. Champ ran straight at it, his hooves kicking up fistfuls of snow, and there were now shouts and cries behind them. A slither of a milky moon lit their way and it shone lonely in the sky, abandoned by all the stars.

The forest rushed closer and Beauty refused to shut her eyes. She stared at it, meeting it headlong with a narrow, challenging gaze. There was a whine of wind and then suddenly they were swallowed whole, and the darkness was all about them.

Part Three

A woman walked out of the glaring sun and into the mountain temple, her red gown sweeping about her sandaled feet. She turned a prayer wheel at the entrance in the direction of the moon, as was customary, and pressed her thumb and index finger together.

Inside, the temple was shadowed and cool. The woman patted her damp brow with the back of her hand and breathed in the smoky scent of incense. It made her nauseated. Everything made her sick to her stomach at the moment, and she swallowed down the bile at the back of her throat with a grimace.

Taking off her sandals, she padded into the inner temple, cooling her feet on the colorful, ragged carpets adorning the floor. She had walked to the temple from the mountain camp, and the rocky passes and midday sun had worn her out. She remembered with a wry smile that she used to be able to hike whole days effortlessly, but things were different now.

She flexed her sore back and moved farther into the temple, passing colorful streamers that hung from the ceiling, ducking under fringes of fabric, and weaving between wooden prayer benches. She could see the golden feet of the goddess's statue at the opposite end, but it would be a while before she reached it. She accidentally knocked an oil lamp off a table and it clattered to the floor.

"Asha?"

She froze. She thought that she was alone and she turned, hoping that it was not the teacher.

"What are you doing here? I thought that this place would be deserted!"

It was the traveling professor from the University of Magic in The Neighbor. The woman smiled, relieved.

"Hello there, Pa," she replied in their Western Realm tongue.

"Oh no, please let us speak in the mountain dialect. I must return home soon and I wish to master it." He spoke haltingly and with incorrect verb enunciation.

"Of course, as you wish."

"Thank you. I wanted to travel to all the temples one last time." He gestured to a pocketbook in his hands. "I wanted to record as much of them as possible so that I never forget."

"I thought that you collected species."

"I seek to understand and record many things." He straightened out his robes. "It is so hot here. Were it not also so beautiful then I doubt that I could stand it. You fair very well."

"I have experienced many climates."

The professor raised an eyebrow. "Well, we might all fair well at a sorcerer's side?"

Asha flushed.

"What are you talking about?" she asked too quickly.

"I have heard rumors."

"A man of learning should know better than to listen to rumors."

"The teacher said something to me once also. He asked if you ever left the camp at night. He asked how powerful you were."

She had wondered if the teacher suspected her. She caught him watching her sometimes, staring into her brown eyes as if he might read her soul.

"You cannot expect them not to be curious," the professor pressed on. "You appeared to them suddenly at night, begging for sanctuary. They are well versed in scripture and they wonder what they house."

"I owe no explanations to you."

He bowed his head. "So be it. I did not wish to upset you, Asha, forgive me."

"All right," she said, and turned to go.

"But I take it that you know the perils of sorcery? You know what you are dealing with? The teacher told me that the scriptures warn—"

"You violate my honor!"

He bowed once more. "Forgive me."

"Leave!"

He did so, glancing back at her dark figure just once. When he was gone, Asha sighed deeply and rubbed her throbbing head. She padded on through the temple once more, her chest heavy.

She reached the feet of the great golden statue of the goddess, and she knelt. From beneath her red gown, she took out an amulet and held it in her palm. Carefully, she pressed the amulet to her stomach as was the custom of the Pervoroccian Houses, even though she was far from her home country.

The baby inside her stirred.

"Great goddess, I pray for my child."

Tears rolled down her cheeks. She was heartbroken and tired with the secrets that she must conceal. In a few days time she would have to leave the mountains; the teacher was getting too suspicious. She knew that she would have to get her child to her sister, Dane, somehow, for she had dreamt it. But she was weary.

"I pray for my love too. Bring him back to me. This child must have a family."

But she knew that it could not be so; her sorcerer had told her as much before he abandoned her in this forsaken place, carrying his child.

CHAPTER TWENTY-THREE

The Beast

Iron gates clanged shut behind them of their own accord, and Beauty and Champ halted before a deep moat. On the opposite bank stood a castle made of coppery bricks and twisting turrets that disappeared into a shifting magenta sky. Champ twitched.

"Steady, boy," Beauty said, but her voice wavered.

She thought that she had heard something. Something like a distant, rumbling roar of a terrifying creature, but she could not be sure. Now she heard nothing.

The castle was some distance away; the moat, meadows, water fountains, and walled gardens stood between them and the great building. The light here was dark and feathery, and it hung in a mist that swirled around the ground. Beauty glanced up at the crescent moon, wondering if it was the same that had watched over her in all her seasons.

For the last half hour, she and Champ had thundered past bracken and woven between trunks in the forest, instinct guiding them. She was no longer cold, though the snow continued to fall; it settled strangely in this place. Icicles hung from tree branches, yet the grand, sculpted fountains spurted water with little trouble. The water droplets even looked as though they might be warm to the touch, and the snow did not cover everything; there were whole orchards and fields left bare.

An echoing clang sounded and a drawbridge lowered, sweeping across the wide, shadowed moat. It hit the ground before Champ's hooves with a bump and Beauty fought to keep him under control.

"Easy, boy. Easy."

She urged him on with her heels and they walked slowly over the drawbridge toward the castle entrance, past meadows of fresh grass, evergreen mazes, and up stone steps. It was silent; there were no rabbits rustling in the bushes or birds singing in the trees. The thought of Owaine kept Beauty moving forward. Without the image of his frail, dying face, she would surely have turned and ran.

As they approached the castle, Beauty saw thick vines covering its red-bricked walls and twisting about its latticed windows. They were studded with thorns, and fat flowers dripped from the vines in bunches. As she drew closer, Beauty realized that these were roses of every color: pink, yellow, orange, purple, blue, green, gold, and silver. They were every shape and hue imaginable and she gasped at the sight of them.

Champ stepped onto the graveled drive before the castle, the stones crunching beneath his hooves, and all of a sudden, every rose turned blood red. A dark shadow darted from a corner and the air was split with the horrendous roar of a beast.

Champ screeched, rearing onto his hind legs, and Beauty lost her seating, tumbling from his back. She smacked onto the hard ground, the wind knocked from her lungs.

"Who dares to pass here?"

The realm swam before her eyes and she wondered if this were a dream. Champ was still whinnying and rearing, his eyes rolling with fear, and for a moment, Beauty thought that she had heard a creature speaking.

"You trespass on this enchanted land!"

She heard it again—a strange sound that was part snarl and part blackness.

Champ's front legs slammed to the ground and the earth shook. It roused Beauty, and she stumbled to her feet as her horse reared onto his haunches once more.

She froze, catching sight of a great beast before her.

It had the body of a griffin bare of feathers, with wings coiled on its back and transparent, webbed skin on its legs. Fangs curved from its mouth and bones jutted from every angle, stretching the skin of its crouched form.

"What do you want here?" it roared.

Its face had something of a lion in it, with matted clumps of fur and a snubbed snout, but most terrible of all were its eyes—hazel and human.

"I . . ."

Beauty felt woozy and faint. Champ was still bucking and rearing beside her, his hooves faltering in the gravel, and he was in danger of toppling backwards.

The beast took a swooping step forward and the blood rushed to Beauty's head.

"No!" she cried, holding out her hands. "Do not step closer!"

Her voice came out trembling and thin, but she was amazed that she could speak at all.

The beast gave a low, rumbling growl, but he moved back. She turned away from him and ran to Champ, dodging his thrashing hooves.

"Easy, boy, easy."

He snorted and bucked, but she placed her hands on his face and he did not rear again. He shook with fear. She whispered and hummed to him, but his eyes rolled and his flanks heaved and foamed with sweat. She remembered the state of Sable at Imwane, and then she thought of Owaine and her panic for his life brought her courage.

"I have come to speak with you," she said, her voice echoing about the eerie grounds.

"How found you this place? How came you to know of me?"

"I am the daughter of a man you have cursed . . . " She stared at Champ's brown muzzle as she spoke, unable to look at anything else. " . . . and I have come to save his life."

There was a crashing snarl that made Champ flinch from her hands and she squeezed her eyes shut, her head throbbing with the sound.

"That thief dies! He pays for the treasure that he stole! A life for a life."

"But he—"

"We gave him food and shelter from the storm and he chooses to repay us with theft!"

Beauty pulled the red rose from where it had tangled in her hair. The thorn had caught her cheek and left a pale scratch, but not even a petal of the flower was dented.

"You mean this? I come to return it to you."

From the corner of her eyes she saw that the shadow shifted.

"It is no use to us now."

"But I have returned it, and you can raise the curse from my father."

A snarl blasted the air, lifting the hair from her shoulders, and she fought to control Champ, who was wild with terror.

"There is nothing I can do. He took a life from this castle and he must repay it with his own. Had he not left, he could have lived here as a prisoner."

There was a moment of silence.

"You cannot lift the spell?"

The beast growled. "Even if I wished to do such a thing, I could not."

"What if . . . what if I will . . . " she swallowed hard and jutted out her chin. "What if I will give my life?" She shuddered.

"You will take his place?"

"He took that rose for me and I will die for him. I owe him at least that much."

The roses covering the castle turned light blue in a flowing burst of color.

"I will move closer to you."

The shadow approached, and Champ cantered to a distance with a squeal, but Beauty stood her ground. Her legs shuddered and she could feel its eyes upon her.

"You are a woman?" it grunted.

"Y-yes. I am different, but I am a woman."

"You are different?"

"My colorings are unusual."

"Are they? It has been a long time since I have seen . . . but never mind." The shadow moved away from her once more. "If you give your life to this place then your father will not die."

"You are certain?"

"A life for a life."

Beauty glanced up and wished she had not. Two hazel eyes bore into her from a horrific, terrifying face.

"What are the terms?" she whispered.

"You will live with us in this castle forever and you will never leave."

Beauty thought of Eli and the State officials and the temple on the hill. Most of all, she thought of Owaine's pale, waning face.

"It is a deal."

The beast made a noise that sounded like a gasp.

"I will return my horse to my father," she said.

"If you leave, you will die. Just as he would have."

She quivered at his roar. "If I cannot leave then my horse must stay."

"So be it. I have stables and he will be attended to there."

Beauty looked down at her silvery hands and felt a sob rise to her throat.

"And where will I be kept?" she asked.

"You shall have your own rooms in the castle."

"Who else lives here?"

"You will see."

A tear escaped from Beauty's eye. "So be it," she whispered.

⚬⚬⚬

The beast stood watching the silvery woman cry.

"Take your horse to the stables," he said. "Then enter the castle. You will be shown to your rooms. And then you must come to see me."

Beauty did not reply.

She walked through the enchanted grounds to Champ's side, half fearful that the beast would seize her from behind. The bay stallion was rigid with fear, the bulging muscles of his haunches stiff and tight, and it took her some time to calm him enough to follow her. She stroked, petted, and sung to him and he caught her tears with his velvety muzzle. After a period of commiseration, both felt strong enough to go on and with his head over her shoulder, Beauty walked Champ to the castle.

The beast was gone. Or at least he could no longer be seen. Beauty felt that he was never gone here and that wherever she stood in these grounds he would always be watching her. She shivered.

A gate at the end of the castle opened. She heard its creaking hinges, and both she and Champ jumped. At first she thought that it had moved of its own accord, but then she saw a movement in the air. The faint outline of some indistinguishable shape could just be made out, and it appeared to be waiting for her. She stared at it for a moment, her heart thumping in her chest, and then it swung the gate again impatiently, as if urging her forward.

She walked Champ toward it slowly, keeping her eyes fixed on its fluid form, but it did not move until she and Champ were through the gate, when it closed it quietly behind them. From then on, doors and gates were opened for Beauty and Champ by a never-ending stream of outlined figures. Some were tall, some were short, some looked as if they could almost be human, while others appeared as if there were barely formed at all. They lead Beauty and Champ into a vast cobbled courtyard, and there was no sound save the *clip clop* of Champ's hooves.

"Easy, boy," she whispered as the double doors of a stable were pushed open.

Beauty led Champ inside a tall brick building with row upon row of wide, empty stalls. It was the largest stable she had ever seen; bigger even than those at Rose Herm. The half door of the nearest stall was swung open to reveal a thick bedding of straw and a full net of hay, which perked Champ up considerably.

Beauty tried hanging around to settle him in, but once he had begun chomping hay, he seemed at peace. She petted and stroked him until the doors of the stable were opened again and she knew that the outlines were calling her.

"All right," she hissed. She turned to Champ and kissed his white blaze. "I'll be back, boy," she whispered.

She heard him snort as she stepped out of the stables and the double doors swung shut behind her.

"Where do I go now?"

She wondered if the outlines could speak. If they could, they did not answer her.

Instead, one opened a gate ahead and Beauty followed her invisible guides to a side door of the castle. Side door it may be, but it was ornate nonetheless, with a marbled arch of carved cherubs that danced continuously from one end to the next, playing harps, horns, and trumpets. Just before she stepped inside, she noticed that the roses of the castle had turned dark blue.

Rose Herm had been excessively grand, but the interior of this castle was more so. There were thick fur rugs, carved stone staircases, dark sculptures, golden tables, gilded paintings, courtyards of lush green grass, balconies, wide quads, and tapestries. Beauty could not take it all in, and the decor flitted before her eyes like a mirage that seemed to evaporate as she passed.

She was led through long, twisting corridors, tall halls, wide galleries, and up a tower. Finally, she came to a sturdy oak door that opened slowly, as if in anticipation, and inside was a huge, tall room that she assumed was hers. Everything was a shade of pink, from the rugs on the floor to the curtains on the bed to the wall-sized wardrobe. It made her feel slightly nauseated.

A few items of furniture trembled as she entered and the door clicked shut. There was too much for her to take in all at once, but a splash of water drew her attention to a tin bathtub set before a fireplace. A china jug hovered just above it, in the hold of some outlined creature, pouring steaming water. After it had finished, the figure set it down neatly on a side table and then flowed through the air toward her.

Beauty yelped and stumbled backward.

"Get away!" she cried. "What are you? Get away!"

She ran to the door and yanked on the handle, wondering what place of the under-realm this must be, but the door would not open.

"Let me out!" She pulled harder, the twisted gold of the handle slipping in her sweaty grasp. "Let me out, please!"

She banged on the wooden panels with her fists, terrified tears falling from her eyes. She wanted to change her mind—she wanted to be away from this dark place.

"Let me out, I beg!" she screamed. "Let me go!"

CHAPTER TWENTY-FOUR

The Enchanted Castle

Beauty lay curled beside the door until she could cry no more. Sobs had racked her body and her hands ached from beating the wooden boards. She was sore, confused, and her silver cheeks were stiff from tears.

Is this a punishment? she wondered.

She looked to the high pink ceiling and felt a long way from the temple and the gods. She thought of Eli, clutching the spurting wound in his leg, and she thought of Owaine, dying pale and weak in the cottage. She felt a long way from all of them.

A sweet perfume wafted through the air and she looked over at the bath. She had not bathed in that way since she had left Sago. The Hillanders washed in rivers and it was always cold, and therefore quick. She realized that she missed the days of soaking in a bathtub.

Glancing about her warily, she saw that the outline creatures had disappeared, so she began to undress. As she peeled off her homemade dress and undergarments, she realized how dirty they were. It was difficult to keep things clean in Imwane, and the outdoor lifestyle of the Hillanders did not allow for mud-free petticoats. Leaving her clothes and boots in a pile on the floor, she stepped into the tub, sighing at the blissful warmth of the scented water.

She soaked for a long time, cleaning her body three times over for the luxury of it. When the water began to cool, she found a pile of fluffy, enveloping towels by her elbow and she reluctantly climbed out and dried herself.

There were bejeweled ivory brushes on a dressing table nearby and she combed the tangles from her hair, peering about the room.

"Where are my clothes?" she asked, noticing that her pile was gone.

An outline creature hovered back into view and she jumped away from it. It whirled over to the doors of an enormous wardrobe and took out a velvet, emerald-colored gown, placing it on the bed. There were jewels about its low neckline that glinted in the light and tiny, neat patterns embroidered across its tight waist.

"I want my dress."

The outline did not move.

"Give me back my clothes!"

In a flash, the dress was gone and her homemade, brown muslin dress with its uneven hem and worn buttons was bundled in a pile beside her.

Beauty changed quickly, regarding the outlined creature suspiciously as it stood on the opposite side of the room.

"Will I be allowed out now?" she snapped.

The door to her room opened very slowly and she stormed through it.

———∞———

When Beauty marched into an ornate dining room, the beast was already there, lurking in the shadows. At the sight of him, she momentarily lost her breath, but she forced herself to have courage.

"Is it necessary to lock me in my room?"

There was a pause.

"What do you mean?" he asked.

"You locked me in my room! I could not get out!"

"I did nothing of the sort," he snarled and his fangs glittered in the firelight.

Beauty folded her fingers into fists to stop them from trembling. "Well, I could not leave."

"That would be the outlines."

Beauty thought of the unformed creatures that guided her about the castle. "They are *your* servants. Tell them I may do as I wish—"

"They are not my servants! I command nothing in this place!"

The hairs on the back of her arms rose at his roar, and it took all of her effort to stop herself from turning and fleeing. The beast was only partially visible in this long, shadowed room, but she could see the faint shaggy outline of his form and his hooded hazel eyes.

"If they are proving trouble, I suggest you try to reason with them," he grunted. "If that does not work, then I have no further advice. They may do as they wish—we are all prisoners here."

Beauty wanted to ask him what the outlines were, but she was scared of the answer.

There was an awkward silence.

"Well, eat then."

She noticed the mahogany table spanning the opposite end of the room with one chair and one place set. Upon the golden cloth sat pies, bowls of vegetables, pans of stew, pastries, casseroles, breads, a whole roasted pig, sauces, and oils. Her stomach rumbled as she approached the chair, her boots tapping on the tiled floor, and she seated herself, staring at the sea of food before her. It was like the Imwane harvest one hundred times over.

"Are you eating?" she asked.

"No."

She moved to take a leg of chicken, but it jumped onto her plate of its own accord and some peas and cauliflower followed it. Too tired to protest, she began eating.

The only sound was the clanging of her silverware, and she felt distinctly uncomfortable with his eyes upon her.

"Do you have to watch me?"

"Yes."

"Why?"

He growled and she kept her eyes down after that, concentrating instead on the exquisite taste of the food. The huge fire in the cavernous fireplace kept the room warm despite its massive scale, and she endeavored to calm herself, though with that shadow hunched in the opposite corner of the room it was not easy.

"What is your name?" it asked her.

She had just moved onto her third course, and his voice took her so by surprise that she almost dropped her gilded glass of juice.

"M-my name is Beauty."

There was a long pause.

"You may call me Beast," he said. "For that is what I am."

"Beast, how came you to live in this castle?"

"Beauty, how came you to think that you may ask such questions?"

Ignoring the rumbling snarl of his voice, his words were surprisingly smooth. He did not have the mind of an animal, clearly, and it made him all the more unnerving.

"I deserve to know if I am to spend the rest of my life like this."

"You deserve nothing! You are a prisoner here!"

She stood, pushing back her chair.

"I cannot spend eternity this way!" she cried. "I should sooner die!"

"You chose this!"

He stepped out of the shadows with one clawed paw and the light revealed his bent, crooked shape.

"No!" she screeched, her hands flying to her mouth. "Stay back!"

"Do I scare you so? Am I such a terrifying, horrifying beast?"

He advanced, the stamp of his paws making the floor shake, and Beauty stumbled away, knocking over the chair in her haste.

"You run!" he growled. "You must run from me!"

He grabbed the tablecloth and tore it away, sending the china, pots, and pans smashing to the floor. The food splattered over the tiles, and he seized a candelabra and hurled it across the room so that it shattered against the wall.

"Run!"

She fled to the door and yanked the handle, but it would not give. "Please! Please let me out, I beg!"

He prowled towards her.

"Please!"

The door opened and she staggered through it. Beast roared a dark, painful moan and she ran blindly down the corridor, praying that he would not follow her. Outlines opened doors for her, leading her down a certain path and finally, she came panting to her room.

She slammed the door shut behind her and said, "Please, lock! Do not let him in," before collapsing on the pink rug. She gasped into it, waiting for her heartbeat and the ache in her chest to lessen.

"I must leave," she sobbed. "I must leave this place! I cannot bear to stay!"

She felt something touching her hair, and she looked up to see an outline edging closer to her with an ivory comb in its grasp. She found that she was actually glad of it after the events in the dining room. Sitting up, she let it brush and braid her hair and then she let herself be dressed in a white nightgown with ribbons and frills.

"I am so tired," she whispered at nothing, and the outline turned the sheets and the quilts of her bed down for her.

She climbed the steps to her colossal bed and slid inside the soft, pink covers. Resting her head on satin pillows, she closed her eyes and fell immediately into a deep sleep.

She dreamt of Imwane. She saw the cottage and Owaine lying on the floor in a sickbed while Isole bustled in the kitchen.

"I be better, my child," Owaine muttered. "I feel much better."

"Yur gone and got a chill, Papa. That girl left yur dying."

"No . . . no . . . yur don't understand."

"Hush up and rest."

"I must go and get her."

"Get her?" snapped Isole. "We be better without her. Them soldiers come for her and the best thing she could of done is disappear. We should be glad she's gone."

"Oh, my Beauty."

"She be here looking after yur? She be here tending to yur while her husband and children home?"

Owaine groaned.

"No, Papa. She ain't. Something strange went on with them soldiers. They come for her, then she go and then . . . " Isole glanced out of the window at the churned, muddy snow. "Then Hally said there be blood on the temple floor and they gone."

"At least they didn't get her."

"Well, she ran, Papa, that's why. Them soldiers could of attacked us, they be so angry that she left and then suddenly, they leave. Like a miracle. As quick as they came. I arrived here from Dousal running all the way for fear for yur, and she's gone."

"I hope they never find her."

"They be hunting her for sure, Papa."

"I hope she is safe."

Beauty awoke suddenly, and it dawned on her that in her hurry to leave Imwane, she had left her amulet behind.

CHAPTER TWENTY-FIVE

The Prisoner

Beauty lay in bed the next morning, contemplating her future. A breakfast tray of buttered toast and sweet tea clattered up to her, but she rolled over.

"I cannot stay here," she said. "He will kill me."

The outline tried to cajole her with some clanging of cups, and eventually the delicious smell of toast encouraged her to take a few bites, but she only nibbled on the crust before casting it aside.

Pale light sifted through the pink curtains and laced blush patterns on the carpet. Beauty climbed out of bed and went over to one of her wide bay windows. She peered out at the snowy, empty grounds with a sense of dread. In the distance, at the castle's boundaries, she could see nothing but the void of the moat and a blurred edge. It was the darkness of the forest mixed with a haze of gray.

"I am a prisoner and this is my cell."

She turned away and slumped back onto the bed. The outline floated over to her with a comb and she tried to ignore it, but then it opened the doors of the wardrobe and pulled out a black riding habit with ermine trim. Beauty glanced at it and a little of the color came back to her face.

"Give me my peasant dress," she said. "I have no need of such a fine garment."

The outline reluctantly replaced the habit and brought out a plain, gray dress. It was plain by the standards of the castle, though Beauty still thought it quite fine, but she decided it would do.

She was apprehensive to leave her room at first, worried that Beast would be waiting in the corridor outside, but the bright light of morning had washed away most of her fears, and though she was still a little frightened, she decided not to spend the rest of the day cooped up.

Outlines led her through the castle's corridors and halls once more and out a side entrance. She briskly walked to the stable, keen to see a familiar face, and Champ whinnied as she entered. There were tufts of hay sticking from his mouth as he chomped on a fresh net, and he looked as though he had enjoyed a peaceful night.

She hugged his nose and nuzzled into his broad chest, glad that he was safe. He snorted in return and chewed at her hair.

"I want to groom him."

By the look of his polished coat, someone already had, but she did not care. A full grooming kit appeared by her side and she set to work. She barely had time in Imwane to run a currycomb through his mane and to brush the mud from his belly, but here she spent as long as she could rubbing his coat to a gleaming bay.

She turned to take a hoof pick and saw a sidesaddle flop over the door. She smiled.

"He does not take a saddle, let alone a sidesaddle."

The stirrups jingled.

"I do not ride on the side. I ride like a man."

The saddle slipped away in what Beauty took to be horror.

"But that is not a bad idea," she added to herself.

She had not thought to ride Champ here, but he would need exercising. She remembered when they used to ride the hills and run freely across the acres of undulating green.

"Come on, boy," she said, slapping his flank.

He raised his head and flicked his ears.

Unbolting the half door, Beauty guided him out of the stables and into the courtyard where they found a mounting block. Once seated, she trotted him away from the castle and pushed him into a canter over the grassy meadows. They raced toward the front gates, pulling up sharply in a cloud of snow before the edge of the moat. The drawbridge was nowhere to be seen and below was a hazy, swirling mist of black water. Beauty stared at the blurry trees on the other side until her eyes ached, then she turned Champ away and they galloped off in the opposite direction.

Snow scattered in clumps as they cantered and Champ never lost his footing. The wind rushed through them and Beauty let go of Champ's mane, stretching her arms wide to feel the surge of air. They galloped for a long time, the meadows going on and on—some covered in snow and some full of fresh green grass—until she finally slowed him down. She thought that she would have reached the boundaries by now. She glanced over her shoulder and she was shocked to see the castle but half a mile away. They had been riding a long time and with Champ's huge strides, they must have covered over double that distance.

"On, boy."

They galloped on and on for half an hour before stopping again. Beauty looked over her shoulder and groaned to see the castle just as near as before. It was all an illusion—they were running and going nowhere. She reached down and patted Champ's neck.

"At least we shall never be lost," she muttered, but she did not feel particularly grateful.

⌘

After two more hours of riding, Beauty returned Champ to the stable, fussing over him for as long as possible. Once she had groomed him three times over and it was well past noon, she was forced to leave him in peace and wander back through the castle. She was idly passing a gallery when she stopped to look at a tapestry.

There were many ornaments and embellishments in the castle that washed over the eye, but Beauty had found that if she tried to stop and look at them closely they became hazy. The tapestry had caught her attention, for it seemed to be the first solid decoration she had found. She halted in front of it, expecting it to blur or grow faint, but it remained crisp.

She stepped closer and reached out a hand to touch it. She could feel the bumps of the tiny stitches beneath her fingers and it smelled of old, musty material. The scene showed a great battle being fought. There were figures with axes lodged in their heads and horses pierced with arrows; there were men wielding swords and soldiers lying dead on the ground. The tapestry was as tall as the wall and the breadth of Beauty's arm span. It was faded a little as if from age and torn in places as if it had been scratched.

A figure in the background of the scene caught her eye and she frowned. It looked like the lyan that had saved her from the Sago shantytowns all those seasons ago. At first she thought that the strange shape of its face could be only a stain on the fabric, but the more that she looked, the surer she became. It was a lyan—a Magic Being. She scanned the rest of the scene and found other creatures: winged horses, trolls, wolf-men, and sprites. It was a battle between humans and Magics.

Beauty was hunting for other creatures in the scene when she was drawn to the figure of a knight in armor. He rode a great warhorse, and when Beauty stared closely she was sure, though the stitching was small, that there was a scar over his eye.

"Did you sleep well?"

She yelped in surprise and turned to see Beast crouched in the opposite corner. He had positioned himself as far away from her as the hall would allow, but she backed up against the wall nonetheless, keen to be farther away from him.

"W-what did you say?"

"I asked if you slept well in your room."

"I slept fine."

It was only then that Beauty realized that it was the first time in a long while that she had actually slept in a real bed.

"Do you want for anything?"

"Only my freedom."

He grunted and caught sight of her trembling fingers.

"You are safe here," he said after a pause. "You need never fear anything, for you are safe in the castle and in its grounds."

"I did not feel very safe last night."

He cast his hazel eyes to the floor. "I am not used to company, but I promise no harm will come to you."

"How long have you lived here alone?" she asked.

"Nor am I used to questions. Do not ask me questions and last night's events will not be repeated."

"That hinders conversation."

He made a low rumbling sound that after a moment she realized was laughter.

"I cannot tell you most of what you ask."

"Why?"

"I do not remember," he muttered, lowering his shaggy head.

"Then say so. Do not shout and rage."

"It is not that easy!"

Beauty flinched and Beast's eyes flashed.

"Forgive me, I have forgotten . . . "

"I will eat lunch in my room," she muttered, edging around him. She had not forgotten the candelabra shattered against the wall the night before.

"I will see you at dinner," he replied, as she hurried away.

That evening, she went down to dinner as commanded, though she did not wish to. With the darkness of night came her fears and she could not forget that it was a terrifying beast she headed to meet, with sharp fangs and claws.

She had spent the afternoon hanging around the stable with Champ for want of anything else to do. On the way in and out of the castle, she had looked for the tapestry again without success. Each time she left her room she seemed to follow corridors and passageways that she had never encountered before.

She entered the dining room with her head bowed and her hands hidden in the folds of her plain, blue dress so that he did not see that they were shaking. Once again, she sat alone at the mahogany table with a feast laid before her.

"Why must you watch me eat?" she asked.

"You wish to spend the day alone? You wish to spend the rest of your days in this castle surrounded by nothing but outlines?"

She did not reply.

"Surely the company of a beast is better than nothing?" he growled. "I did not think that the daughter of a farmer would be so demanding."

"I am not the daughter of a farmer."

"The thief that stole my rose said he was a farmer."

"I am his adopted daughter, and do not call him a thief!"

"Then who is your real father?"

"If I am not allowed to ask you questions, then you are not allowed to ask me any."

Beast bared his jagged teeth and snarled. Beauty gasped, dropping her spoon, but he turned away from her so that he faced the huge fireplace, and they waited in silence until he had calmed himself.

"Forgive me," he muttered.

She turned her attention back to her dinner and heaped glazed gammon onto her plate instead.

"Where does all this food come from?" she asked, before quickly adding, "Is that a question that I am allowed to ask?"

"You may ask it, but I cannot answer it, for I do not know."

"Do you hunt in the woods?"

"No, I do not leave the castle."

She paused. "You cannot leave, or you choose not to leave?"

"I cannot leave."

Beauty fell silent, suddenly realizing that she was not the only prisoner here.

CHAPTER TWENTY-SIX

The Forbidden

The days passed and Beauty tried to settle in. The fact that she would never leave the castle had not yet sunk in, and she did not know whether it ever would—it seemed an impossible thing. She wondered often if Beast would one day get bored of her and cast her from this place, but as time passed, she became sure that he was truthful when he said that it was not him who kept her here. He seemed more like her cellmate, not her guard.

She spent her mornings leisurely, which was a novelty in itself. She woke late and took her time with breakfast before visiting Champ in the stables and riding him across the grounds. She would then try to amuse herself until dinner, when she would meet Beast in the dining room. This was the ominous task that lingered at the end of each day. She did not feel that she could relax until it was over with, and then she would sleep and the whole routine would begin again.

She was beginning to feel periods of ease in Beast's company, but she was never a wrong question or a sharp word away from inflaming his temper, and she had not forgotten their first meal. He proved a difficult companion, but as long as he stayed hunched in the corner of the room, hidden by shadows, then she found that she could eat near him without worrying that he might suddenly attack her. She did not realize that he, too, was making an effort in their meetings until she came down one evening and he stood as she entered.

He had never done this before and she stopped short, the sight of him balancing on his hind legs almost absurd. She wanted to laugh, but she saw his lips curling back into a snarl and decided quickly against it.

He dropped back to all fours, his hazel gaze falling to the carpet.

"Good evening," she muttered.

He grunted and she sat at the table, busying herself with filling her plate. She had learned that if she spoke to the pots and pans, then they would give her whatever she wished, and so lately she had been asking for her favorite dishes from Sago. She had not eaten a proper omelet since she left—Owaine had tried to make some in their first seasons in Imwane, but they had not tasted the same—and recently she had been gorging herself on the delicious variations created by the castle's invisible cooks.

"Did you have a good day?" asked Beast.

"Yes."

Glancing up at him, Beauty noticed with surprise that he had combed the matted knots from his face and his dark fur was clean and wispy. She did not know whether to be pleased or alarmed.

"Are . . . are you well?"

"Yes."

There was a moment of silence until Beast asked, "Would you care for more drink?"

It seemed like a line that he had not said for a long time. It was as if it had suddenly popped into his head from the past and he instantly regretted it. He shifted away from her, further into shadow.

"Yes, please. Um, thank you."

The decanter refilled her glass.

"What is your horse's name?" he grunted.

"Champ."

"How long have you had him?"

"Since he was a colt."

"Where did you get him?"

Beast's questions continued until Beauty realized that he was attempting to make conversation. The shadows flickered when he spoke, as if he were fidgeting, and she was not sure if she felt grateful or panicked by his efforts.

"I am full and a little tired," she said finally, standing.

"Goodnight, Beauty," he said as she walked to the door.

She shivered and did not reply.

———⊶∞⊷———

A few days later, she was walking back to the stables after eating lunch in her room when she stopped short.

"Take me to the front of the castle," she ordered.

She desired to do something other than hang around the stables for the rest of the afternoon, and she had not explored the front gardens since her arrival.

Outlines led her through a series of gates to the graveled drive, and tiny stones crunched beneath her boots as she stood before the front of the castle. It was very silent. A dot of red caught her eye, and she saw the rose that had been her downfall still lying perfect on the ground. She picked it up, touching the fading scar on her cheek where its thorn had scratched her, leaving a silver line.

Its scarlet petals were un-dented and still fresh. Its scent was strong and sweet, and its full head radiant. She tucked it into her hair, looking over her shoulder at the roses covering the castle. They were a mixture of blue and purple, but she did not know what the colors meant.

Turning, she followed a path through an avenue of overhanging trees, their branches frosted with snow. When she reached the end, she found a flowerbed full of spring blooms, its soil clear and brown. She thought about last night at dinner when she had asked Beast about the strange climate here.

"Why are some of the grounds covered in snow while others are not?"

She had been thinking of her daily rides with Champ across white and green meadows.

Beast had moved his shoulders in what could have been a shrug. "It is always partly winter here."

"Always?"

"The seasons are the same. There is always snow."

Beauty had known better than to ask why. Instead she had slumped back in her chair, wondering at an existence forever surrounded by whiteness.

Now she wondered about it again as she continued through the grounds, peering into walled gardens full of exotic plants and passing headless, bare statues that made her blush. She dipped her fingers into one great fountain that had golden horses and mermaids erupting from its center and found that the water was warm. She lost herself in an evergreen maze and then sat for a while on a stone bench laid before a symmetrical, still pond. Finally, she came to the deep, misty moat and she was about to turn and head back when she saw another walled garden.

She gasped and stumbled toward it, wondering if it were a trick. It was filled with red roses. They climbed the walls, they trailed the ground, they grew from bushes and even on trees. There was no other plant but roses and all of them were blood red.

Beauty staggered among them, their scent charging the air. They were all perfect and all frozen at the height of their splendor, but there was one that drew her eye in particular. It grew in the very center of the garden, emitting from the ground in a tangle of purplish thorns, and it was the biggest and most breathtaking of them all. Beauty recognized it immediately from her dreams and she stepped toward it.

There was an earth-shattering roar and Beast flew into the garden, his teeth bared.

"Get out!"

But Beauty was too intrigued to be afraid this time and she held her ground.

"What is this place?" she asked.

"I said get out!"

"What is that rose?"

"Get out before I tear you to pieces!"

"You will not—you said that I would be safe here."

Beast roared, his fangs glinting in the winter sun. She had never seen him in bright light and he was all the more terrifying, but she was determined not to flee.

"You cannot stay here!"

"Why?"

Beast paced in a circle, the muscles in his haunches rippling. He was evidently fighting to control himself.

"You may do great damage," he growled.

"To you?"

"No, to yourself! My damage is already done."

"What do you mean?"

"Go from here, please."

She hesitated.

"Go!"

She turned and ran to the castle, now covered in orange roses.

Later that evening after she had bathed, the outline that occupied her room did not lay out a dress for her as usual. Instead her nightclothes were placed on the bed.

"I have not eaten dinner yet," she said, frowning.

The outline did not move. Beauty had grown accustomed to its fluid form, and sometimes she thought that she could almost read its actions. Right now it appeared angry.

"I cannot go down in my undergarments!" she insisted.

The outline ignored her so she went to the wardrobe and took out a plain, brown frock. As she was about to leave the room, she turned back and glanced at it.

"I am sorry," she muttered, and then she left.

She was led reluctantly to the dining room by other outlines, but when she entered, she found that it was empty. She looked to the corner that Beast normally occupied and was surprised to find that she was disappointed upon not seeing him there.

"Beast?" she called. "Beast, where are you?"

After waiting in silence for a while, she finally sat at the table and ate a little, but she felt uneasy.

"Beast? Please come in. I am . . . I am sorry about before. Beast?"

A door opened and he entered, his shaggy head turned away from her. He stalked to his shadows and curled there, staring at the carpet.

"You never told me that I could not go to the walled garden."

"You did not leave when I asked you to!" he growled.

"I was curious."

There was silence.

"Owaine took my rose from there, did he not?"

The rose was in her room now, resting on her dressing table as perfect as ever.

"Yes."

"He took it for me. They are so rare in Pervorocco, they are so—"

"Yes."

She finished her broth. "I miss him."

"You said he was not your father."

"No, he was better. He was my friend. I do not know who my father is."

She wanted to ask if he knew his parentage, but she suspected that the topic was off limits.

"He would never have taken anything from you if it were not for me," she added. "He is a good, kind man, and he has only ever tried to make me happy."

Beauty was shocked to feel tears welling in her eyes. She dried them quickly.

"I suspect a man would do a lot of things to keep you happy," Beast rumbled quietly.

"Are you still angry?"

"I am not ecstatic."

She knew that she had hurt him in some way. Trespassing in his walled garden of roses did not make him angry; rather, it made him sad.

"You must promise never to go there again," he growled.

She jutted out her chin.

"I am immovable on this. It is not just for my sake that I ask it."

She thought of the outlines that occupied the castle.

"All right," she said. "I promise."

There was a pause.

"I did not want you to see me in daylight yet. It is a wonder that you did not flee."

She blushed. She had not considered that he kept to the shadows for her sake.

"I have seen you before."

"Not like that."

It was true, but she would not admit it.

"Light or dark, it makes no difference to me," she said, though neither of them was convinced.

She pushed back her chair and walked across the room.

"Goodnight, Beast," she said as she passed through the door.

"Goodnight, Beauty."

The next evening, he stood closer to the fire as she ate, his fangs and claws glinting in its amber light, and Beauty pretended that her knees did not tremble.

CHAPTER TWENTY-SEVEN

The Library

A moon-cycle passed and Beauty looked down at her hands one day, scarcely recognizing them. The silver skin was no longer hard and peeling, but soft and supple. She had the hands of a lady now, not a laborer. She touched her palms, feeling the smoothness of them, but it mattered little to her; she would trade them in a second for her old life. She thought wistfully of Imwane every day. She missed it dearly, and she found that she even missed Isole and the villagers. She could not put into words how much she missed Owaine. It was too painful for her to dwell on it.

Champ was the only one who shared her heartache and she told him at length about it on their rides. He flicked his ears as she spoke while they cantered across meadows and zigzagged through orchards in the mornings.

Despite this daily exercise, Champ was getting rounded from all the food on offer at the castle.

"A little less of that," Beauty said one afternoon as a fresh hay net appeared on a hook in his stall. "The Hillanders would not be calling you warhorse if they could see you now," she said, slapping his ample rump.

Champ chewed indigently.

Without him, Beauty knew that she would be lost and bored at the castle. In the afternoons she often found herself idle. If she did not return to the stable, then she had little else to do accept wander the ever-changing corridors or stroll through the eerie grounds. One day she was doing just that when she called, "Beast?"

He appeared in an instant by her side.

"What is wrong?" he asked.

They were standing in a snowy patch by the evergreen maze at the front of the castle and Beauty noticed that there were flakes in the tufts of fur on his cheeks.

"I just . . . just wondered where you were."

They shuffled their feet awkwardly and she wished for a moment that she had not called for him.

"Is there anything I can do?" he asked.

"No, not really. I just wondered what you do all day in the castle? I never see you when I walk around."

"I thought you would not want to see me."

She blushed.

"I just wonder where you go. That is all."

"I stay out of your way, but I am never far. If you need me, you may call me and I will always hear it."

She had guessed as much. She felt watched always, sometimes by Beast and sometimes by the castle itself.

"But, will you tell me what you do? Surely that is not a question out of bounds."

"Well, often I read. Have you seen the library here?"

Beauty at once wished that she had not asked. "No."

"You must! It is the only good thing about this place."

"Oh, I—"

Beast's body shifted back. "Do not worry, I will not make you visit it with me, but you should ask the castle to take you there. I will try to make sure that I am away while you explore."

"That is not necessary," she said before she could stop herself.

"You will come with me now?"

"Well . . . I suppose so."

She could not very well summon him here and then reject him, though she wished they could do anything other than visit the castle's library.

"This way." Beast motioned with his paw for her to walk in front of him.

"Surely you should lead the way?" she said. "I have never been before."

"It is better that you do not see me move, it may unnerve you."

Beauty did not need to be told twice and she obediently walked ahead of him.

"Take us to the library," he commanded in a rumble as they entered a corridor.

Outlines began directing them down passages and through halls with hazy ornaments.

"The things in this castle, they do not belong to you?" Beauty asked as they passed a huge, carved urn.

"No."

"Are they real?"

"They do not look it. But that is what is wonderful about the library; the books there feel real and worn."

They climbed up a flight of narrow, twisting stairs.

"Have you seen every room in this castle?" she asked.

"I do not think that is possible."

"How long have you lived here?"

"A long time."

"Have you—"

"The library will find any book you could possibly want, all you have to do is ask for it. I have never seen every book in the library either, but I suspect that that has more to do with its size than anything else."

Reaching the top step, Beauty glanced over her shoulder at him and wished she had not. She lost her footing, stumbling a little, and he pretended not to know that he was the cause. His face took her by surprise sometimes. Listening to his voice, she could almost imagine speaking to a man.

The outlines led them on until they reached two wide double doors. As they approached, they were thrown back to reveal a yawning hall stuffed with bookcases. There were books in the walls, in piles on the floor, and on the ceiling. Beauty gasped, for it truly was spectacular.

"Ask for a book," said Beast. "Any book!"

Beauty did not think that she had ever seen him so animated. She muttered a title under her breath and a slim volume flew towards her. She opened her old nursery book with a smile, turning to an illustration of a troll.

"I had this when I was younger," she explained, turning a few more pages.

"Ask for something else," he urged her. "Test it—it has everything."

She licked her dry lips.

"Um . . . "

"What else did you used to read?"

She stepped away, looking at the floor.

"Nothing," she said quietly.

"You do not like to read?"

"It is not that. I . . . " She clenched her fingers and jutted out her chin. "I cannot read."

"You were never taught?"

She swallowed hard. "No, I was never taught to read."

"Would you like me to teach you?" he asked, adding when she did not reply, "You may say no if you wish."

"Can I be taught?"

"Yes."

"Will you be patient?"

He made a growling, crashing sound like a chuckle. "Yes."

"Then I suppose so. Yes, I should like to be taught to read."

He stalked over to a table and crouched in front of it, then motioned for her to sit on the chair opposite. She had never been so close to him before, and she could feel the warm gusts of his breath and the heat of his body. She hesitated just a moment before taking the seat that he offered.

He barked a sound and a book flew from a shelf to his hands.

"This is a favorite of mine and I think that you will like it."

He raised his great paw and turned to the first page with incredible delicacy, using the very tips of his claws.

"You do that very well."

"I have had a lot of practice."

He pushed the book toward her and she stared at the dashes and dots.

"I will say the words and you will repeat them after me," he said. "If you see a word you recognize, then interrupt."

"But these markings make no sense."

"They will in time. If I am to be patient, then you must be patient also. Besides, I do not think it will take you long to pick up the skill."

She hoped that he was right.

"Once upon a time," he began, hovering his claw over the markings.

"Once upon a time," she repeated.

———◦≫◦———

After that, Beauty met with Beast every afternoon in the library and they would read together for several hours. Sometimes she would get frustrated and stomp off through the maze of towering bookshelves until she had calmed down, but Beast always tried hard to contain his temper during these lessons. She only discovered how hard he tried when she came back to their table after a tantrum one afternoon and found the book in front of him torn clean in half.

"Did you do that?" she asked.

"Unfortunately, yes."

"Was it because of me?"

"Do not worry, this library is good at fixing itself. I am sure that I have torn this book at least once before."

"But it is one of your favorites."

"I know, but it will be mended tomorrow. We shall carry on our lesson then."

"No, we can read another book."

"It is probably best—"

"But I want to read another."

He saw her pleading face. "If you wish it."

He called down another book and Beauty was more careful to control her own temper after that.

As Beast predicted, she learned quickly and could soon read whole paragraphs with just a few corrections. One day, she insisted they read late into the evening, she was so gripped by the story's plot.

"Beauty, you must ready yourself for dinner."

The library was dark and the candles in the golden chandelier had lit themselves.

"But we need to find out if she loves him too."

"You should take the book to bed with you and finish it before you sleep."

"But then you will not hear it."

Beast paused, his hazel eyes locking with her own.

"I have a better idea," she said. "I will take it to dinner and we can read it together then."

"If you wish it."

Once she had reached a competent level of reading, Beauty wanted to learn to write and the library produced a quill and ink for her.

"It is harder than it looks," she muttered, scratching the nib over the parchment.

"I do not doubt that you will master it soon," said Beast, encouragingly.

If she was not reading or writing, then Beauty liked to wander through the bookshelves, Beast following at a distance. Sometimes she would try to count all the books, but that was impossible, for there were volumes hidden in the most unlikely places. Often, she simply liked to pull out books at random and leaf through them. One afternoon, she saw a yellow spine in a slot on the wall high above her head.

"That one!" she said to the library, pointing, but it brought down the book below it. "No, that one—the yellow one!"

When it brought down the book next to it instead, Beast suddenly jumped onto the wall, climbing up the rows of books with his claws. He grabbed the desired volume and carried it down, landing with a crouch on the floor beside her.

"T-thank you. I wish that I could do that." She was a little breathless.

"I have read that book before," he replied.

"Yes?"

"It is about the Southern Realm."

Beauty took it back to their table and they began to read. It conjured a dry landscape of sand and rock, where the days were blistering and the nights were cold. As she read, she forgot the snow and the castle and lost herself in the words. When Beast had taught her to read, he had given her a kind of freedom—a way to endure the prison of this enchanted place.

"Is this what the Southern Realm is really like?" she asked after they had reached the end of the chapter.

"Yes, it is hot and desolate. There are deserts there."

"You have been?"

He shifted. "A long time ago."

"Is it like Sago?" she asked.

"It is a drier heat. When have you been to Sago?"

"A long time ago."

They read another chapter before stopping again.

"How well do you know the realm?" he asked.

"Not well at all. I know Pervorocco and The Neighbor, and I have heard of the Wild Lands. I did not realize that there was more."

"There is much more."

He led the way through the maze of bookshelves to a section in the right wing of the library.

"Maps," he said to the air and a chest of scrolls shuffled up to them. He carried a few back to their table awkwardly in his paws and unrolled them.

"This is what we know of the realm so far," he said. "It is likely that there is much more that we have never found. The Wild Lands, for instance, are ungoverned and could be large or small for all we know."

Beauty stared at the jagged shapes and expanses of sea.

"The Scarlet Isles," she read, running her finger over the words to say out the sounds. "The Jade Rivers."

She swept her hand over the golden parchment, following the illustrations with her finger, and suddenly her hand bumped with Beast's paw. "Oh!"

"Sorry, forgive me."

He quickly stepped away from her. His fur had felt bristly and the bones of his paw hard, as if she had touched Champ's hoof.

"No, do not worry," she said, and they both turned back to the map.

CHAPTER TWENTY-EIGHT

The Voices

As Beauty rode Champ through the grounds one morning, she realized that she had been at the castle for almost two seasons. The thought caught her by surprise and, sensing her shock, Champ skidded to a halt in the middle of an orchard. Beauty glanced at the crooked, leafy branches around her, which were hung with russet apples, and could scarcely believe it. Back at Imwane, it would be summer and there would be rainbows arching over the hills and children playing on the hillside. Hally would hold a feast in the barn to celebrate and they would sing Hilland songs and drink ale.

She looked over her shoulder at the castle, as far away as it was ever going to be. The rest of the realm was carrying on without her. Come autumn, the horses would be taken to town and sold and then new steeds would be caught and the cycle would begin again. She wondered if Owaine would ask for a village lad to help him since he was too old to train them all alone. She wondered if this new lad would whisper soothing words to the horses and make them into perfect rides. She wondered if Imwane, Owaine, and all of the Hillanders would eventually forget her.

With a gentle squeeze of her knees, Beauty turned Champ away and they galloped back to the stables, her head full of memories. Life at the castle was not terrible; in fact, she almost had everything that she could ever desire. But she did not have her freedom.

She was in a bad mood for the rest of the day and Beast suffered at their meeting in the library that afternoon.

"Is this book boring you?" he asked.

"No."

"You do not seem very interested."

"I am tired." She shut the book and pushed it away.

"Is something troubling you?" he asked.

"No."

"Beauty . . ."

"I do not remember agreeing to be hassled continually with questions! That was not part of our deal."

Beast sensibly moved himself to the other side of the library.

"Perhaps you should go to bed early tonight," he said as he retreated. "If you are so very tired."

"Yes! Perhaps I should!" She got up and stormed from the room.

"I shall see you tomorrow!" she shouted. "Like I shall see you every day for the rest of my life!"

She paced her room for the remainder of the afternoon and evening. Several times she walked over to the windows and looked out at the misty void of the moat and the iron gates that imprisoned her.

"I just want to see the other side," she whispered. "Just for a moment."

But all she saw was a haze of gray and black.

She snapped at the outline in her room as it undressed and bathed her that evening, complaining when a comb found a tangle in her hair and yelling when the water in the bath grew too cold. She would not eat dinner and climbed into bed too early and tossed and turned for an hour before she slept.

"I wish to dream of Owaine," she said to herself. "Please."

But she did not. When she first came to the castle, she had dreamt of him often. She had seen him in the cottage regaining his health and she had seen him walking through the village, asking if anyone had heard news of her, which they had not. Then the dreams had changed. She closed her eyes now, thinking of lush green hills, waterfalls, and lakes, but her head conjured the sticky heat of Sago and its close reek of sweat and people. She wanted to see the cottage and the temple, but instead she saw Rose Herm's drawing room and Ma Dane's study.

She had never dreamt of the past before and it confused her. It could not be the present or the future, for she knew that after the turmoil of the Magic Cleansing, Sago must be a different place. She did not understand much of the powers she possessed, but she knew that they always meant something—her imprisonment in the castle proved that much. She wished to understand herself more; she wanted to be able to harness her gift and direct her own dreams, but she did not know how. She had even tried to look for a book about it in the library once without success.

"I wish to know about Magics," she had said to the air.

There had been silence.

"Why do you seek such knowledge?" Beast had barked.

"I am curious."

"You will find no books on such things here."

She did not mention it again, but dreams of her past came faster and more vivid with each night. When she finally slipped into slumber that evening, after twisting her bed sheets into knots, she dreamt of Ma Dane.

Beauty saw a mob dancing and shouting in the streets of Sago, baying for blood, and she saw a string of starved women dressed in rags. Blood oozed from their backs where they had been flogged and filth was smeared across their faces. They were chained at the ankles and some were missing their hands. At the very end of the line crawled a woman that could once have been Ma Dane. She was shriveled and gaunt now and her head was shaved to dark stubble. As she was led to the stake she was whispering, "Asha? Asha, will you save me?"

There were men in gray uniforms watching and carrying out the spectacle. They occasionally beat the crowd or jeered with them. Beauty knew that Eli was there, but she could not see Pa Hamish Herm-se-Hollis and suddenly it occurred to her that he could not be there, for he was already dead. She instinctively sensed that he had died the moment Eli handed Ma Dane over to the State.

The women were pulled screaming onto their stakes and there was much sneering and taunting from the crowd. Ma Dane resisted the least of all of them and once she was secured, the fires were lit. The next scene was the dream that had haunted Beauty's childhood—the knowledge of her aunt's death—and she awoke.

Her pink room was dark and felt empty. Her sheets were messy, her pillows were on the floor, and her body was wet with sweat and tears. Her chest heaved with the shock of the vision and she gasped for breath. The image of Ma Dane's poor, crippled body came to her mind and she suddenly forgave her for the seasons of abuse in her childhood, when she never thought that she could. She would wish that fate on no one.

Beauty lay still for a moment, wondering if that was the dream's purpose. She had begun to feel differently about Ma Dane since she came to the castle—she had begun to feel differently about everyone. She no longer hated Isole, but pitied her instead. She realized that the Hilland villagers did not despise what she was; they feared what they did not understand. She was slowly changing.

She did not have long to contemplate this revelation before the stillness of the room struck her. By now she would have expected the outline to begin rearranging her pillows, light the candle beside her bed, and straighten the sheets.

"I would like a glass of water," she said, but nothing happened.

The room felt strange—unoccupied. She did not feel watched.

Slipping out of bed, she padded to the door and slowly turned the handle. She looked down the long, empty corridor.

"Beast?" she whispered.

He did not appear and she was sure that he could not hear her.

She walked down the corridor, following it into a hall and then up a twisting turret. She did not know where she was going, but she felt that something was wrong.

There were no outlines to direct her and she rambled through the castle's never-ending depths. At one point, she opened a set of double doors and gasped, finding herself in a ballroom of magnificent décor and proportions. After staring for a moment at its tall, painted ceiling, she turned and continued her search.

"Beast?" she called another time, but still she heard nothing.

None of the candles were lit and she fumbled in the dark, her heart thumping in her chest. As she stumbled through a drawing room and across another hall, she heard voices and froze.

"I cannot keep it from her much longer."

That was Beast's rumbling growl. He was standing in a quad below and one window of the hall was ajar. Beauty edged closer to it, pressing her ear against the pane.

"You must," replied another voice. It was light and sharp and it seemed to come from the air.

"But she will guess!"

"You must deny all knowledge."

"I cannot keep her here. I cannot subject her to my torture."

"She took the rose—she took the life."

"*She* did not take the rose."

"No matter! You remember the spell, do you not?"

"How could I forget?" snarled Beast.

"Without just one rose—without just one life, we die. All of us." Beast growled.

"We are lucky to still be here after all this time," said the voice. "There are evil spells in this castle that try to—"

"We are not lucky, we are cursed!"

At Beast's roar, the window in the hall slammed shut and Beauty jumped away. The castle was breathing again and the rug beneath her feet was pulled out, knocking her to the ground. She heard high-pitched laughter and staggered to her feet. This was not the presence that guided her about the castle each day; this was not the friendly outline that waited on her; this was altogether different. The hairs on her arms tingled and she ran.

Doors slammed in her face, the corridors twisted away from her, and she heard high-pitched laughter all around. Archways became walls and passageways led to dead ends. Beauty felt something pull at her hair and try to trip her feet.

"Beast!" she cried. "Beast!"

He was there and instantly she felt safe again.

"What are you doing?" he asked.

"I—I woke and my room felt empty. There were no outlines—I could not see them anywhere."

"Where have you been?"

"I just stepped out of my room," she said, as she did not want him to know that she had heard him in the quad. "I called for you, but you did not come."

"Forgive me, Beauty."

"I do, but I felt something else just now," she whispered. "Something that was not the outlines."

"It is the evil in this place."

"There is evil here?"

"Where there is good, there must be a balance of evil. I am sorry that you had to feel it tonight, but do not fear. It is gone now."

"Where has it gone?"

"Back to its corners. You may return to bed safely."

She noticed that the candles around them were being lit by the comforting, pale shape of an outline.

"Will you accompany me to my room?" she asked.

"If you wish it."

She stepped close to him and he instinctively moved away.

"No! Stay near. I am scared."

"If you wish it."

They walked through the corridors to her room and its door opened for her as they approached. Inside she could see that her bed had already been straightened and there was a mug of steaming tea set on her bedside.

"Do you feel better?"

She nodded.

"Good night, Beauty."

"Good night, Beast."

Part Four

The battlefield was awash with bodies and blood gushed in great, scarlet streams. The air was saturated with the moans of the dying, the crack of bones, and the terrified shouts of soldiers. They did not call it the Red Wars for nothing.

They had taken up position on this barren stretch of wasteland the day before. It was cold and boggy here and the men, who had been trained in Sago, were not accustomed to the weather. They had marched straight from the capital—called as emergency back up— and had not had time to acclimatize. Many were sick and sniveling before they had charged into battle that misty morning. They were all dead now. Dead or had deserted.

The general sat on his horse before the battlefield. All of his troops had been wiped out, but there were reinforcements coming now. He had thought that he could go ahead and push these evil creatures back before they arrived, but he had not understood their tactics. He felt the loss of his men deeply and knew that he had been too rash, too hasty. But how was he to know what these *things* could do? How was he to know that they could break every bone in a man's body just by wishing it to be so?

He waited with his horse until the second unit of troops arrived. It was beginning to snow by then and white flakes fell to the ground, turning to red slush. The men quaked when they saw the carnage laid out in the field and he did not blame them.

"General, where are the rest of your soldiers?" asked their leader.

"Gone," he said.

"Gone?"

"I am the only one left. I was lucky that my horse carried me to safety and none of those under-realm things could get their claws into me."

The troops muttered and shuffled their feet, their armor clanging.

"Quiet!" yelled their leader. "General, what do you advise we do?"

He looked across the expanse of death to the distant horizon where the creatures had retreated after massacring his troops. He knew the Forest Villages well—he had been posted here before on various expeditions—and he guessed that they must be hiding in woodland a mile or so away. During his first visit here, he had received the scar that made him renowned in a small battle with some Magic outlaws in that woodland. He touched the silver slither that cut across the middle of his eye for luck.

"I suggest we attack immediately," he said. "They will not be expecting it."

But the Magics were expecting everything. When the State army marched across the battlefield and through scrubland to their camp in the wood, they were waiting. There were trolls and griffins and fey, but there were humans, too, and they were the worst of all: Magic Bloods. They were the worst because there was no telling what they could do. Some of them could simply destroy you with a blink of their eyes or send you half crazy with visions.

The general watched as the State men were butchered once again. They ran across the open scrubland, their axes and swords raised, only to fall prey to the creatures standing in the fringes of the wood, watching them come.

"Charge!" he yelled, gathering a bundle of men and leading them running for the woods. He heard the terrible crack as those around him had every bone in their body broken, and the screams as some of them began tearing out their own eyes due to horrific visions, but he pushed onward.

Suddenly he was in the woods, and he saw the startled gaze of many Magic Beings before his horse disappeared from beneath him. He scrambled to his feet, alone in a glade of tall, yellow trees and there was snow at his feet. He circled about, thrashing his sword through the air, knowing that this was a vision and what he saw was not how things were. At any moment he expected to be attacked.

"Halt, I wish to speak with you."

He jumped at the sound of the voice, which seemed to come from all around. Out of the corner of his eye, he saw a figure approaching him, a man as tall as himself with white hair, dark skin, and eyes that sometimes looked silver, sometimes gold, and sometimes violet.

"I will fight you to the end!"

"That will not be necessary, general," said the dark man. "We have won."

"You have not!"

"We were always going to win, it is written in scripture. That is the problem with your race. You think yourselves above the gods and that is why you always die."

"My race? It is your race who are scum!" He spat on the ground and swished his sword so that the air hummed.

"Why do you hate Magics so?" asked the man, stepping closer. "Do you fear them?"

"I fear nothing."

"You should fear me."

"I do not. I stare straight into the eyes of death. If I die, then I die honorably."

"There is no such thing as an honorable death."

The general could feel the hilt of his sword growing slippery in his grasp.

"I will make you a deal," said the dark man. "If you call off your army, if you demand that the State bring peace between Magics and humans, then I will let you go. You are an infamous general and I know that they will listen to you."

"I thought that you had won this battle! You lie, and I have no desire to make deals with the likes of you! I would rather die."

"You will not die."

"I do not care! Come and fight me, you demon thing! Come and fight me, you beast!"

The man raised his hand and he smiled.

"Beast?" he said. "I am not the beast."

CHAPTER TWENTY-NINE

The Thaw

One afternoon, Beauty entered the library and Beast was not there. She wondered if she should call him, but if he was busy then she did not wish to disturb him. He often came a little late and she did not like to think herself so spoiled that she could not wait.

She walked over to their table and touched the book they were currently reading that sat on top of a pile with a ribbon through it, marking their place. They had paused on a cliffhanger and she could not wait to read the next section. She was sorely temped to begin now, but she liked to see the look on Beast's face when the plots unraveled themselves, so she forced herself to wait.

Instead, she began strolling through the bookshelves, mentally noting other volumes that she would like to read. She had asked Beast once if he thought that they would be able to read all the books in the library, and he had replied that he supposed they could if they were here for eternity, which had not been the answer she desired.

She passed deeper into the library, running her fingers along the spines, and it was as she moved between two cases that she noticed the chest of maps lodged in one corner. She remembered how one day Beast had shown her drawings of the whole realm and she wished to look at them again. She wondered if she could copy one onto a piece of parchment. She could write competently now, but she had not yet tried to draw.

Opening the dusty chest, she began hunting through the scrolls. It was only when she caught sight of an unrolled piece that she realized these were not the maps. She frowned, picking up the parchment that had caught her eye, and tried to read what it said. There was writing scrawled all over it in thick calligraphy and she remembered the scrolls that the preacher used to carry around with him in Imwane. Her fingers trembled as she tried to make out the swirling words.

The gods did build the hills for those,
That does good deeds for one they chose.

She gasped and rocked back onto her heels, clutching the parchment tightly and humming along the Hilland tune in her mind as she read the words:

They shelter with old spells and might,
For one who comes to them to fight.

They know not what that thing might be,
It comes to keep their people free.

Beauty frowned, for the words were different from the verses that she knew. She read them quickly, her mind swimming with the tune of the song.

It shall lead the Magic to task,

And wage war with a silver grasp.

Deaths shall rein and family ties
Will be broken by one with violet eyes.

Then the writing stopped. She turned it over, but the ink was faded and she could make out nothing. Her heart thudding, she scrambled through the other scrolls in the chest, wondering what she had happened upon.

Violet eyes . . . silver grasp . . . war.

Suddenly, she heard the doors of the library opening and the tap of Beast's claws against the floor.

"Beauty?"

She threw the parchment back into the chest and slammed it shut before hurrying through the bookshelves.

"Forgive me, I lost track of time," said Beast when she appeared. "Is something wrong?" he added, noticing her flushed cheeks.

"No, nothing at all."

She was surprised to find that it saddened her to have to lie to him, but she knew that he would not be happy to hear about the chest of scripture. They must both have their secrets.

"Are you sure?"

"Yes."

She picked up their book, settled herself in a chair, and began to read aloud.

———⊗⊗⊗———

The next day, before she went to the stables, Beauty asked the outlines to take her to the library. Once there, she weaved between the bookcases to see if Beast were present, and when she was satisfied that she was alone, she retraced her steps from the day before.

But the chest was gone.

Thinking she might be mistaken, Beauty tried another section, but still she found nothing.

"Where is it?" she asked the air, but received no answer.

She wondered if the outlines had hidden it from her. Or Beast.

Violet eyes . . . silver grasp . . . war.

The words ran through her mind, but she dismissed them.

I am here for eternity, she told herself grimly. *Those words mean nothing to me.*

She left the library and went down to the stables, hoping to ride away her worries. Champ was pleased to see her and they went clattering out of the courtyard and into the grounds of the castle at a gallop. As usual, they raced through snowy meadows, jumped over fences, and thundered across lush green grass. Beauty was beginning to shake off the eeriness of what she had read when Champ abruptly skidded to a halt.

Clinging to his mane to stay astride, she whipped her head around, wondering what had spooked him. Before them she saw the deep, smoky moat and on the other side of its bank was a high stone wall.

She slid from Champ's back and waded through the snow to the edge of the moat. Its bank was steep and the dark, misty water in its depths swirled and gushed strangely. She quickly stepped back.

"Beast!"

He was there before she had finished speaking, a dark figure crouching in the snow.

Champ tensed and his ears flattened.

"Steady, boy," said Beauty, moving to his side. She patted his neck to reassure him and whispered soothing words.

"If I had known your animal were here then I would not have answered your call," Beast growled. "It is cruel to subject him to me."

"I would not have called you but . . . " She pointed to the moat and the wall and he started in surprise. "What is it?" she asked.

"It must be the boundary of the castle."

"I have never come across it before."

"Nor have I."

They were silent for a moment, looking at it.

"Does it go on?" he asked.

"I do not know."

Grabbing a chunk of Champ's mane, Beauty led them along the length of the moat. The stallion quivered and skirted a little to have Beast so close behind him, but he otherwise behaved himself.

"It continues," she confirmed.

"The castle has never had borders before," muttered Beast.

"Is this good or bad?"

"I do not know."

Beauty sighed.

"For once I wish that you would tell me something," she said. She stared into his human, hazel eyes and he looked away.

"I am surprised at your animal," he said. "To stay so close to me he must be a brave creature."

As if he knew that he was being discussed, Champ nudged her with his nose, knocking her over face-first in the snow. She scrambled back to her feet, her cloak covered in white flakes, and laughed. The high peal echoed across the grounds, bouncing through the stillness, and the icicles that hung on a tree beside them shivered and fell. They hit the earth and shattered, melting to water.

Beauty gasped and Champ shied away.

"What happened?" she asked.

Beast watched her closely.

"I do not know," he replied.

CHAPTER THIRTY

The Ball

The season shifted to winter, but the snow at the castle continued to thaw. Beauty noticed it disappearing as she rode Champ each day. It was gradual, but eventually whole fields that had once been covered were clear and she no longer had to wear a cloak when she stepped outside.

Without the miles and miles of limitless fields to gallop across, Beauty was forced to circle Champ around the grounds several times, following the boundary of the deep, misty moat. Even then, he was never worn out. Once, she tested him and rode and rode until evening, but still, he was not even out of breath.

Meanwhile, with Beast's guidance, she was steadily working her way through sections of the library. After reading about the Western Realm, Beauty was anxious to learn more and she asked for book after book that described its hot, rocky landscape until she had almost exhausted the archives.

"See, I knew that he would die at the end—did I not tell you so?" she said, snapping a volume shut one evening.

They were in the dining room and Beauty had insisted on finishing the book that they had been reading that afternoon, as she could not bear to wait until tomorrow to know what would happen.

"You did, yes," said Beast. "But it was a foregone conclusion."

"What makes you say that?"

"He loved her. If he did not die saving her then his love would be fake."

"I suppose."

Beauty pointed at a dish of roasted potatoes and a selection jumped onto her plate.

"Soon I will have been here four whole seasons," she said, keeping her voice light and her eyes down.

Beast was sitting before the fire and he shifted.

"Do you miss your family?"

"I miss my father."

She had dreamt of Owaine recently. She had seen him walking about the village, rubbing his tired eyes and looking often to the forest over his shoulder.

"We should do something to mark the occasion," said Beast.

"I do not think it necessary."

There was silence.

"What was the best birthday that you ever had?" Beast tried again.

"I never had one, and besides, this is not a birthday. I do not know when my birthday is. I lost count of my age a long time ago."

She remembered Eli's ball at Sago and the dresses and the dancing.

"What is it?" asked Beast, seeing the change in her expression.

"Nothing, I . . . I just remembered a birthday party I went to a long time ago. It was a ball in Sago. It was beautiful."

"Then we shall have a ball."

"We cannot."

"Why? We have a ballroom—"

"I know, I have seen it, but . . . "

"Yes?"

Beauty wanted to tell him that she did not wish to celebrate the anniversary of her imprisonment here. She wanted to tell him that every night she prayed that she would be free of this place. She wanted to tell him that she always hoped that one day she would leave. But she did not want to hurt him.

"All right," she said at last. "We shall have a ball."

Lately the outline in Beauty's room had been taking more and more liberty with her wardrobe. At first Beauty had insisted on wearing plain dresses in plain colors, but she had gradually relaxed her ways, and now she spent most of her time in comfortable but ornate gowns. With the prospect of a ball, however, the outline became carried away.

"No!" Beauty cried the evening of the event as it presented her with a pink, frilly thing. "I am not wearing anything as ridiculous as that!"

The pink, frilly thing was replaced by a glittering blue gown of silk, with a wide hoop and a plunging neckline.

"Absolutely not!"

Beauty was not looking forward to the ball. She was going along with it for Beast's sake, but she hoped that it would be over soon.

"Yes, I suppose that looks all right," she muttered as a blush-colored gown edged to her. It was strapless and the skirts were wide, but not restricting, while the ruffles were pretty without making her feel silly.

"This will do," she said as the outline fastened it in place.

For the next half hour she argued with the outline about various hairstyles and extravagant jewels until finally she was ready to leave. She was walking out of the door when she suddenly stopped short.

The red rose was lying on her dressing table where she kept it, as perfect as always. She liked to hold it sometimes and smell its sweet scent when she woke in the morning; for some reason it comforted her. She took it now and slid it into her white chignon. It nestled in the crook behind her ear. Then she left.

Her skirts swished as she walked down the long corridors and candles lit themselves at her approach. A set of double doors appeared and she braced herself, wishing that she could meet Beast in the library instead and they could forget that she had been trapped in this place for a year.

The double doors were thrown open to reveal a dazzling sight. The ballroom's huge, domed chandelier was lit and hundreds of candles flickered in its holders. They cast dancing lights on the painted ceiling that was clouded with dark shadows and thunder. The walls were covered with gold filigree that laced its white hue and the floor was a mosaic of shimmering crystal.

Beauty stood at the top of a grand, sweeping staircase and Beast was below, watching her. She felt too exposed and she wriggled in her gown.

"Do you like it?" he asked.

She tried to muster up as much enthusiasm as she could.

"When I was younger, I always wanted to walk down stairs like these," she called.

She thought back to Eli's ball at Rose Herm and she remembered all the girls traipsing down the stairs while they were announced—all except her. She did not envy them anymore.

"I am pleased," he replied in a rumble, and he bared his sharp teeth in a grin.

Trying not to trip on the netting of her skirts, Beauty stepped awkwardly down the stairs in her soft slippers. When she reached the bottom she laughed, feeling silly, but Beast's face was serious and he was trying to balance on his hind legs again. Occasionally he would have to steady himself with his front paw, and Beauty wanted to ask him to stop trying so hard, but did not wish to offend him. She knew that he was only trying to please her.

"This is all very lovely, thank you," she muttered.

Beast dipped his great, shaggy head.

"Come and eat," he said.

There was a table of magnificent cakes and desserts set out in the far corner and Beast ushered her toward it.

"I chose your favorites," he said.

"I believe it is taller than me," she replied, looking at the various layers of a towering iced sponge cake. She cut a slice and held the plate out to him.

"No, it is for you, Beauty."

"I cannot eat even a quarter of these lovely things. You should have some too."

"It is better if you do not see me eat."

"What if I insist?"

"Then you will regret it. It is not a pretty sight."

She ate the dessert herself, but she was not very hungry.

"Should you like to dance?" asked Beast and an invisible orchestra began to play.

"No. . . no, thank you."

"You do not have to dance with me, you can dance by yourself."

"No." Beauty looked longingly behind his head at the double doors. "Let's go to the library," she said.

"The library?"

"Yes. I want to know how that book ends."

"But Beauty . . . "

She grabbed his paw, feeling the bristles of his fur, and tried to guide him to the exit, but he stood still, staring at her silver hand on his own as if he could scarcely believe it.

"Come on," she said. "We can take some of the cake with us and—"

"You look very beautiful."

Her violet eyes met his hazel gaze. She could feel the heat of his body under her palm and she could feel his gentle gusts of breath that tickled her cheeks.

"Beauty, I—"

Suddenly, she noticed a scar over his left eye and she frowned. She had never been so close to him before and it was hidden in the fur of his face, almost completely obscured. She pulled away from him, stumbling on her long skirts.

"You are him!" she gasped.

"What do you mean?"

"You are the man with the scar! The man that I have dreamed of and the man from the tapestry!"

"I am a beast."

"Why must you keep things from me?"

"Please—"

"Why did you hide the chest of scripture from me?"

"What are you talking about?" He tried to step towards her, but she backed away.

"Do not come any closer!"

"Beauty, you know I will not hurt you."

"You hurt me all the time by keeping me here!"

Tears of frustration were clogging her chest and she tore the red rose from her hair and threw it to the floor.

"How can you expect me to live with something that I do not understand?"

Beast bowed his head.

"I am sorry."

"Yes, I am sorry too! I am sorry that I ever came to this evil place—I am sorry that I ever met you!"

She fled the ballroom.

CHAPTER THIRTY-ONE

The Chapel

After a lonely night of interrupted sleep and bad dreams, Beauty awoke miserable, and even riding Champ for several hours through the grounds did not improve her spirits. She ate lunch in her room and then sat on one of the large window seats, staring out through the crystal glass.

The grounds were a mismatch of melting snow and greenness. They were as beautiful and cheerless as ever, which only deepened her dark mood, and even the outline floating china teacups of syrupy sweetness into her hands could not raise her to a smile.

"One day I will die here and no one will know," she said to the air, biting her thumb.

The tea tray clattered.

"Perhaps I am already dead."

She thought of her last night in Imwane, though the memory was blurred with age. She remembered Eli in the temple and the rifle in her hands, but she could recall little else. She tried not to remember any of it, but it haunted her often.

I took a man's life, she would sometimes remind herself, but surrounded by this enchanted place, it did not seem real. Nothing seemed real.

At mid-afternoon she found that she was chilled right through and she was forced to move to the armchair near the fire to warm herself. The room fussed over her numb fingers and blue lips, but she paid little attention. In her mind she could only see Beast's expression as she ran from him. The hurt in his hazel eyes burned her with guilt.

After an hour she stood and walked to the door of her room.

"Take me to Beast," she said to the air.

The door did not open.

"Take me to Beast, please." She reached out her hand and pulled on the handle, but it would not budge.

"Take me to him! I demand it!"

After a long struggle, the door eventually gave way and an outline led her down a long corridor. It twisted around several passages and then guided her up and down various flights of stairs before trailing her through additional halls.

"Stop it!" she puffed at last. "I need to speak with him and I do not care what you think!"

Two double doors beside her creaked open and she was bathed in the soft glow of candlelight. A long, thin hall stretched before her with black-and-white stone in kite-shaped tiles. Wooden seating lined either side and there was a golden dais at the opposite end with various statues and figures carved around it. Before the dais knelt the huge, dark form of Beast.

Beauty's boots tapped on the floor as she approached him, and she glanced above at the painted ceiling and tall windows that looked over nothing. She waited for some time behind him, her hands clasped.

"Beast?"

She saw his shoulders twitch. He grunted quietly and then turned to her.

"I am sorry, I did not mean to interrupt. I came to find you—"

"What is it that you want?"

She paused. "This is a beautiful place, I have never seen it before."

"If you wish to find places in the castle, you must ask to see them."

"What is it?"

"A chapel. It is a place of worship made in the form of those in The Scarlet Isles."

"Similar to a Pervoroccian temple?"

"I suppose."

Beauty studied the carved walls that were set with jewels and the engraved plaques written in a language that she did not understand.

"They pray to the same gods?" she asked.

"Mostly."

"I was taught that pomp and ceremony were unnecessary—you would be better praying by yourself in the hills."

"It helps some people."

"I did not mean . . . " She sighed and dropped her arms to her sides. "Beast, I am sorry about last night. I find it . . . " she trailed off. "It is difficult to . . . " she failed again.

"I know. I do not want to keep you here."

He looked away.

"Do you come here often?" she asked.

"Every day."

"I did not know."

"I did not know that you cared."

She approached the dais and then knelt on the floor, pressing her hands to the stone tiles. It was not the same as Imwane's temple, but it was better than nothing. She had missed the soothing balm that the services there had brought her. Closing her eyes, she thought of Eli and she prayed.

"How did you find it?" Beast asked as she stood.

She shrugged and wrinkled her nose. "It was all right. It feels a little cold and impersonal to me."

"I think the people of The Scarlet Isles would accuse you Hillanders of the opposite."

She smiled, for it was the first time that anyone had called her a Hillander.

<hr/>

Beauty began to join Beast each day at the chapel before breakfast.

"You do not have to do this," he said once. "I forgive you for that night, Beauty. You did nothing wrong."

They were kneeling together before the dais.

"I am not doing it to please you."

"If you wish it," he muttered and they closed their eyes.

She truly did miss the temple on the hill and this was the closest that she could get to it at the castle. She often wondered as she knelt whether she would ever return to her temple at Imwane.

"I notice that there are no books on scripture here," she said to Beast one afternoon in the library.

She had been thinking recently of the chest of scripture and the words, *Violet eyes . . . silver grasp . . . war* weighed heavily on her mind.

"No, you will find nothing like that here," said Beast.

"Why?"

"Because it is like Magic."

He would say nothing more and she knew that she would not find that chest of scrolls again.

The days turned to moon-cycles and suddenly it was spring. Beauty had lost count of time by now and she would not have noticed the change of season had the grounds of the castle not completely cleared of snow. Whenever she broached the subject with

Beast he became closed and secretive. He had said that there was always snow at the castle—that was part of the enchantment—yet now this was not the case. She knew that this had something to do with her presence, but she could not fathom what it was.

She was marveling at the bright, light grounds one day when she came across Beast quite suddenly, lying in a patch of sun before a pond.

"Oh! I am sorry," she said. "I did not realize that you were here."

It was funny to see him stretched out on the grass. He quickly scrambled to his feet when he heard her.

"Beauty, forgive me, I—"

"No, there is nothing to forgive." She giggled and he looked down at his paws.

"The grounds are so lovely," he said.

"Shall we walk about? It is too good to waste."

He waited for her to lead the way as she usually did, but she stood still.

"Is something the matter—"

"I do not think that you move so horrifically as you believe that you do. You should not worry about upsetting me. I do not fear you."

He tried to balance on his hind legs, but Beauty placed her hand on his shoulder to stop him. It was the first time that she had touched him since the ball and they both shivered.

"You do not need to do that," she said.

With her hand still resting on his shoulder, they followed the graveled paths around the gardens. Beast shuffled his paws at first, but gradually he relaxed and they walked side by side.

"Everything looks so much better!" she cried as they passed emerald lawns and blossoming fruit trees.

"Yes, you are right."

As they came to one apple tree, he caught his elbow on a branch and sent a cascade of pink, feathery blossoms floating through the air. They caught on Beauty's loose, white hair, almost making a crown about her head.

"It even smells different!"

She was right. The atmosphere was not so heavy or so thick. Beast bared his teeth at her in a smile and then suddenly they heard it: a sweet song that broke the silence.

It was the gentle chirping of a bird. They looked around but could not see anything, though they could still hear the lilting melody of its tune.

"I have missed that sound," she whispered.

"And I."

They waited until it faded to nothing and then they strolled on, marveling at the splendor of spring until it was time to go to the library. Thus, another ritual was added to Beauty's days. She awoke to pray with Beast in the chapel, then rode Champ for several hours before strolling the grounds with Beast until they found their way to the library. They finished up their day together at dinner.

"I feel like a fine lady now," she said to him once, and she was about to add that she wondered if she could ever return to the hard life of labor when she realized that she would never have to. The thought saddened her deeply, for she had seen the life of luxury in Sago and she had seen the life of work in Imwane and she knew which she preferred.

Beast asked her once if she would not prefer to spend more time alone. She was seated at the table, eating an exotic dish that she had asked for after reading about it in their latest travel volume and she had almost gulped the whole meal, it tasted so nice.

"Why do you ask?" she replied between mouthfuls.

There was silence and she paused, glancing over at him. He was crouched on a rug before the fire and his expression was pensive. Though his features were mostly covered with fur, she had learned to read his moods.

"Do you wish to spend more time alone?" she asked with a sinking feeling at the pit of her stomach.

"Beauty," he said at last. "You are not here to please me. You must not humor me with your company; you should do as you wish."

"But I do wish to spend time with you!"

"You are sure?"

"Yes."

He did not look completely convinced.

"Beast, you have taught me to read and you have lavished me with pretty things, but I am most grateful for your company in this lonely place—do not deny me of it, please."

"I would never deny you anything."

She glanced down at her plate.

"Beauty, I . . . I . . . "

"Yes?"

"I am very grateful for your company also."

"I am glad that is settled," she said with a smile, but Beast turned away and stared into the fire.

CHAPTER THIRTY-TWO

The Nightmares

With the joy of spring came the horror of nightmares. The first occurred after a blissful day, when Beauty and Beast had taken their books from the library outside and had laid on the grass beside one of the fountains to read. Beauty still sometimes found a word that she did not recognize and she preferred reading aloud so that they could share the story. She had climbed into bed later that night with her head full of the tale they had been reading—about a ship sailing to a distant land, carrying a boy who sought adventure— but as she fell into slumber that image had quickly disappeared.

Instead, she saw Owaine lying shivering in his sleeping closet with the doors unfastened. Sun streamed through a window of the cottage, yet he hunched in the shadows. His face was pale and drawn and his hands shook. He coughed and she awoke, her cheeks damp with tears.

"What ails you?" asked Beast the next day.

She sat next to him beneath a willow tree, wringing her hands in her skirts. He was reading aloud from the book since she had said that she would rather not, and the tale that had so gripped her the day before now barely held her attention. Instead, she was staring off into the distance, not hearing a word.

"I had a bad dream," she whispered, working her fingers into knots. "I dreamt that my father was dying."

"It is just a dream."

She turned to face him.

"It is never just a dream for me," she said.

He started with a grunt and was speechless for a moment. "You . . . you have never told me that before."

"You have never asked."

The next night she dreamt of the cottage again, and she saw Owaine even weaker than before. The life seemed to be ebbing from him slowly and deep pain was etched across his face. He coughed blood into his hands and could barely move. Watching him was torturous and Beauty awoke with blood on her own hands, having bitten her lips as she slept.

"Is it true what you said to me yesterday?" asked Beast abruptly the next morning.

They knelt before the golden dais in the chapel, their hands pressed to the ground. Beauty had been praying fervently for Owaine and she jumped at the sound of his voice.

"About my dreams?"

"Yes."

"It is true."

He sighed and rocked back onto his hind legs. "Then you are a Magic Blood?"

"I suppose I must be. I told you that I do not know my true parentage. I know nothing." When he turned from her with a growl she asked, "You did not suspect with my appearance?"

"What do you mean?"

"Well, I do not look like other people," she said with a blush. "I look peculiar."

His hazel eyes searched her. "You do?"

"Yes."

"I had noticed nothing." He stood and stalked from the room.

"Where are you going?" she called.

"I must think!"

That night she dreamt of a bare, desolate place. Skeletal figures crept about the streets, rubble choked the squares, and bodies littered the shantytowns like wood chippings. Beauty saw Sago as she had never seen it before. The people were like savage animals that stooped in corners and the temples were destroyed. Added to the stench of grime and muck was the reek of death, and the air was constantly filled with wails of pain and screams of horror. It was calling her back to it, but she knew not why.

That morning, Beast did not join Beauty in the chapel. He had not been in the library yesterday either, or at dinner the night before, and Beauty wondered if she had offended him with her secret. Unable to stand being alone for much longer, and with the image of her nightmares haunting her, she ran to the stables. She had not dreamt as vividly as this since she had been tormented by the image of the red rose.

Champ placed his great bay head on her shoulders and snorted as she sobbed into his silky coat.

"He is dying and something is changing," she whispered. "I feel it."

She stayed with him for the rest of the day, until hunger pangs spiked her stomach and she was tired of standing. She entered the castle exhausted, not wishing to sleep tonight, for she knew that she would dream again and she dreaded what she would see.

"Beast?" she suddenly cried, her voice breaking. "Beast? Please . . . "

He appeared and she sighed, rushing towards him, but stopping short at the last second.

"Where have you been?" she gasped.

"I told you that I needed to think."

She rubbed her silvery, wane face.

"Is my being a Magic Blood so very terrible?" she asked.

"I thought that it mattered, but it does not. Forgive me, Beauty, for I have been foolish. It is a prejudice from long ago that often still haunts me."

"You do not like Magics?"

"I am a Magic now," he growled. "But yes, there was a time when I did not like them. I hated what I did not understand, and I was jealous of their gifts."

Beauty swallowed hard. "Beast . . . would you . . . may I . . . what I mean to say is that I cannot sleep tonight alone. I do not wish to, I mean. I am scared."

He frowned.

"You would like me to stay near you?" he asked.

"Yes, please."

"As you wish it."

That night, she climbed into her bed and Beast entered her room, sitting awkwardly in the chair before the fire, keeping his eyes turned away from her.

"You are sure you do not mind?" she asked quietly as the covers of her bed pulled themselves around her.

"No, I do not mind. Your dreams must be very terrible if you feel better with me here."

"You make me feel safe," she whispered before she dropped off to sleep.

She dreamt of Owaine again and she saw life leaving him. His chest was racked with coughs and shivers, and his face was pale and bloodless. He lay alone in the sleeping closet of his cottage and no one came to aid him. She saw a shadow appear at the door, but he cursed at it and it disappeared.

"Go away yur evil things!" he cried. "Yur people sent away my Beauty!"

She had never seen him so angry and his face was contorted with bitter hatred.

"Beauty!" he gasped at the ceiling. "Beauty, where are yur?" He choked and his breath wheezed and then he lay still.

"No!" Beauty screamed, sitting up in bed.

Beast was by her side in an instant. He reached out to take her in his arms, but stopped, his claws just grazing the skin of her back.

"What is wrong?" he asked. "What is the matter?"

Tears flowed from Beauty's eyes and she clenched her fingers around her pillow.

"My father!" she cried. "Owaine, my papa—he is dead!"

"Are you sure?"

The fire was still lit and before it was an upturned book, which Beast had been reading before she woke. The heat of the fire made the room feel stuffy and close.

"I have dreamt it, so it must be," Beauty moaned, raking her fingers through her hair. "He died alone. He died calling my name."

"Are you sure that is what you saw?"

But she did not hear. Burying her face in her bed sheets, Beauty sobbed violently.

"He cared for me!" she cried. "He saved my life."

"Beauty . . . " Beast was rumbling. "Beauty, please."

Finally, he laid a paw on her shoulder and she raised her head. Her violet eyes were red with pain, and for a moment he could not speak.

"I have a way that you can know for sure if he is dead," Beast said suddenly.

Beauty caught her breath. "You do? How?"

"I will show you."

CHAPTER THIRTY-THREE

The Corridor of Mirrors

As she changed out of her nightclothes, Beauty saw through the windows of her bedroom that it was dark outside. It must be almost midnight and the scene below was pure blackness. Beast was waiting on the other side of her door as she readied herself and she hurried, desperate to see what he would show her.

The outline in her room dressed her in a simple, elegant gown of dove gray and began fussing with her hair before she batted it away.

"I must go," she said irritably. "It is not the time for that now."

She opened the door to find Beast crouched in the corridor and he turned to her slowly.

"Are you ready?" he asked.

"Yes."

He led the way and no outlines opened doors for them and no torches flickered to life as they approached. He was showing her something that they did not wish her to see. She knew that he was doing some great wrong and she burned with guilt, but the thought of Owaine dead in the cottage was too much.

"Careful here," said Beast, lifting up his candelabra to throw dim light on a flight of twisting stairs. "It is uneven."

They climbed higher and higher until Beauty's legs ached. They climbed higher than it seemed possible that the castle could reach until suddenly Beast stopped.

"What are you showing me?" Beauty whispered, afraid.

"Something that I should not."

She placed her hand on his arm. "Beast?"

"It is all right. I know what I am doing."

He pushed open a door and she gasped. Before them stretched a tall, long corridor lined with mirrors. The floor was polished marble, the ceiling shimmering gold, and chandeliers dripped like jeweled bouquets from one end to the other. The mirrors were set into the wall and edged with gold; they reflected each other from one end to the next.

"These are the only mirrors in the castle?"

"I do not wish to see myself."

Beast led the way into the corridor and the door shut with a bang behind them. Beauty looked into the first mirror, but she saw no reflection. It was a vacant shimmer of nothing.

"I do not—"

"You must tell it what you wish to see."

Beast hunched himself against the wall on all fours, but Beauty did not notice. She stepped toward the mirror, whispering, "I wish to see Owaine."

Her voice echoed about the corridor and all of the mirrors rippled, their surfaces merging with colors. Suddenly, she saw the cottage reflected in all of them and Owaine lay on the floor before the dying fire, coughing.

"He is alive!" she gasped, pressing her fist to her mouth. "You are right, Beast. My dream was wrong."

Beast groaned.

In the mirror, Owaine's body jerked and shivered feverishly. His brow was slick and his eyes were wide and bloodshot. He did not have long, that much was clear, and Beauty yearned to comfort him. She stepped toward the mirror, trying to reach inside and pat his pale, withered cheek, but she touched cold glass instead.

"Oh, Papa," she breathed.

"You should go to him."

She spun around. "What?"

"I said that you should go to him. He is sick and he needs you."

"Beast—"

"Go."

Beauty could scarcely believe what she was hearing. She had desired her freedom for so long that she could not fathom it.

"You set me free?" she asked.

"I am permitting you to leave."

She clasped her hands to her chest, unable to hide her happiness. She could return to Owaine; she could be with him before he died.

"I will return right away," she promised.

"You do not have to."

"But I want to."

She walked over to him and laid her hands on his great, furry shoulder.

"I want to come back," she said, and when he did not reply, she added, "Beast, what will this cost you? I know it is not you that keeps me here."

"Just go!" he growled. "Go before anything tries to stop you."

She jumped back from him.

"I will return," she said. "I will."

"Go!"

She ran to the door and then stopped. Turning, she ran back to him and lightly kissed his cheek.

"Thank you," she whispered and then she ran from the room.

There was no time to take anything, she could tell that much, so she went straight to the stables, sprinting through the dark courtyard to Champ's stall. He snorted as he saw her, startled.

"Come on, we're leaving," she hissed.

She swung open the half door and it tried to stop her, but she yanked it hard.

"He said I could go!" she cried.

Champ clattered into the cobbled courtyard and she used the mounting block to climb onto his back.

"Imwane will get a mighty shock when they see us," she whispered, a smile playing across her lips.

He flicked his ears as she nudged him forward and they cantered across the front gardens of the castle to the smoking moat. There, Beauty pulled him up short and stared at the blurred darkness that awaited them on the other side. She looked over her shoulder at the castle, which was bathed in the filmy white of the moon and covered in roses as black as death and pain. Beauty suddenly understood what their changing colors meant.

"Do not be sad, Beast," she whispered. "I will return. Watch for me in the mirrors."

A drawbridge appeared out of nowhere and it slowly lowered through the mist. As it hit the ground on the other side with a bump, the iron gates creaked open. Beauty looked once more at the castle before galloping Champ into the forest. As the gates clanked shut behind them, an anguished howl tore through the night's silence.

<hr />

Beast crouched in the corridor of mirrors, his shaggy head bowed. He finally knew what Beauty had done when she came in the place of Owaine to the castle—now he, too, was about to give up his life for one he loved.

A shimmering glow of light caught his attention and he turned to see the mirrors rippling. He hoped that Beauty would reach Imwane in time.

"Show me Beauty's father," he said, and the surfaces of the mirror swirled.

The image of Owaine in the cottage vanished and it was replaced with the view of a craggy mountainside bathed in moonlight. There was a figure walking across the narrow path alone, his long cloak pulled about him, and he felt the eyes of the mirror on him. He turned, wondering who dared seek him out, and Beast saw the man who had cursed him all those seasons ago. He threw back his head and roared.

Part Five

A great and terrible beast raged. Standing before a smoking, dark moat he threw back his head and roared to the moon.

"Calm yourself," said a voice from the air.

He turned and looked at a pale outline. It had once been a soldier of his, but now it was only a faint shadow like the rest of his army.

"How can you bear it?" he snarled. "How can you accept this?"

"I do not remember. None of us remember."

"You were once great soldiers!" the beast growled. "You were once strong men!"

The outline rippled.

"We only remember the curse," it said. "We only know that we are here to guard and serve you."

The beast roared.

"Memory is my torture," he said. "I wish for your blissful ignorance."

"There is nothing we can do—"

"I know that!"

"We must live here for eternity, our hearts bound like the red roses to the earth."

"You think I do not remember this?"

"If one of us tries to leave, then he shall die," continued the outline. "The castle must always carry a thousand lives."

The beast turned and swiped at the outline, but his claws fell through the shape like water. He looked at his paws and roared, disgusted with what he had become.

"I wish to die! I would kill myself if I knew how."

"To do that you must give your life to another," said the outline.

"You leave and then I can give my life to you."

"But my only wish is to serve you."

The beast howled.

"Go and be a man again!" he shouted.

"I do not remember how."

The beast paced before the moat, his shaggy head bowed to the ground. He did not know how long he had been imprisoned in the castle. Perhaps it had been five seasons; perhaps it had been twenty. He saw a mound of snow and he clawed it.

"I am sentenced to be this way for eternity," he growled.

"We share in your curse."

"I pity you all."

CHAPTER THIRTY-FOUR

The Blackness

Beauty crashed through the forest, clinging to Champ's mane. They were surrounded by blackness that smothered them. Branches clawed at her cloak and face, and brambles tore at Champ's feathered hooves, but they galloped on, fighting through the shadows. Then she saw a dim halo of sterling light ahead and guided Champ towards it. Suddenly, they broke into the moonlight and the green, clear space of the hills. Beauty saw Imwane lit in the milky light of the stars and it was as if she had never been away.

"Owaine!" she yelled, but the village was silent.

Champ ground to a halt outside the door of the cottage and Beauty threw herself from his back. She burst inside and found a dying man lying before the ashes of a fire.

"Papa, it is me!" she cried, taking his chilled fingers in her own.

He roused himself and his brown eyes slowly opened.

"My child," he wheezed. "My Beauty, I be dead?"

"No! No, I am really here. It is me."

She could not bear to let go of him, but she did so only to light the fire. She grabbed a fur from a chest in the corner and threw it over his shivering body.

"How did yur get away?" coughed Owaine. "What did that creature do to yur?"

"Oh nothing, Papa. Beast is kind, he is not as he appears—"

"Kind? How could—"

"Hush, Papa, hush. Save yourself."

She filled a mug with water and brought it to his lips, but he pushed her hand away.

"No, child, I be too far gone for that. I be leaving."

"Papa, you cannot!"

"I be seeing my wife soon. I been waiting for this day a long time and it's my time, see. I be old and not much good for else. The winter were hard and there were lots of sickness. I be just so glad to see yur again, Beauty. I must be dreaming for sure."

"No, it is really me." She bent her head and kissed his cheek. "See? Did you feel that?"

"Then perhaps yur are real."

She smiled and a tear slid down her cheek.

"Beauty, I be so sorry for what I did to yur. Not a day go by when I don't hate myself for what happened—"

"Hush, Papa. You saved my life. I had to escape Imwane."

"I ain't been able to step in the temple since for shame."

More tears flowed from Beauty's eyes. She knew how Owaine loved the temple and she knew that it must have pained him dearly not to attend.

"Would you like to go there now?"

"I can't . . . "

"You can. I can take you."

She helped him stumble to his feet—he weighed almost nothing. Pulling more furs over his shoulders, Beauty almost carried him outside to where Champ was waiting. Owaine's head lolled against his chest and he groaned softly as she placed him on Champ's back in front of her, so that she could hold him still as they rode.

"As gentle as you can, boy," she said.

Champ was placid as he carried both of them up the hillside, and he even stooped a little as they dismounted. Owaine's legs buckled when he touched the ground, and Beauty had to almost drag him through the doors of the temple. It was as cool and quiet as always inside.

"I ain't fit to be in the likes of here," he muttered, his eyes flickering.

Beauty looked to the center of the temple, where she had stood seasons ago with a rifle in her hands.

"Nor I, Papa," she said. "But you did nothing wrong. You have no shame."

She propped him against one of the gold-flecked walls and pulled his furs tighter around him.

"Where is Isole?" she asked, unable to keep the anger from her voice. "Who has been looking after you?"

"Isole gonna have a baby and says she can't make the trip here from Dousal. The villagers tried to care for me, but I wanted none of their help. I deserved no help."

"That is not true!" She hugged him, being careful not to crush his fragile body. "Papa, you did the right thing."

"I be glad to be leaving this realm, my child. My only worry is yur."

"I will be safe."

"Yur will?"

"I have dreamt it," she lied.

The corners of his mouth lifted in a smile. "I be watching yur from the next realm, my child."

Beauty grabbed his hand and kissed it, her teeth clenched to stop herself from yelling out her pain. For as long as she could remember, she had loved only one other person in the whole realm and he was about to be taken from her. She wanted to beg him to try and stay; she wanted to force him to stay, but she knew that it was not what he wished. He was ready to go.

"You have done everything for me," she whispered, forcing back her tears. "You should never feel shame."

She began to sing quietly, her voice husky:

> *There was a time when the hills were young,*
> *When creatures ran free as these songs were sung.*
> *Back when the realm was a different place,*
> *And we were all of the same race.*

Her voice echoed about the temple and Owaine's lips quivered in time to the beat.

> *The time comes and we are called away,*
> *We are all claimed by the gods someday.*
> *They will decide when we must go,*
> *To the realm of the high or the realm of the low.*

> *We know not where we shall find ourselves,*
> *The pattern of our lives begs and tells,*
> *Of the new realm that we shall know,*
> *A place where we will—*

Owaine slumped against the wall, his last breath whooshing out of him with a sigh. Beauty held his lifeless hand to her cheek and cried. She did not know how long she stayed there, weeping and moaning, but suddenly she felt that she was not alone. She turned to see the preacher.

"My child, it's been a long time since we met."

His face was shadowed and she could not see his expression. She wiped the back of her hand across her eyes and said, "My papa is dead."

The preacher walked over and bent, closing Owain'e lifeless brown eyes. He placed his palm on top of the old man's head and muttered something under his breath.

"He's in a different realm now."

"How do you know?"

"Did yur learn nothing from the ceremonies I gave?"

"Of course, but why should I believe you?"

"Yur shouldn't. Yur should know it, and I knows yur know, Beauty."

She glanced back at Owaine and a whimper escaped her lips.

"Will you help me do the rights?" she asked.

"What about his other daughter?"

"She is with child and will not come. Well, will you help me?"

"As you wish it."

Dawn was breaking outside and as rose-colored light slipped over the horizon in a sheer mist, Beauty collected Owaine's bed sheets from the cottage and the preacher helped her swaddle his body. They worked silently, and after they had wrapped and anointed him with prayers they carried him to the next valley and burned his body at the peak of the highest hill—an old Hillander tradition.

Beauty stood at a distance with the preacher, watching as smoke and ash fluttered away. She clasped her hands and bowed her head, remembering all the wonderful things Owaine had done for her.

"I suppose it's useless asking yur where yur been all this time?" said the preacher suddenly, looking at her fine, embroidered gown.

"You would not believe me."

"I think I might."

"I have been in the forest under an enchantment."

His face remained impassive.

"And what will yur do now?" he asked.

"Soon I will return but . . . "

"But?"

"I have something I must do first."

"There be a thin line between the work of evil and the work of good," he said. "Some folks misunderstand the good, for a good must be magnificent if it is to win against an evil."

"What do you mean?"

"Magics can be good and bad—they just the same as humans. But humans fear them, even those that are good, for they are different."

She watched him turn and walk away from her, confused.

"You are not shocked to hear where I have been?" she called after him. "You believe me?"

"I suspected as much."

"How?" she shouted for he was far from her now.

"I've read the scriptures!"

Then he disappeared.

"So have I," she muttered under her breath.

<hr />

Later that morning, Beauty looked down at her hands and saw that they were shimmering silver. They had looked like that once before, when Eli had appeared, and she ran to the cottage window for fear, but she saw nothing outside except the usual scene of Imwane. She turned away, her chest heavy.

She was packing a saddlebag with provisions. Her instinct told her she must go to Sago, though it was the last place she wished to be. She had hoped that she could rest in Imwane for a while and pretend for a few short days that there had been no castle, no Beast, and no death, but she knew she could not.

Once she was packed she climbed the attic stairs to her bedroll. She had been without her amulet for a long time and she was glad to be reunited with it once more—she needed the strength and the guidance that it gave her. But when she walked through the dust to her bedroll, she found the rusty nail empty and her amulet gone.

She spent the next hour turning the cottage inside out searching for it, but it was nowhere. Panic mixed with grief made her angry and she began breaking things in her haste: smashing plates, knocking over chests, and splitting tools. Her brow was damp and her vision blurring. Suddenly, she felt the wooziness of a vision. She glanced down at her glittering skin and let it wash over her.

She saw her amulet held in olive, manly hands. A thumb with a ragged nail smoothed across the engraved rose and a voice whispered, "Beauty."

Abruptly, the vision left her and she gasped at the figure in the door.

"Beauty? Be that yur, child?"

It was Hally, and he surveyed the shimmering, silver woman before him and the destruction of the room with a gaping mouth.

"Yes," she breathed. "It is I."

"W-where have you been?"

"Away. I returned to be with my father when he died."

"Owaine be dead? I been checking on him every day though he always tells me to leave."

"Yes, he is dead, and the preacher helped me send him on. It was on the peak of the next hill if you wish to anoint him."

"That I do."

Beauty grabbed the saddlebags that were packed and waiting on the table. She was suddenly anxious to leave.

"Where is Sable?" she asked.

"She died a season back, child. I never seen such a change in a horse so quick."

Beauty bit her lip, feeling weary of death.

"Yur went so sudden," said Hally. "Them State men came and then that eve yur were gone and they be hunting all the houses for yur."

"I am sorry."

"When they found we did not have yur they left."

Beauty wondered if she should ask about Eli, but she thought it best if she did not.

"Now I must go again," she said and she hurried past him out of the cottage.

"Will yur return?" called Hally.

"I do not know."

She ran up the hillside and found Champ grazing beside the temple where she had left him. If she looked across at the next hill, she could still see tendrils of smoke leaking into the pale blue sky. She pressed her hand to her chest and muttered another prayer for Owaine before vaulting onto Champ's back. As she turned him in the direction of town, she saw that a crowd had gathered in the valley below and they shielded their eyes against the springtime sun and waved to her.

They saw a shining, silver woman astride a warhorse, and they made the sign of the gods as she disappeared.

CHAPTER THIRTY-FIVE

The Return

Beauty rode Champ at a gallop through the Hillands and into the Forest Villages. They did not stop—they did not need to. Champ's hooves barely touched the ground as they galloped faster and faster until they were moving at an impossible speed. Nobody saw them. Occasionally a lonely walker would blink and think that a silver shadow flew by, but he could never be sure.

Beauty's skin shimmered as they ran. She knew that she was doing something with her gift, but she did not know what it was or how she was doing it.

"What have I done to us?" she whispered to Champ that night, when she finally stopped to rest in a shepherd's hut.

She had brought Champ into the hut with her for fear that someone might see them, and they were tight for space. She had laid here once before, many seasons ago, when Owaine rescued her from Sago and changed her life for the better.

"Goodnight, boy."

Champ snorted.

"Goodnight, Beast," she whispered, hoping that he was watching in the corridor of mirrors.

Beauty set out her bedroll by Champ's feet and lay on the cold, hard floor. She barely needed to sleep, for she did not feel at all tired, but she made herself lay there out of habit, recounting memories of Owaine until dawn.

Seeing Champ as invigorated as she was the next morning, Beauty wondered if she should bother stopping at all the next night, and when it came to it, she did not. Neither of them ate or drank much—it was as if they did not need to. Nor did they sleep over the next three days. They were preoccupied with just one thing: getting to Sago—and they would not be distracted with anything else.

They passed the Strap cities and then Beauty would not stop for fear of catching unwanted attention. Sensing her anxiousness, Champ picked up the pace and the crowded, bustling cities became a haze of colors and loud noises. They charged onward into Sago, dodging travelers on the streets and catching glimpses of ruined mountains of rubble and homeless, starving people. Beauty remembered how afraid of the shantytowns she had been in her childhood and how terrifying Sago had looked in her dreams, but she would not turn back. Though she longed to run back to the hills, she knew that she must go on.

Her amulet seemed to shine like a beacon above Sago, and she thought of nothing else as they neared the capital. It was somewhere there, she could feel it, but Sago was a huge, dangerous place and she worried if she would ever find it. She knew not what situation she was rushing into—were there still rebels in Sago? Was the city deserted? She could be sure of nothing.

She was over its borders before she knew it and suddenly she pulled Champ to a halt. They had arrived. As soon as they stopped, the heat hit them with a stifling punch. Champ began to pant immediately and his coat darkened with sweat for the first time.

Beauty threw back the hood of her cloak and laid a shimmering palm on his neck to reassure him.

The air smelled thick and salty as it always had, with a new tang of smoke that warned of death and despair. The sun was orange and blistering, the heat muggy and humid, and the sea beside them was a calm stretch of azure. In the distance, Beauty could hear gunshots and screams, but there was no one around that she could see.

She turned to look at Rose Herm in all its ruined glory. The boulevard was a wreck of remains. There were shells of houses, blackened from within, and flattened mansions that showed the deep scars of war. Beauty remembered the grandeur and the splendor of Rose Herm. She remembered once when carriages had flocked to Ma Dane's doors and guests had sipped syrupy tea in her drawing room, and something-se-something and someone-se-someone had marveled at the magnificence of it all. She bowed her head.

There were smashed windows, broken doors, destroyed gardens, and dark shapes hanging from trees that she did not wish to look at. Rioters had come here, she could tell that much, and they had pillaged and raided the mansions. They had been angry and desperate—drawn to cruelty by the brutality of the time.

Beauty slid from Champ's back and pushed open the rusty gate of Rose Herm. It creaked and she held it open for Champ to follow behind her. Together they trudged across the dead, yellow gardens that were dried to dust, and as they passed a broken fountain, Beauty remembered hiding from Nan in it. She remembered leading Comrade from the stables to whisper her secrets to him all afternoon, and she remembered the time that she had counted all the zouba trees in the grounds and carved a "B" on each of them. She paused as she reached the stone steps to the front door and she looked up at the mansion that had once been her whole realm. She had been to many places and seen many things since she left it.

I was not happy here, but I never wished it like this, she thought to herself. *I never wanted to see it destroyed.*

She was about to enter Rose Herm when a flash of gray caught her eye. She gasped, thinking that a State official had discovered her, but instead she saw a woman walking through the rubble.

"Hello," said the woman, straightening out the gray folds of her dress as she approached.

Beauty glanced around, worried that this was an ambush, and Champ pressed himself close to her side in case she wished to flee.

"I warn you, I have no sticks," she said as the woman came closer. "I have nothing of value to give you."

The woman was but a step from her now and Beauty could see her dark brown hair flecked with streaks of gray and her large, brown eyes. She had a strange expression on her face; it was a mixture of joy and awe.

"You look so like him," she whispered and her voice was almost familiar.

"Like who?"

"Like your father."

The woman reached out a hand, but Beauty flinched away from her.

"What do you know of my father?" she snapped.

But the woman seemed barely to hear her.

"I dreamt that you would be here," she murmured fervently. "But I did not know you would be so powerful. I never guessed that things would turn out this way. He did not tell me that it would be like this."

Beauty looked around her once more, afraid.

"I do not understand you," she said, taking a hasty step back. She wished that she had thought to bring some kind of weapon with her—she had no way of defending herself.

"You must come with me," said the woman. "It is not safe here and we have much to speak of. You must come with me."

"Who are you?"

The woman blinked as if she did not understand.

"My name is Asha," she said. "I am your mother."

CHAPTER THIRTY-SIX

The Attack

Beauty looked around the dark, dusty room. They were beneath a pile of rubble in what used to be one of Sago's thriving squares, and Asha was lighting an oil lamp.

They had hurried here from Rose Herm, scurrying down backstreets and darting through the safety of the smoky gloom of destruction. Beauty had been sure that someone would see her shimmering skin, but when they had come across a stream of bony, dirty people walking on the opposite side of the alleyway, they had seemed not to notice her. Their desperate, dull eyes had slid over the silver woman and her warhorse without surprise. There was some Magic involved, Beauty realized, and she wondered whether it was herself or Asha that was conjuring it.

They had reached a square and Asha had guided her to a decrepit building with scorched windows and bloody walls. It looked like every other building they had passed, but Champ had been placed in a stable at the back, where Asha had promised he would be safe, and

Beauty had followed her down a hidden flight of stairs at the side of the torn structure to a small basement full of boxes and tables.

"What is this?" she asked as the oil lamp's dim light lit the room.

"This is where we meet. It is a safe house, and others will join us shortly."

Beauty faced the woman who claimed to be her mother. She had nothing and everything to say to her at once, but right then, she could only stare. Asha looked like a typical Pervoroccian. There was something of Ma Dane about her features, but she could not be more different from Beauty.

"I suspect you are wondering why you have never met me before?"

"That and many other things."

Asha's brown eyes searched Beauty's silvery face and there was sorrow in their depths.

"It . . . it takes my breath away to see you," she admitted. "You look so much like your father; it is uncanny. I have not seen him since your birth."

"And who is my father?" Beauty was surprised that she could speak at all. Her throat felt dry and tight.

"You have not met him? I was sure he would come to see you by now."

"I have never met either of my parents. One stands before me now but—"

"You do not believe me?"

"It is hard to believe."

Asha sat in a wooden chair, motioning for Beauty to join her, but she kept her distance instead.

"You are stubborn and you get that from him," said Asha. "I know many things about you that only your mother would. I know that you dream at night and that your dreams come true. I know that you are a House of Rose by birth and that makes you strong and proud. I know that you are the daughter of a sorcerer and a foreteller and that you can do extraordinary things."

"That proves very little."

"You have never dreamt of me?"

Beauty felt instinctively that she had. Asha's voice was familiar to her and so was the outline of her face, but she would not admit it.

"I have no mother," she said. "I was born in a paupers' hospital and my mother was not there. She abandoned me."

"It had to be that way, Beauty. That is how I dreamt it—you can understand that, surely? When you dream it, it has to happen."

"And did I have to grow up in cruelty? Did I have to flee Sago for my life? Did Ma Dane have to die?"

At the mention of her sister, Asha's face went pale.

"I do not see everything," she whispered. "I am not as powerful as you."

"What makes you think that I am so powerful?"

"It is your birthright and it is written in scripture, but I do not need to know it for I can see it. You are glowing before my eyes. He does that sometimes, when he has cast an enchantment."

Beauty thought of the castle and Beast.

"I have . . . I have cast no enchantments," she said.

"You will do it without realizing."

Beauty remembered standing in the temple, struggling against Eli's grasp. She remembered the rifle in her hands though she did not remember taking it from him.

"You have the power to do everything that I can do and more," continued Asha. "You have the power of a sorcerer."

Beauty placed her hand on a table to steady herself.

"Whatever is happening to me now, I did not cast it. I have come from a castle in a forest and this is not my enchantment, it is not something that I have—"

There was the sound of footsteps on the stairs and she stopped.

"Do not fear," said Asha. "It is safe. Those are friends."

The door opened and several men and women hurried into the room. They were of various ages and ethnicity and they regarded Beauty with interest.

"I did not think that she would really come," said one.

"I did, I dreamt it," said another.

Beauty fidgeted under their gazes and felt beads of sweat trickle down her back. It was even hotter down here than it was in the boiling streets. She wished that she could go to the stable and be with Champ.

"Let me explain," said Asha, trying to take her hand, but Beauty would not let her.

"We are working to evacuate Magics from The Neighbor and Pervorocco. Though most left at the beginning of the Magical Cleansing, there are still many in hiding that fear for their lives."

"If they have not already been captured, tortured, and killed," added one man.

"We are trying to take them to the Wild Lands," continued Asha. "Once we are there we can regroup and fight back."

"It is the second bout of the Red Wars," said a woman.

"The Red Wars never ended," someone else replied.

Beauty glanced at each of them in turn, her chin jutted out and her arms folded.

"What is this to me?" she asked.

"We are taking you to the Wild Lands."

"What if I do not wish to go?"

Asha frowned. "You must," she said. "It is written in scripture—you will lead our battle."

"What scripture is this?"

Asha began to mutter the verses and the other Magic Bloods joined in:

The gods did build the hills for those,
That does good deeds for one they chose.

They shelter with old spells and might,
For one who comes to them to fight.

They know not what that thing might be,
It comes to keep their people free.

It shall lead the Magic to task,
And wage war with a silver grasp.

Deaths shall rein and family ties
Will be broken by one with violet eyes.

When the time comes, it will lead,
To keep those with Magic freed.

Beauty's body shook and sweat dripped down her spine.

"And what if I will not do it?" she said. "What if I refuse?"

There was a long silence.

"The ship leaves Sago's docks tomorrow," said Asha. "And you will come with us."

CHAPTER THIRTY-SEVEN

The Magic Bloods

Beauty sat with her back to Asha and the other Magic Bloods. They would not let her leave and see Champ so she was sulking. If she was as powerful as they said, then she supposed that she should be able to do some sort of Magic to force her way out, but she did not know how. Instead, she sat with her head in her hands.

They were talking logistics, but she understood little of what they spoke of. She did not wish to leave Pervorocco. She had promised Beast that she would return and compared to the darkness of Sago, the enchanted castle did not seem so terrible. She tried to think of Beast, wondering if he was watching her in the corridor of mirrors, but her instincts told her nothing.

"Beauty?"

It was Asha, and she sat in front of her daughter so that Beauty could not turn away.

"Where is my amulet?" Beauty asked.

"You do not have it?"

Beauty was about to explain what had happened with Eli in the temple, but then she thought better of it.

"I left it in Sago before the Magic Cleansing," she said instead.

"But I entrusted it to you!"

Beauty shrugged.

"The Houses are the ancient people and those with Magic Blood have ancient Magic," hissed Asha. "When a member dies, they pass their amulet onto the next generation."

"You are not dead."

Asha sighed and raked a hand through her hair. "I might as well be. When I gave birth to you I gave you everything, do you not see? My amulet—my ancient Magic—everything! If it were not for him then I would not be here. Oh, Beauty, he said that you should have it with you always!"

"Who is *he*?"

"Your father." Asha had dropped her voice.

"What is my father's name?"

"No one knows that. Even I do not know that."

"Where did you meet him?"

"I trained as his apprentice. I left Sago to travel the realm and find teachers when I was young. There are distant countries that know far more than we do, and I found your father on one of my journeys. I was very lucky."

Beauty snorted.

"I have always watched over you, Beauty. You are my daughter."

"I cannot do what you want me to."

"You can and you will, Beauty. There is nothing to be afraid of."

When Beauty did not answer, Asha left her and went back to her meeting. The Magic Bloods talked long into the night in whispers until finally Beauty was handed a bedroll and told to make herself comfortable on the floor.

"I will know if you try to run," said one man. "I am a sensor and I feel things before they happen."

She gave him a withering look before rolling over.

"Goodnight, daughter," whispered Asha, extinguishing the oil lamp.

She received no reply.

Beauty was surprised to find that she was tired for the first time in days. Yawning, she closed her eyes and slipped instantly into a troubled sleep. She saw a man with dark skin and white hair smiling at her and then she saw her amulet and it was held in the hands of someone who she knew—someone who she feared. She felt footsteps and she saw gray shadows.

She woke suddenly, knowing that something was wrong and there was no time to run. Others were waking around her with startled grunts and cries.

"How did we not feel them?" cried someone.

"How did they get here without us noticing?"

Asha sat up, her face pale with fear.

"I did not dream it!" she hissed. Her eyes fell on Beauty. "Did you know?"

But Beauty did not have time to reply. The door burst open and gray men ran down the stairs and into the room, holding rifles and swords. The bang of gunfire exploded and smoke clogged the air. Blood splattered across Beauty's face as the man next to her was shot three times in the head. She screamed, but her voice was drowned by more shouts and cries.

"Beauty! Get out of here!" she heard Asha yell.

A gray man caught sight of her and swung his rifle in her direction. Before he could take aim, a command was shouted and he shrieked in agony. He crumpled to a pool of skin on the floor, every bone in his body smashing in an almighty crack.

There was more gunfire and more yells as State officials fell to the ground, destroyed, and Magic Bloods were shot through again and again. Red blood streaked the ceiling and stained the floor. Beauty could taste the metallic stickiness of it in the air. She ran to the stairs, taking advantage of a moment when the State officials were preoccupied with a Magic Blood throwing visions at them from the middle of the room.

As she was about to flee, something grabbed her arm and dragged her back, smacking her hard against the wall so that the breath was knocked out of her.

"I have found you, Cousin!" hissed a voice in her ear.

She looked up at Eli. His handsome face was twisted with rage and he hobbled unsteadily on his right leg, which was wooden from the thigh down.

"You thought that I was dead!" he yelled over the gunfire and wails of pain. "I have spent seasons searching for you! I dreamt that you would be here!"

He had a rifle cocked over his arm, and hanging from his neck were two amulets. Beauty made a grab for hers, but he stopped her, breaking her fingers with his fist. She yelped and tried to dart away, but he grabbed her hair and pulled her back.

Before them, the State officials were shooting blindly around the room, unable to see due to the visions they were experiencing. Some were crying with fear as dark monsters from their nightmares jumped at them and tried to tear them apart. Occasionally one of their rouge bullets would hit a Magic Blood and they would yell, their wound spurting and gushing, before they collapsed in a heap on the floor.

"You will not get away this time, Cousin!"

Beauty tried to tear herself from him, but she could not. She struggled, her limbs thrashing and her heart racing.

"I have found you! I have found you and you will not escape!"

The ground began to tremble and then it began to shake. Both the Magic Bloods and the State officials cried in surprise, distracted by the shifting of the earth beneath their feet.

"Beauty!" Asha screamed.

And suddenly the basement caved into itself with a bang.

CHAPTER THIRTY-EIGHT

The Dead

Beauty struggled to the surface, pushing debris and bricks out of the way. Her eyes and mouth were covered with dust and her ears were ringing. As she wriggled through the rubble, pieces of wood and bricks slammed her body and created deep, mauve bruises. Her broken fingers throbbed and her head ached with a dull, incessant pain.

Finally, she felt the clammy air of Sago on her cheeks and she gasped in a lungful, coughing and spluttering. She rubbed the dust and chippings from her eyes and looked at the crater that she stood upon. Around the square, several other buildings had fallen and there were mounds of rumpled remains everywhere.

Beside her, a hand was sticking out from beneath a fragment of wall. Lifeless.

She felt something against her chest and looked down to see her amulet. She did not remember grabbing it before the basement caved, but she was glad to have it all the same. Her skin was still shimmering silver and the amulet seemed to warm against it. When she touched the engraved rose at the center, a shiver ran through her.

She must leave.

A shrill whinny sounded through the echoing silence, and Beauty ran to the stables behind the fallen building. Champ and the stable were still intact and she cried out in relief, throwing open the door to let him canter out.

She was desperate to leave and she calmed him quickly, the eerie, deserted silence pressing on her as she did so. With her body still bruised and aching, she climbed upon his back and clung to his dark mane. She did not need to tell him where they were headed—he seemed to already know. She looked one last time at the crater where the basement had been and then she turned Champ away.

—✦—

They galloped out of Sago so quickly that even if Beauty had had her eyes open, she would have seen nothing. She wove her fingers into Champ's mane and trusted him to carry her away, shutting her eyes to the death and destruction she had witnesed. Her cheeks were stiff with splatters of dried blood and her head pounded with pain, but she pretended not to notice. She had to return to Beast—that was all she knew.

Night came and went and still Champ galloped onward. During the next day, Beauty found some of her strength returning and she sat taller, taking an interest in where they traveled. By the glimpses she stole of the crowded streets and many inns that they passed, she guessed that they must be leaving the Border Cities. She remembered how once Owaine had been so excited to return to his hills, and she remembered how she had not understood what he found so beautiful in their green, rolling isolation. She understood now.

If I can just reach the Hillands, everything will be all right, she told herself. *I just need to reach it.*

On the third day, Champ began to slow. It was subtle and he still traveled at an impossible speed, but Beauty noticed it. She looked down at her hands embedded in his mane, and she saw that they were not shimmering as brightly as they had. The enchantment was fading.

"Go, boy!" she urged, and he tried, but he could not travel as fast as before.

On the fourth day, they were forced to stop when evening fell. Both felt drained though they pretended not to notice, and they made camp beneath a tree in a wood.

"We can reach the Hillands tomorrow," said Beauty, her voice tinged with hope. "Do not fret, boy. We will be there tomorrow."

But the next morning they were weary. Beauty looked at her hands and they glowed only faintly. She hoisted herself onto his back, ignoring her tender muscles, and urged him on. They were in the midst of the Forest Villages and she prayed that they could reach Imwane by nightfall.

"We are almost there, boy," she whispered.

The day was hard. Champ galloped as fast as he was able and Beauty rode him with all the strength she had left, but they only reached the edge of the Hillands before nightfall and they were forced to stop due to sheer exhaustion.

Beauty collapsed onto the ground, too tired to even unpack her bedroll, and Champ lay on the grass, his nose tucked under him. They did not even eat; they just slept deeply under the scatter of stars until dawn. When she woke, Beauty knew that something was wrong. She could feel it like a pull across her chest. She opened her eyes and whispered, "Beast."

Her sense of dread only increased throughout the day as they fought their way across the hills. Champ's bay coat was soon black with sweat and his mouth foamed, while Beauty was almost delirious with pain. Her broken fingers were now puffy and bruised and she had deep scratches on her arms. But she refused to stop.

As the sun was setting and casting jets of amber and gold across the horizon, Beauty and Champ tumbled down the hillside into Imwane. A few villagers sat outside their cottages and they watched with amazement as the great warhorse thundered over the valley and straight into the forest, a silver woman slumped on his back.

Hally, who stood on the threshold of his house, made the sign of the gods and all of the villagers copied him, holding their hands to the sky long after Beauty and Champ had disappeared.

The forest was the worst part yet. Champ stumbled through the bracken and vines, and Beauty was clawed and pulled from his back by the thick branches. Often she tumbled from his shoulders and had to wrench herself astride him once more. Both were exhausted and lost. Before, they had needed only to ride into the forest and they would be pulled toward the castle like a magnetic force, but now there was no such guidance. The light was disappearing and frustrated tears began to collect in Beauty's eyes.

"Beast?" she cried, but there was no answer and the forest seemed to swallow her voice.

An hour later, she saw a glint of dull silver through the trees and she rode Champ toward it at a lackluster trot. A pair of rusty, iron gates appeared and Beauty cried out, stumbling from Champ's back in haste. She fell against them, for they would not open of their own accord and they creaked as she tripped into the grounds.

"Beast?" she called, but there was no one.

She saw broken fountains, dried and cracked. There were weeds in the flowerbeds and fractures in the paths. Trees bowed with fruitless, gnarled branches and meadows lay barren and black. The moonlight fell dimly on this dead place.

"Beast?"

She ran to the forbidden walled garden and peered around the archway. She gasped, for every rose had been destroyed. Their red petals lay like a crisp carpet across the ground and crackled beneath her feet. Bare heads withered on shrunken stems and brown leaves curled. At the center of the garden, the magnificent rose that had so awed her was gone. Its stem was cut clean.

"Beast?" she cried.

Champ hunched over by the gates, too tired to go on, and Beauty left him to rest. She ran through the grounds by herself, approaching the castle at a frustratingly slow pace, for she was weary and ill.

"Beast?"

The castle was dry and dead looking. Its silence was tomb-like and the roses covering it were black; they hung from the vines in rotten clusters that dripped to the ground.

Beauty ran to the great double doors and heaved at them with all her might. They shifted eventually, though she was forced to pause and catch her breath from the struggle. She allowed herself a moment of rest before she hurried into the dark, foreboding silence.

"Beast?"

She stumbled down a passage, opening the doors herself.

"Take me to the corridor of mirrors!" she said, but there was no one to hear her. "Take me to the corridor of mirrors!"

There was no sound.

She dragged herself up flights of stairs, across one bare quad and through various passageways, but she recognized nothing—every room looked the same. She could feel no presence in the castle, either good or bad. Just death.

"Beast!" she screamed. "I did not mean to be gone so long," she shouted in a hall that echoed. "I always intended to return! I promised that I would return!"

She ran deeper into the castle, following different routes wildly with little success. At one point she fell to the floor and lay there for a long time, sobbing into the embroidered carpet. It took all of her willpower to pull herself back up and go on.

She prayed as she searched, pressing her thumb and index finger together as she ran from room to room. Then, suddenly, she saw it. It was a passage that she faintly recognized and she cried out in surprise, hurrying through it to the flight of stairs at the end, hoping that this was it.

"Beast?"

She climbed the stairs and fell through the door at the top. A dark corridor opened before her and, peering through the gloom, she saw two walls of mirrors smashed to shards that glistened in the darkness. At the opposite end, a huge form lay on the floor, a dying red rose clutched to his chest.

"Beast!"

CHAPTER THIRTY-NINE

The Spell

Beauty ran to Beast's body and threw herself on the ground beside him. His features were set and stiff, his eyes shut tight, and there was a terrifying stillness to him.

"Beast? Please, wake up! Beast?"

She pressed the bristly fur of his cheek gently at first and then she stroked it, praying that he would awaken to feel her touch. But he did not. She took hold of his shoulders, bending over him, and tried to shake him, though he was heavy and she had no strength left. Shards of mirror fell from his fur and crunched on the floor, but he did not move. She stared at his dark lids longingly, wishing that she could see his familiar, hazel eyes. Sobs of despair tore at her throat and a great pain slashed her heart.

"I said I would come back! I was always going to come back."

The rose across his chest was wilting and its fragile, blackened head rested upon his heart. Its petals curled at the edges and there were three purple thorns upon its dry stem. Beauty snatched it away.

The thorns bit into her palm, drawing beads of red blood that stained her silver skin, but she did not care.

"I have kept my promise!" she screamed, ripping the stem in half. "I have come back!"

She shredded the petals and threw them to the floor. Then suddenly, Beast stirred and she rushed to his side, holding him.

"Beauty?" he growled, his eyes opening weakly.

"Yes! Yes, it is me. Beast, what has happened? Why are you—"

"The roses . . . my army." His eyes were flickering, his jaw going slack.

"No!" Beauty cried. "Stay with me!"

"It is the curse," he croaked. "No one may leave."

Beauty bunched her hands into fists around his fur.

"You took my place?" she said. "You took my place in the curse?"

"Beauty . . . I love you."

"I will not let you die for me."

"I wish it," he sighed and fell back against the marble floor, his eyes dim.

"No!"

Tears trickled down Beauty's cheeks, washing away the blood and the dirt of the journey. She sniffed, her lips trembling and her heart breaking.

"You cannot leave me! I will not let you!" She shook him, but he did not stir.

"Please," she whispered. "You do not understand what you have done for me—what you have taught me."

She rested her head against his chest and held him tightly.

"You cannot leave me, for I love you too."

She sobbed into his fur, drenching it with her tears, and then she felt something pushing against her collarbone. Looking down she saw her amulet and she touched the engraved rose at its center. She un-looped it from her neck and placed it on Beast's chest, tears coursing down her cheeks.

"You cannot leave, for I love you too," she repeated. "I give you my life, for I love you too."

An explosion cracked the air and she was knocked back. White light rushed around her and she screamed, shielding her eyes from the brightness.

"Beast!"

But she could see nothing. Magic surged over her, touching her cheeks and hands with its warmth, and the ground shuddered. Above her, at the top of the room, Beauty could just make out a ball of light that was sometimes gold, sometimes silver, and sometimes violet.

"Beast?" she cried again and then there was a thunderous roar. Shards of glass and red rose petals swirled through the spinning air and there was an almighty crash before a ripple of light poured through the room. The mirrors reformed themselves and the windows before her were thrown open to reveal a balcony, upon which stood a man.

Beauty climbed to her feet, clutching the wall for support. Her fingers were no longer broken and her body no longer ached. She looked around the corridor fervently and she called out: "Beast?"

"Beauty."

She looked at the man standing on the balcony and she caught her breath. He was tall with broad shoulders and brown hair. He wore a white shirt with loose, velvet trousers and he had hazel eyes.

"It is me, Beauty," he said, leaning against the stone balcony for support since his legs trembled and buckled. "It is me."

She stared. Then he staggered and she rushed to his side, steadying him. She felt the heat of his skin, smelled the musty scent of his body, and saw the gentle hazel of his eyes, the left of which was slashed with a scar.

"It is you," she whispered.

She glanced at her hands and they were shimmering silver— her whole body was radiating with glittering light and she appeared so strange against the olive tint of his skin. Beast tried to take her fingers in his own, but she pulled them away.

"Beauty?"

She would not look at him for shame. She felt as if she had been called down to the drawing room at Rose Herm once more for the handsome guests to gawk at.

"Beauty, I am the same," he said and his voice rumbled with familiar inflections.

"You are not. You are a . . . man."

He stroked her silvery cheek and drew her to him. She tried to turn her head away, but he wrapped his arms around her shoulders. Bending his head, he pressed his lips to her forehead and smoothed her white hair.

"I meant what I said before," he growled. "I love you."

A shrill whinny sounded and they leaned over the balcony, hands entwined. Champ was rearing below, his bay coat shinning, and behind him stood an army, shaking and flexing themselves as if after a long sleep. There were red rose petals at their feet, and over the horizon, gold, silver, and violet light seeped into the sky, rushing to the corners of the Hillands and settling over the villages as the dawn came.

"I believe this is yours." Beast took the amulet from beneath his shirt and placed it around Beauty's neck. It felt warm against her skin.

"I gave it to you," she said. "It is ancient Magic. I believe that it holds my life."

"But you are still living and I think you will need it for the times ahead."

Beauty thought of the scripture. "I am to fight for the freedom of Magics."

Beast pressed his cheek to her own.

"Wherever you go," he said, "I shall be by your side."

Acknowledgments

A huge thank you to everyone at Sky Pony Press, particularly my lovely editor, Julie Matysik. Massive thank you, as always, to my wonderful agent, Isabel Atherton, for her dedication, support, and insight. Hugs and kisses to every one of my friends and family who were subjected to first drafts and tears: Mum, Dad, and James. Lastly, special thanks to Lydia—there are no unicorns, as promised.